1:05 a.m.

C.M. Moore

Yearning for a normal life, assassin Karmen-Marie has had enough—enough of surviving contracted hits, and enough of the post-apocalyptic world. Forced to take one last job, Karma sets out across the frozen landscape of Earth.

Rea MacBain's job is to ensure the safety of Earth's precious few water purification plants. He believes his abusive past must stay buried under the snow that encases his domain.

A single bullet will send Karma and Rea in a direction they'd never expected. Ice-cold assassin's blood drives the woman sent to kill him, yet it ignites the fire which thaws Rea's heart.

www.trollriverpub.com
1:05 a.m.
An Ice Era Chronicle (Book 1)
Copyright © 2016 C.M. Moore
ISBN: 978-1-939564-95-5
Cover Design: FrontBrush
Editors: Carol McKibben
Boomy Patiño Plunket

Dear Reader,

Connor and Monica have worked very hard on this particular piece of entertainment. This book was brought to you by hard labor and love. Please respect an artist's work for the enrichment we try to bring you. I humbly ask that you don't outright steal this child born on paper and brought to you by love. If you come by this book by nefarious means, and you are simply unable to give the change in your pocket for the purchase price, then take it with my blessing. But if you can purchase it and would like Connor and Monica to continue to bring you great books, please purchase a copy to support them.

Thank you,
Troll River Publications

Join the fun with for giveaways, updates, and new release opportunities at:
http://eepurl.com/bApcwD

Dedication:

I dedicate this book to my backyard. The area is a mud pit with dead tree stumps and weeds. One day, I hope to have a patio. Here's to dreaming…

Acknowledgements:

To my better half, without you, this book wouldn't exist.

To my fabulous four: April, Lyn-z, Sarah, and Kat. Some of you read this bad boy TWICE! You're awesome.

To Cez Apello and Diana De Brito, the love scenes and fight scenes needed you. Your patience with me was very kind.

To the Trolls in the Troll River Publishing House, your wisdom and insight were easy to swallow. Thank you for letting me gulp from your well of knowledge.

To the New York City Writers Guild and my group at the Wounded Warrior Project Writers Retreat. Your encouragement was uplifting. Especially my mentor David Crabb. (I know you told me to abandon fiction and write humorous memoirs, but I just couldn't. Please don't hold that against me, David.)

To Kay and Stephanie, for all the help with the MRLs.

And finally, to my daughters, Capi and Sam... I appreciate that you were quiet when I wanted to write. You are wonderful girls, and you will one day be wonderful women.

To all of you, thank you.

Chapter 1

Place: Old United States of America, New York City
Time: 1:05 a.m. Ice Year 1

Blood splattered on his ice-coated pack of playing cards.

Freeing the ace of hearts, Keith glared at his blindfolded captive while he wiped off the card. When the deck was clean, he set the pack down between the neat row of different-sized knives and his old clock receiver. The time blinked at him: 1:05 a.m. He leaned his hip against the stainless-steel table as he eyed the man who was tied to the chair in the middle of the stark room.

The prisoner flexed in his seat in fear and pain. Sweat trickled down the side of his face. Keith considered the blindfold. The eyes never lied. He might remove the cloth once they got started again. Not really interested in torture today, he flipped on his radio.

While listening to the only radio station available, he picked up his favorite knife—the one with the jagged hook on the end.

"Welcome to CNN-Fox News United, Full Spectrum. This is Ethan Robinson, and this is your Eye on Ice. It is currently five minutes past one," the radio announcer began in a monotone voice. "The United Nations announced today all government officials would like to celebrate Ice Year One or I.Y.1."

"What a…" Keith paused. "What is the word… stupider?" Keith muttered to the man, who was gagged.

He didn't expect an answer. His prisoner was choking on the cloth shoved into his mouth. Keith reached for a whetstone and focused on sharpening his knife to a razor-fine edge.

"Scientists have announced the beginning of a new era. They are urging all citizens who have not found safe underground homes to continue to move south. The weather along the Equator continues to be a stable fifty degrees. In other news today, the Canadian Prime Minister announced this day to be a holiday for all former United States citizens. Our new leader has high hopes for smoothly joining the U.S.A., Canada, and Mexico during these hardships. After much political debate, the United Nations has agreed on naming our new joint government The Confederate Territories of North America or C.T.O.N.A. Spirits remain high as a celebration of the holiday begins with…"

Keith got up. He switched off the radio in a huff. While shaking his head in disgust, he returned to circling the large man tied to the chair. The failed assassin flexed his muscles, testing the strength of the rope. Keith huffed at the stranger much like he'd done at the radio. The announcement of a new holiday annoyed him. He had too much work to do today to let any of his men off to celebrate this joke of an event. There were no celebrations anymore as far as he was concerned. People should just start accepting that. They should be concerned with making food and basic survival. Not drinking, clinking glasses, and saying "Thank God, I didn't freeze to death after that meteor hit."

Irritated, he sank his knife into the arm of his victim, who was now struggling. The blade sliced cleanly through the skin. To his credit, the prisoner didn't make a sound.

Keith pulled the knife out roughly and smiled. His prisoner hadn't made a sound *yet*, he corrected. By the time he was done, Keith would know everything he wanted to know. That's how it always went.

The white metal door from the hall was thrown open and squealed on its hinges. The worn knob clattered against the wall with a loud bang. As his eyes grew wide at the interruption, Keith spun around to see who'd dare bother him. Fletcher, the young man he planned to train as his second in command, stepped past the threshold.

"Kazimir, I need to speak to you. It's urgent."

Furious, Keith shot Fletcher a look that caused the boy to wince as if he'd yelled. All of Fletcher's tall, sinewy frame flowed with catlike grace into the room. His black skin, hair, and eyes looked like a shadow against the stark walls. When Fletcher saw the hard expression on Keith's face, he took a step back.

The bloody knife he was holding sailed toward the table when Keith threw it. His face showed a menacing scowl at the unwanted intrusion.

"I told you not to call me that." He pinned his second-in-command with a look sharper than any knife he owned and he spoke with a perfect American accent. "We changed our names to fit in. It's Keith Davis. If you call me Kazimir Denisov again, I'll ship you to Russia in pieces. I did not have to save you when we met at that mass of confusion on the Equator. You would do well to remember that."

Keith went over to the table and shoved the radio back into the corner. He looked for the knife he'd thrown. When he couldn't find his blade, his fingers grasped his machete instead.

"I'm sorry, Keith. I'll remember in the future. Keith Davis." Fletcher nodded. He repeated the name a second time, but an uncomfortable silence finally won out and settled between the two men.

Keith scratched at his beard as he regarded his would-be second. The boy looked and acted nothing like him. Maybe he was wasting his time trying to mold him into someone useful.

He took a deep breath and decided to let the boy be for now. Even though Fletcher was in his early twenties, until the kid started behaving like an adult, Keith was going to consider him a child. He wouldn't explain again why they had to have new names since leaving the pandemonium on the Equator. If Fletcher still didn't understand that they'd lose everything they'd built because they weren't American, Canadian, or Mexican, then he'd never get it. Russia didn't have the building resources the old U.S. did, and he wasn't going to go back there to start all over. It would be terrible luck to be sent back.

Keith waited for Fletcher to tell him what was so urgent, but the boy's eyes were riveted on the blood pooling on the floor. He also waited to see if Feliks would remember he was supposed to go by Fletcher now. Feliks was close enough to Fletcher, so he couldn't understand why the kid couldn't remember it.

"Fletcher!" he snapped out when his patience ran out. "What the hell do you want?"

"Right, your daughter's here."

The silence which followed that statement was larger than the room itself.

Finally, Keith found his voice.

"That is not possible." Keith was so flabbergasted his fake American accent faltered. "You are mistaken." He stopped himself from swearing in Russian and regarded Fletcher.

The boy was back to looking at the blood seeping from the cut in his detainee's arm. His eyes were drinking in the sight like a thirsty traveler. Fletcher might one day be more than he could handle, but for now, Keith was happy Fletcher could embrace the shadier side of his business.

"Should I tell her to go? I didn't know you had a kid." Fletcher finally lifted his eyes to Keith's face. Across his features was a clear question of what to do. Keith reminded himself that Fletcher was young. For now, if he could control his temper, then maybe he wouldn't shoot him.

Keith smoothed his graying beard and flattened out his unruly hair. He didn't know why he was bothering to adjust his looks like a teenage boy insecure about his appearance. He gave up trying to tame the curly locks. This young woman probably wasn't his daughter anyway. He hadn't seen her in over a decade, and he doubted she could track him. A nagging thought clung to his brain. What if this kid was her? What would he do then? He was much too old for surprises.

"Send her to the adjoining office. Then leave us. And remember your name is Fletcher Davis. You are an underground builder. Try and be... what's the word... professional."

"My name is Fletcher Davis. I'm a builder," Fletcher repeated. "I can do professional." His hand went up to the design he'd shaved into the side of his head. His fingers ran over his scalp like he had thick hair. Keith was trying to take the kid seriously, but when dealing with his nonsense, it was close to impossible. Fletcher would never be able to run the legitimate side of the business, but he might one day become an excellent assassin. That's why he kept him around, at least for now.

As his would-be protégé vanished out the door, Keith took a moment to remember his first love, Marie. He'd only stayed married to her for a short time, but because of her, he'd moved to the United States right after the meteor hit. His life would probably be fairly different if they'd never met. That's what he called the luck of the draw.

Keith closed his eyes and considered their ridiculous whirlwind romance. Marie was a silly, optimistic woman. She never believed the planet would turn so cold so fast. During all of that was when his baby Klaudia was born.

"Do you think it is really her?" Keith looked at the man bleeding in the chair. The prisoner flinched when he heard Keith's voice. He shook his head as if answering.

Keith recalled the child vaguely. It was because of his little girl that he got roped into going to the United States. Marie wanted them to create an underground home for the kid. Everyone was constructing underground homes like some kind of fad. So many men headed to the heart of C.T.O.N.A. thinking they could survive the cold. Building underground homes back then wasn't as easy as now. When the construction started, most of the equipment was still above ground. They were all fools, Keith included.

"Keith?" Fletcher interrupted his thoughts when he ducked his head back in the door.

"What now?"

"She won't go to the offices. She says she wants to see you now. She used your real name." Fletcher looked like he was confessing a grave sin.

Keith turned his head toward the metal door that connected to his outer office. He tipped his head to the side as he considered whether this girl was really his child.

Keith could interrogate her. That was normally how he obtained information. Well, he *could* torture her, but he wasn't going to. His eyes went to the forgotten assassin in the chair. He might need his fillet knife. He looked around for his sharp weapon while he tried to decide how best to handle his current situation.

"How old is she?"

Fletcher paused. "I don't know. Younger than me, I guess."

If Keith was doing the math right, his child should be about seventeen. Marie had left him for some banker who had a spoiled little boy, Tad or Tom, he couldn't remember. Keith did recall that was about the time when Marie changed Klaudia to Karmen-Marie. His ex-wife had perverted her name so Klaudia would never be tainted by the kind of life he'd chosen to lead. Marie always believed he didn't have what it took to raise a baby girl. He agreed.

"Did she say her name was Karmen?"

"She told me to tell you her name was Klaudia." Fletcher was distracted again by the blood. Keith paid him little attention. Instead, he chuckled at his ex-wife. Marie thought changing his little girl's name would hide her from him.

"Is she a threat?" Fletcher asked suddenly, like the thought had just entered his head. "I could kill her."

Keith guffawed, but it was a dark sound. "I don't find a lost little girl a threat. If she was going to kill me, I doubt she'd walk in the front door and introduce herself."

Fletcher nodded.

"She said her parents died of radon poisoning. Maybe she's just confused as you said, lost. I'll just kick her out."

Keith had heard that Marie's banker took the first opportunity for a subterranean house. The fool led them both to their graves. Bankers knew nothing about radon poisoning underground.

As for his little girl, last he'd been informed, she was living with her uncle. He thought she was safe with Marie's brother.

"Wait. Did she say how she found me? How she knew my name?" Keith fired the questions at Fletcher before he turned to exit. In the kind of work he did now, it was good to never have anyone know his name. Keith had changed his name so many times that it was unlikely for her to have been able to track him down. If this were really his daughter, then he'd have to find out how she got here. Keith looked down at a bloody footprint. Maybe he didn't really care. Kill her or not kill her, that was really the only important question.

"She only said this area of underground building was underdeveloped. The ice on the surface of the planet made it hard to get here. She said she's not leaving until she sees you."

Keith nodded. In this area, the ice was also worsening, and housing was scarce. The wind generators on the surface weren't even built. In this region, they still used oil hauled from Canada, and big equipment was hard to operate.

"Go back. Tell her to wait in my office. I'll handle this myself." Keith gave a dismissive shake of his head. Fletcher gave him a curt nod in response, and then hurried back out the door. In his haste to do as he was told, he left the door slightly ajar.

If she'd honestly found him here by herself, Keith would be impressed. She'd be his kid to have that kind of ingenuity, tenacity, and grit. He appreciated grit almost as much as luck.

Keith hadn't even taken a single step to close the door when Fletcher's head popped back into his line of sight.

"Sir, she won't go to the office. She won't listen to me and… fuck… she's here." Fletcher's head disappeared for a second and then reappeared. She must be directly behind him. Keith thought for only a moment.

"At least I know she's smart. I wouldn't listen to you either." Keith reached for the door.

If it were his girl, this would be a good test. If it wasn't his kid, then he'd kill her. No loss. Afterward, Fletcher and he were going to have a *talk*.

"Fine, let her in." His hand gripped the doorknob, and he opened the door all the way. Its hinges protested like the barrier was trying to stop him. Keith looked down at the blood splatter on his pants and shirt. Let's see how much grit she has.

Before Fletcher could step aside, the boy stumbled and glared behind him. The young women who'd just stomped down the hall had used both hands to push his second-in-command to the right of the door. A pretty amazing feat as Fletcher clearly outweighed her by fifty pounds.

The expression on her face was a mixture of challenge and anger, and she had his dark brown eyes. There was no doubt in his mind. This was his child. She was a blend of familiar attributes of his ex-wife and himself, yet a stranger.

Her eyes went to the bleeding man in the chair, and she tossed her long dark ponytail over her shoulder. While staring at the blood on his clothes, she didn't say anything. Keith crossed his arms and absorbed the fact he was staring at his very grown-up little girl.

"I guess you go by Karmen-Marie now." He frowned. She appeared to have grit. "This looks like my luck of the draw." He spoke more to himself, but he was sure she caught his words. She curled her hands into fists. Maybe she thought he was going to kick her out, or maybe kill her. He wasn't sure either way. He had no idea why she'd be here. In his line of work, when people showed up surrounded by mystery, it was never a good thing.

Kicking her out was the best option. Even if she died in the snow, he didn't care. He didn't know how to raise a teenage girl, even one who wasn't squeamish when she saw blood. He could kill her, but that didn't sit well with him. What happened to her didn't matter, as long as she was gone.

"Fletcher, get rid of her." Keith inclined his head at the door.

Her eyes flashed. The girl's reaction told him she didn't like that command. Keith opened his mouth to clarify that when he said "get rid of" he didn't mean to have her killed.

Before he could explain to Fletcher, she took a belligerent step in his direction. Her glittering brown eyes stopped him from speaking. Her eyes reminded him of his when he was mad. She tipped her chin up, and her back stiffened ramrod straight. She was here, and she was staying, unless he killed her. He wasn't going to. Keith could read in her face that she knew she was safe too.

"I'm staying. Just try to get rid of me. You know what people say," she said defiantly. "What goes around comes around."

Chapter 2

His palms stung when they hit the cement floor. He could hear his father's large black army boots grind into the cement near his head.

"Get up."

Rea pushed with both hands and only made it to his knees. Pain was beating at him where his father's fist had just been. He forced back tears. His girlfriend was gone, his friend Eric had left, and his mom was dead. He didn't want to get up. Why bother when his dad would just knock him down again?

The blood in his mouth gathered over his tongue, and he spat some of it out. A mixture of saliva and blood clung to his lips. The tip of his father's boot crushed his fingers. Rea gritted his teeth. He wasn't going to cry or admit he was hurt. He was already a disappointment, and he wasn't going to add to it.

"Get up, fucking lazy piece of shit." Rea didn't have time to move. His father's foot met with his ribs. Air whooshed out of his lungs. "I told you to be at training at seven. You'll train with my old army squad, or I'll throw you out into the snow."

When his dad crouched next to him, Rea could feel his hot breath on his neck. "I wish you'd died in the Oil Wars instead of your brothers. If your mother were alive, she'd say you were worthless."

His father's voice was cold and calculating on that last sentence. He said it like it was a fact. Rea knew it was a lie. He had a unique ability he'd only ever told one person about. His father didn't know. Rea knew when someone was lying. He felt it in his gut. His mom would've been proud of him. Proud that he kept living every day when so much was gone. When the world was covered in ice, and so many people had died, she'd asked him to keep going. He was trying.

Blood decorated the cement floor of his bedroom. Rea pushed again with his hands and finally came to stand once more. His father stood in front of him and smiled. He crossed his arms over his massive chest, and the action pulled at the fabric of his army uniform.

"You're no fighter, Joseph-Rea MacBain, but you will be. By the way, today is a holiday. Happy Ice Year or some shit. I got you something."

Rea was more prepared this time. His father's huge, meaty fist came toward his face, and this time, he ducked. He stumbled forward and almost nose-dived into the little table next to his door. His balance was still off. That's what happened when you got hit in the face multiple times. Quickly, Rea used his tongue to check if he still had all his teeth.

After he had righted himself, he moved to the pathetic kitchen area of his bedroom. He looked for the best place to run. His dad was in front of the door that exited out into the underground base hallway. No escape there.

His father chuckled. "You look like someone fucked you up."

Rea refrained from saying anything. There was no point. When his mother died, his father had gone crazy. He was always a mean son of a bitch, but now he was truly out of his mind. His old army buddies couldn't see it, but Rea knew it was true. Maybe living underground is what had gotten to him.

"I got a surprise for you."

All the muscles in Rea's body poised to dash away. Those words were normally not a good omen. Last time his dad said that he'd told him his girlfriend had left. Rea pushed that heartbreak out of his mind. So what if she was gone? If she didn't care anymore, then neither did he. All he cared about was surviving his father until he could leave here too. Maybe she was smarter than he was. Nothing had stopped her from going. Not even him.

Rea's father turned away from him, and a tiny bit of the tension lifted from Rea's shoulders.

His father's massive six-foot frame lumbered over to the door that led out into the base they had built together.

He threw the wooden door open. Standing in the doorway was a skinny kid that had to be a few years younger than Rea—maybe fifteen or sixteen.

As the boy stood there, he trembled visibly and pushed his glasses up his nose. The action seemed like a nervous tic. He was also playing with the buttons on his huge knee-length down coat. His tan-colored hair matched the jacket exactly.

"This's Adam. Keep him out of my way. I've a meeting with the underground builders. I'll see you at seven, tomorrow."

Rea's father's harsh words accompanied his stomping to the door. The young boy paled, and his eyes went wide. Rea made a mad rush toward the boy and stepped between his father and Adam. The kid, maybe out of a sense of self-preservation, stooped behind Rea. His father's hand struck Rea upside the head before he strode out of the room.

Rea's shoulders slumped with relief at his father's exit. He felt like the air around him was easier to breathe without his dad around. He rubbed his ear where his father had hit him.

He didn't acknowledge Adam but instead lifted his palms to look at the scratches on his hands.

"You should wash your hands and clean the cuts."

Rea looked up. The boy had taken a few steps into the room and pushed up the big black rimmed glasses that were perched on his narrow nose.

"Whatever, Adam."

"My name's Gears. I don't go by Adam." The boy went over to the sink, and to Rea's amazement, took off his coat. He threw it over one of the chairs by the table. He was wearing another layer underneath. That jacket came off next. Rea gaped.

After the layers of fabric had been removed, Gears shook off a backpack that he'd hidden under them. The zipper on the first pouch was tugged down, and the kid produced a pink rag. He used the sink to wet it before coming over to stand directly in front of Rea.

"My dad just called you Adam," Rea pointed out when he recovered from the way Gears seemed to have made himself at home.

"Yeah, but I go by Gears. That's what my dad used to call me." Tears welled up in the boy's eyes, and Rea looked up at the ceiling, pretending like he didn't see it.

"You can call me Mac."

Rea stood perfectly still when Gears grabbed one of his hands. The kid began swabbing at his palms. When Rea got his shock under control, he tried to tug his hands away from Gears' grasp. The boy wasn't strong, but every time

Rea got his hand away, Gears snatched it back again. He wasn't a quitter, that's for sure.

Rea had the choice to either hit the other boy or give in.

He gave in.

"It's okay. Don't look worried. I'm a doctor. I'll have you fixed up in no time," Gears kept dabbing at the scraps on his palms.

Rea couldn't help the smile that kicked up one side of his face. He raised one eyebrow and kept his hand held out in front of him.

"A doctor, huh? Yeah, right. How old are you?"

Gears glared at him. "I'm fifteen, but I'm real smart."

"You couldn't be that smart if you ended up here."

"I'm here because my dad served with your father in the U.S. Army." Gears let go of his hand.

"There is no U.S. anymore. There is no army. All that is left is—" Rea abruptly stopped talking. Who cared? No one gave a shit anymore that the U.S. lost to Canada when the Canadians were the only ones left with oil. The war had been short. Canada had taken over Alaska; then the U.S. had fought to get it back. Everyone started to die when they couldn't last in the overwhelming cold. Canadians and Americans alike didn't make it. The ice didn't take sides.

Rea sighed. None of it mattered now. All that mattered was survival.

"I know that." Gears pushed his glasses up. "What I meant was before, when our parents were younger."

Rea nodded. "Okay."

He wasn't sure what he should do with this kid, but Rea was a problem solver. He figured he should find him a place to sleep. One of the areas of the base that wouldn't cave in. Underground living was hard in that regard. That was a good idea. Well, he would also warn him to stay out of his dad's way. He'd have to make sure he was safe until he got the hang of living on the base. Rea figured he could keep an eye on him until he found a new place to live. Everyone he met moved on, and this boy would be no different. He'd just help him out until he was ready to find a new home.

"My parents are dead. My mom was killed in an avalanche and my dad died in the Oil Wars."

Rea stared. He hadn't asked, but Gears seemed hell-bent on sharing with him.

"A lot of people died," Rea responded. He wasn't sure what he was supposed to say. He was never good at dealing with people's feelings. Sometimes the right words eluded him.

Gears frowned. He placed his backpack on the center of Rea's bed on the other side of the room. He began rummaging in the many pockets. He then went over to Rea's fridge and got out ice.

"You're probably in a bad mood because you don't feel good. I know I'm not in the mood to talk when I'm feeling under the weather."

Gears handed him the ice and gestured toward Rea's face. Rea took a deep breath and didn't even try to hide his amusement. He slapped the ice to his fat lip. Who even said "under the weather" anymore? That was funny and odd all at the same time. What was up with this kid?

"I came here after the UN asked for a treaty," Gears tossed that out as he walked back over to his backpack. "I told your dad I could make clean drinking water for the base. I'm going to stay and do that."

"Okay."

Gears didn't look up at him. Rea figured he missed the crystal clear look of confusion he shot at him. How did someone make water? What was wrong with the water they had? Was it not clean? Rea guessed that if he asked these questions Gears would be here all night explaining it to him.

He shrugged. It wouldn't be so bad to have Gears around. He could keep him company for a short while. Rea was alone most of the time, so a few hours of someone to talk to would be okay with him.

Gears unzipped a side pocket of his bag. He pulled out what looked like small brown bandages. Rea studied the tiny adhesive rectangles. He hadn't seen those since he was a child.

After the meteor had hit Earth, medical supplies had become scarce. Only a few brave men were willing to scour the surface for items to retrieve out of the ice. Just after his father and an underground construction company had begun to build this base, that was maybe the last time he'd seen anything as simple as a Band-Aid. His mother used to give him a Band-Aid when he was little.

Gears took out a round bottle of rubbing alcohol next.

"I don't need that." Rea had the urge to back away, but he wasn't a coward. He could handle one nerdy boy playing doctor. Besides, it had been a long time since anyone had tried to help him. The last person who'd wanted to help him had left him when he needed her most.

Forget it. He was stronger now. Strong enough to forget her.

"Yes, you do. If this gets infected it will get yucky." Gears poured some of the clear liquid on a cotton ball. He then took Rea's ice pack out of his hand.

"Yucky? Is that a fancy medical term, Doctor?"

Gears laughed. "Yes, it is. And I'm not only a doctor. I'm a scientist too."

Rea bit his tongue from the sting when Gears began wiping his hands. Even with his eyes watering from the pain, Gears made him smile.

"I'm going to make sure all the men around here have clean drinking water, and I'm going to care for people," Gears spoke to Rea's hands while he cleaned them. "My dad told me once that one day we'd need someone like me. I'm always helping. I know a lot of things."

Rea wanted to say that he doubted very much if this guy knew anything, but he didn't. He just listened. He figured this boy needed someone to talk to. Gears was younger than him, and his parents had died. The boy needed him. Rea wasn't going to admit he needed a friend too.

Tomorrow he'd get him settled on the base and just keep an eye on him until he left. It was the right thing to do. His mom would be proud of him for that.

Chapter 3

11 Years Later...

"Damn, my luck is running low today," Karma muttered as her phone slipped out of her hand. It sank into the oil-filled ocean water lapping against her small one-man inflatable boat.

"You'd think the residents would give a fuck about Florida. No wonder no one lives here."

Swearing silently, she dug out another phone and typed in the current year, Ice Year Twelve, and the time. It was 1:05 a.m. The phone took a few minutes to connect to the nearest cell tower that was working. When all the things on the screen looked right, she tied off her boat. Satisfied her new cell would update, she shoved it into the hidden pocket of her black one-piece body suit. She pushed the worn green sack onto her back as she climbed up through the hole in the floor above her to her temporary hideout.

As soon as she was inside the forgotten seaside bungalow, she paused. Her hands carefully removed her pack, and she found a safe place to set it down. She checked her cell again. Her phone was loading all her information.

She breathed a sigh of relief that her phone was still working here in Florida. As she moved on, it would be out of service because of the ice knocking down yet another service tower. She glanced down at the blinking screen. She'd use the cell for as long as she could, but she'd have to trash it before leaving her decaying ocean lair.

After she'd pocketed her phone a second time, she looked around the small damp room she'd just entered. Her eyes accepted the darkness like it was daytime. It was a strange gift, an added ability, but she never questioned it. Instead, in the dark, she was simply pleased that she could double-check all entrances were safe, and all her traps were still in place.

When she finally completed her task, she picked up her bag. She proceeded down the narrow hall to what some would've once called the kitchen. When she reached the small, moldy room, she dumped her bag of canned food on a short metal table. She then looked around for her stepbrother.

It had been one month since Tad had appeared on her doorstep. She had to admit it was so far so good. That's what made her nervous. She was waiting for everything to fall apart. When it came to her wayward sibling, trouble was always something to expect.

When Tad was nowhere to be found, she headed to the main living space of the dilapidated house.

As she entered the living room, the building swayed. The structure had long ago become a dangerous place to be in, which was precisely why she liked it. The house was once a fancy place for the rich on a beautiful coast near the ocean. Now, it was on worn stilts above the murky black water. This was no place anyone would venture, which meant no one would come looking for her here.

Karma found her favorite seat situated over a decent place on the floor. The chair looked inviting, and she sank down on to the cushion. She hadn't slept in two days, so the idea of some well-deserved rest was too tempting to pass up. She'd look for Tad later, and she hoped he hadn't gotten into trouble wherever he was.

Her eyes drifted shut. She relaxed, thinking all was secure for the moment.

A scratching noise drew her attention only seconds after she had closed her eyes.

Karma rose, gliding through the hallway, making sure to stay on safe patches of tiles. Her small, lightweight form moved like a dancer, hopping gracefully from safe hardwood to reliable carpet.

She'd never fallen through the rotted floor, but the idea of being dumped into the disgusting water below didn't appeal to her. She wasn't even sure she'd be able to swim in the swill.

Karma moved swiftly. She constantly scanned the area, looking for the noise that had stalled her sleep. As soon as she came upon him, she almost stumbled and lost her balance. Her eyes rested on her stepbrother's battered form. Sadly, nothing about this situation shocked her.

She was almost pleased Tad was so beaten. The odd angle of his arm prevented him from climbing up from his boat into the house. He was trying to pull himself up on the stilts, and failing. If he'd advanced, he'd have set off one of her traps and a smoke bomb. As it was, with his arm broken at his side, he was struggling to lift his body.

Karma quickly dismantled anything that would harm him. She reached down to help him from his boat through the rotting hole. She left his rickety wooden raft in the water and took on as much of his weight as she could. Tad was a skinny man, so she didn't have to fight under his weight. For now, she ignored her own exhaustion.

"Tad, what the hell did you do? You've got the worst luck in the world, you know that?"

The words slipped from her lips before she could stop them. She ushered him into the chair she'd just vacated.

"I really have done it, Sis." Tad gave a shrug with his good shoulder. He winced, but Karma didn't feel bad for him.

"You only call me 'Sis' when you're about to tell me something that's really going to piss me off. Tad, eventually, you're gonna have to grow up. You threw away every cent your father left you, and now what? You think I'm going to help you forever? I can't even help myself," Karma spoke angrily while she located her first-aid kit. "I thought you came to me to get your shit together. That's the speech I remember getting."

Karma didn't wait for a response to her diatribe. Instead, she started mending Tad's shoulder as best she could. She didn't really expect an answer. Tad was spoiled and selfish. He'd end up giving her a line of excuses she didn't want anyway. Besides, what Tad did with his life wasn't really any concern of hers. She wasn't his keeper, and she wouldn't want the job even if it were offered.

"I need money, Karmen-Marie. This might be over my head."

Karma's head snapped up. She looked more closely at her stepbrother. He always asked her for money, but the way he was asking now made her pause. She could see him perfectly in the dark. His features were twisted in pure fear.

"Over your head?" she asked quietly while she used a bandage to close a particularly ugly cut. Tad grimaced, but she assumed his scrunched-up face was caused more by the idea of talking to her than the actual injury.

"I was so bored sitting around here. I know you said it wasn't safe to go exploring, but I didn't see anything around here to be worried about. Besides, you know how I get. I can't just sit around like you."

"So?" Karma asked when Tad paused.

"So I went out for a while. Then I ran into a friend of mine. It's a guy I knew a while back. He's cool."

Karma knew Tad had no friends, so the person he was referring to must've been a drug dealer or a thief. Not the best of company, but who was she to judge. Even with the knowledge this guy was probably bad news, she refrained from saying anything. Karma was afraid Tad wouldn't continue, and she needed to know what kind of mess he'd made. She should never have expected Tad to be able to wait here for her. What had she been thinking? Oh yeah, she remembered what she had been thinking. She had thought it'd be nice to get food.

"My friend and I, we started partying at a place which he said was on the level. He knew I didn't have any money. He didn't care. We were having a good time, but then I guess I blacked out. I don't remember some of it. When I woke up, I was at another guy's house. We were playing poker…"

"Let me get this right. You got stoned. You passed out. Then you began playing poker with strangers? And at some point, you thought 'what a great idea?' Tad I swear, this is the stupidest thing I've—"

Tad cut her off before she could finish. "I was having a good time," he whined.

"You're a terrible poker player. And a stupid drunk. Are you out of your mind?" Karma barely refrained from slapping him.

"I know." Tad actually seemed a tiny bit contrite, which cooled her temper.

"Is that it?"

"No," Tad muttered miserably. "I pissed someone off. Then I remember some guy saying I owed him money. He beat the shit out of me."

"This can't be the first time that's happened," Karma responded dryly.

It was becoming incredibly difficult to care about Tad as this story continued, but Karma promised herself she'd listen and stop interrupting. She needed to know everything. If Tad had told someone about her, or if someone saw where they lived, it would mean it was time to get moving.

"Aww, come on, Sis. I was having a good time."

That was it. His perpetual "I was having a good time." Karma gave an exasperated exhale. He probably deserved his beating, yet no matter how much he received, his "good time" was always more important. Why was she patching him up? She was wasting her time and her luck with him.

Karma decided it was time she removed herself from her stepbrother's life. She'd let him make it, or not, by himself. She'd take care of whatever he needed one last time, and then cut him loose. Besides, she was tired of living in a house suspended above stinking water. If she moved on, she'd have to do it alone. It was safer that way. Being alone was safer even if it was lonely.

"Let's start with how much you need, and who do I pay?"

"Me," a deep voice spoke from behind her.

The hair on the back of Karma's neck stood on end at that distinct sound. A voice that was chillingly familiar.

She straightened her spine slowly and turned around to face her enemy. It was a real testament to how tired she was that she not only hadn't heard him and his cohorts approach, but she'd also forgotten to hide the boat and reset the traps. She was kicking herself for her brainless actions, but she figured she didn't have time to dwell on her mistakes.

Karma regarded the two men standing next to the tall figure in the center of the doorway. She eyed the shorter men speculatively. They weren't her immediate threat. She then turned her full attention on Fletcher.

Fletcher Davis was as perfect as always. He was exactly as she remembered him when she left. He was tall and elegant with unblemished black skin and beautiful straight white teeth.

Carefully, Karma inched her hand toward the gun that was nestled along her spine. Fletcher gave her a bright smile because he had her trapped. There was no point in pretending otherwise. He moved with casual grace an inch closer. Karma continued to watch him warily. She'd always thought it was a shame that a man with the face of an angel had the soul of the devil.

Fletcher flashed another mock smile and slapped at his dark chocolate-colored skin as if to kill a bug. It was to show her what he thought of where she'd ended up. Karma was again reminded of how immaculate he was. She must look like a lost waif from the Mexican border.

"Really, Karma, I'm stunned to see you living here. You truly must be in love to stay in such trash." Fletcher's eyes raked her stepbrother and then moved back to her. "I guess some people truly do get what they deserve, but I'm sure you've heard that before. What goes around comes around, right?"

The smile drained from his face. He ran his right hand through his short, shiny black hair. Karma recognized that action. She glided skillfully in front of Tad. She waited for Fletcher's next maneuver, which was always the same. Now he'd pull out his weapon.

Karma didn't have to wait long. She pulled her own handgun almost as fast, but still found herself looking down the barrel of Fletcher's .45. She kept her hand steady and tightened her grip on her own .22 Magnum revolver. The other men in the room also produced their own weapons, but she dismissed them. She kept her focus on Fletcher.

"You know, you're getting awfully repetitive in your old age. You should learn some new moves."

Fletcher smirked. He lowered his gun from pointing at her forehead to aiming at her middle. It was better than before. Her barb at his age had the effect she wanted. He was only thirty-four, but she always pointed out he was older than her, even if it was only a handful of years. She had to keep him off balance while she came up with an escape plan.

"You don't like my moves? I can solve that. The position by my side still happens to be open. You could come back to me and teach me all the moves you want. I always did think it was a shame that you and I weren't fucking. I know your dad would've loved to have us together." Fletcher paused. "We could've ruled the world," he added.

Comments like that infuriated her like nothing else could.

"You don't know anything about my father, so don't even try to pretend with me. You only ever wanted me because you wanted to control the family. I was your ticket to controlling The Seemyah."

Karma spat the words, forgetting for a second her precarious position. She cursed herself silently for her rash comments, but she didn't backpedal. Instead, she drew her other Smith & Wesson from the holster on her thigh. She aimed it at the blond inching his way closer to her from the left.

"Ruling the world and The Seemyah are the same thing, or don't you remember?" Fletcher taunted. He must've loved that he'd agitated her.

"Enough, Fletcher, what does my stepbrother owe you? I'll pay you. Then you can get the hell out." Karma couldn't believe she was about to pay this handsome piece of shit any of her money, but she had decided to save Tad's ass one last time. For what it was worth, she figured of all the times his butt needed to be rescued, it was now.

"I don't know, Kar." Fletcher acted like he was contemplating what she said. He slapped at his skin again. "Your money might not be good enough for me. Besides, I'm not buying this whole 'save the brother' angle you're trying to feed me." Karma saw Fletcher gesture to one of the men to take a step closer to Tad.

"Stepbrother," she corrected.

Fletcher continued like he hadn't heard her. "I'll say your bleeding *stepbrother* here finally gave me a way to find you. I'll give him that much. I've been searching for you for over a year now. You could elude The Seemyah, but not me."

He practically sang the last of his words, and it caused dread to fill her, Karma hid her reaction. It did gall her that Fletcher had found her, but she couldn't put the blame squarely on Tad's shoulders. It was long past the time to move on. She hadn't heeded the voice in her head that always protected her. She'd used up all her luck staying here.

Karma made a sweeping motion with her arm. The blond surfer guy moved back from Tad. She regarded Fletcher once more. His black eyes looked like pools of oil. Maybe she should choose her next words more wisely.

"Keeping in mind that I'm not for sale, what's it you want in exchange for my stepbrother's debt to you? The one you claim he has."

"I'm working for someone currently, and your brother is simply the answer to a problem."

The words shot through Karma's skull at a lightning pace. If Fletcher was working for someone outside The Seemyah, it could only mean trouble. What game was he playing? She shouldn't dwell on the past, but she wished she'd stayed hidden. This kind of shit was exactly why she left The Seemyah in the first place. She no longer wanted to live a life always wondering if she was going to live or die. What was wrong with wanting a normal life?

Irritation bubbled up inside of her. She wanted to be left alone. Not trusting Fletcher had become an art form, yet somehow she was going to be dragged into his crap again.

"If you took a job outside The Seemyah, then they'll kill you. It'll save me the trouble."

Fletcher chuckled.

"I liked the work in The Seemyah, but like all people, I have a price. I can see by your defense of this man you seem to have a price also."

Karma's eyes jumped to Fletcher and then to his surfer boys. She tried to see beyond the room to the third man who'd be waiting in the hallway. Fletcher always worked the same. He never traveled alone, and he always had a backup plan. There was always a third man waiting for a perfect time to ambush.

"What do you want? What're we talking about here?" she asked impatiently.

"I have an offer for you," Fletcher spoke absently, but he wasn't bluffing well. What he was about to say was important. "I took a job outside the family, and I'm finding it hard to accomplish on my own. If you manage a simple target, I'll walk away from your brother—"

"Stepbrother," she corrected.

"No monetary exchange. I can even promise you I'll never tell the family where I found you. You can believe me when I say, after I leave here, The Seemyah will have bigger problems than looking for you anyway."

For the first time since all this began, Karma heard her stepbrother stir behind her. Tad seemed to understand some of the exchange. She'd never told him about her life, that was true, but then again, he'd never asked. Her life choices weren't a topic she'd wanted to share anyhow. He probably only had a vague memory of her as a child. She'd never told him she'd become Karma, a cold-blooded murderer. They hadn't seen each other much in all these years.

Tad's voice came out thin and wispy from behind her. "What does he want you to do, and what's a Seemyah?"

Even if those were the only two things he asked, Karma could feel the barrage of other questions behind them.

For the hundredth time in the last month, she wished Tad wasn't around. It wasn't like she had to defend her choices to him, or anyone for that matter. At the same time, Karma really didn't want to discuss this in front of Fletcher. Her decision to live with her father and embrace the life of an assassin wasn't a topic she ever wished to discuss, actually. She'd paid the price to be with her dad, and well, what goes around comes around. She did deserve the life she had. If her father were still alive, he'd have said it was the luck of the draw.

Sighing with resignation, Karma chose to explain even though she wasn't inclined. The only reason she made up her mind to talk was to show him she didn't care what he thought of her. She didn't care if Tad judged her. After they had parted ways, she didn't plan on seeing him again.

"Fletcher is currently a freelance killer. For some reason, he's being a baby about a job. Seemyah was my father's word for family, and it's what my dad called all of us who worked together. It's some sort of Russian-American word he made up. Anyway, in exchange for your life, Fletcher wants me to take out a target that he and his men can't seem to get," Karma said the words bluntly. She waited for some dramatic response from her stepbrother. She might as well tell him what was going on. Besides, unless she made a deal, they'd both be dead soon, anyway. Her body suit was made of durable material, but the fabric wouldn't be able to stand up to four men unloading their full magazines at close range.

Tad's sharp intake of breath told her he understood, but to her shock, he remained silent. Karma never took her eyes off her opponent. Instead, she decided to get some details. She really didn't want to take the job, but it looked like she didn't have a choice.

Since her father died and she'd left The Seemyah, she hadn't killed anyone, and she liked it that way. She wanted her freedom. Why Fletcher had decided to seek her out was strange. Maybe he came to her because he couldn't go back to The Seemyah. When she left, no one was willing to give their allegiance to Fletcher, especially since she refused to marry him. A rumor was out that it was Fletcher who'd killed her father. Those whispers had been the second driving force to have him ousted. Was he still working for them? She really didn't know for sure either way.

"Suppose I take the job. Who's the hit and how much time do I have?"

"The target is some crazy recluse who lives in one of the Northern Earth Dens. He's in an area of the ex-United

States that's still partly accessible from the surface. And as for time—I'm afraid my boys wasted a lot of it. You only have three days. I want you to check in with me. I need confirmation by 1:00 a.m. That gives me time to contact the client." Fletcher paused. "We couldn't get into his place. It's harder than I thought." Fletcher appeared slightly embarrassed. Normally, she'd have made fun of him for that, but because of the timeline, she was reeling instead.

"You can't be serious. I've recon to do, weapons to get, and logistics. Three days, my ass."

Fletcher's laugh nauseated her. Karma had never before wanted to shoot someone as badly as she wanted to kill him.

"I've the entire job set up. I'll download all the information to your cell, and you can go over it on your trip there. Your phone will work until you get to the old Texas area. Once you get to Dallas, the snow and ice will get thick. Your phone will become a paperweight. My boat is waiting, and I have all the ins and outs set up. All you have to do is go there and do what you do best. Kill people."

Karma hated when he sounded smug. She also hated that it was true. She was good at killing people. After this, she was going to go somewhere and never be tied to anyone or anything again. She'd get a job she actually wanted. Maybe she could get a nice relaxing hobby too. Well, maybe she'd kill Fletcher first, but then she really was quitting.

"I don't like prepackaged murder. I work alone. You of all people know that. I can't trust your info or the fact you supposedly left The Seemyah. Besides, has it occurred to you maybe I don't kill people anymore?"

"As for The Seemyah, I've no ties to the family anymore. When I couldn't have you, I couldn't have them.

And you don't have to kill anyone if you don't want to." Fletcher's voice turned soft, and he took a step back from her. "Here are your options. We have a gun fight right here, right now, and you'll probably escape, and you can probably hide again, but I can guarantee you that your so-called brother here will die."

Tad gasped. She had the urge to shush him.

"Or you can do this job for me," Fletcher continued. "And, when you're all done, you can both walk away alive."

Karma took a quick glance at Tad sitting behind her. His face was swollen and his arm looked horribly twisted. He didn't look good. She remembered how her mother got all excited when she found out she'd finally have a little boy to love. Her mother had loved her shiny new husband, and his boy, from the moment they met. For her mother, she figured she could risk her life to save Tad. It was the least she could do to make up for some of the mistakes she'd made. There hadn't been a lot of love between Tad and her over the years, but after all this time, she could do this for him. She'd risked her life for a hell of a lot less noble reasons.

"Fine," Karma sighed. "I'll give you my cell, and you can download the specifics, but while I'm gone, I don't want one hair on his head disturbed. Got that?"

Karma eyed Fletcher while she put her one gun back into the holster on her thigh. She then tossed her phone to him. He caught it with an easy sweep of his arm and finally put his weapon away. Once his gun was no longer pointed at her, his disciples followed suit.

As Fletcher took out his phone and started to download information at a snail's pace, she put her other weapon back in the pocket at the base of her spine. Since the ice seemed to have damaged everything beyond the Equator, the towers and the satellites were slow.

When Fletcher finally finished with her phone, he threw the cell back to her, and she caught it. She looked down at the information and swore.

"The mark is on a water treatment compound underground? Those places are fortresses!"

"I told you it was in the NEDs. Northern Earth Dens are underground. You know that." Fletcher picked a piece of lint off his coat and didn't look at her.

Karma shook her head. "Dad used to say the guy who runs them is out of his mind. I saw those bases once a long time ago. They're a maze. They say that man was military trained, and better armed than the U.S. Army was before it was disbanded. This is a suicide mission. You're setting me up."

"I thought you said my men and I were babies."

"It's a setup by The Seemyah because I left and didn't take my father's position when he died. You and The Seemyah just want to see me die so I never cause problems."

"If I wanted to see you die, I'd kill you right now, and I don't want The Seemyah anymore. I want something better. Anyway, the story is there's an old guy who's building water treatment bases all over the C.T.O.N.A. The Canadian government lets him because without him we'd have no clean drinking water. The Canadian government is all about the water bases in the NEDs because they're part of the whole rebuild-and-survive initiative."

"Don't bullshit me, Fletcher. Canada has been running the old U.S. and Mexico since we lost in the Oil War. They've no reason to try rebuilding anything in the C.T.O.N.A. They like everything the way it is, and water treatment plants are a necessity. Everyone dies without water, ex-Americans, ex-Mexicans, Canadians, everyone. Besides, it's not new information that water bases have been appearing. They're the only safe places to live. People are flocking to them. They're going to be underground cities one day."

Karma glanced again at her phone and read the first name that appeared on the screen. It was only one word— Mac. She considered the name. It seemed familiar, but she couldn't place it. When nothing came to her, she went to study his stats. Every line was blank.

"What the hell, Fletcher? You've got nothing on Mac? And who are these other guys that you sent me info on?"

"I forgot how annoying you are to work with. Scroll down and you'll see the two men that need to be left alone. There can be no mistakes and no accidents. Mac dies, and the other two will be left for me to handle. Besides, Bennett isn't even on the base. He travels a lot. Just take care of Mac."

Karma gave Fletcher a curt nod and kept reading. She was a professional, so it was completely offensive that Fletcher would even imply she'd make a mess. She didn't comment on the insult and instead looked at the next name. The next one also had a familiar ring. Eric Bennett. This young man had pages of data. He was a thirty-one-year-old wealthy heir with a house on the Equator, and that was the first thing she noticed. Only the super-rich could afford a house above ground in the last remaining areas with no surface ice. If this guy had so much money, why would he be hanging out in a frozen country like the C.T.O.N.A.? Why would he be in the NEDs? The Northern Earth Dens weren't the safest places to be unless you were on an already established water base. This didn't make any sense. Was Bennett the client? Was that why he was trying to make sure that he was safe while the hit went down? Why did his name seem familiar? Maybe she'd worked for him on another job.

Karma's inner voice screamed setup again, even though she didn't say it out loud. There seemed to be too many pieces to this puzzle. If her dad were here, he'd deal her into a hand of poker and tell her to check her luck.

"I want Mac dead. I just found out he's building a new compound. A new compound should be easy to get into. When it's still under construction, it's weaker. I'm sure someone as good as you will have no problems. Just check in when you're done."

"At one?" Karma replied distractedly. Already her head was filling with her plan to get into the base. She'd need a few items.

Fletcher shrugged. "For you, princess, since we've such history, how about I give you an extra five minutes. 1:05 a.m."

"I don't give a shit about the time. I'll be done with it long before that. Just keep your fists off Tad while I'm gone."

"Your brother will stay with us. If things don't go well, let's just say it won't be pretty. I'll send you a picture."

"Stepbrother," she sighed. "And after this, I'm out, Fletcher. I mean it. I'm not killing anyone else. I left The Seemyah. I'm free to do whatever I want." After her confident statement, Karma realized that might not be entirely accurate.

"Yeah, right, whatever you say," Fletcher responded, unfazed. He flashed another one of his dazzling smiles.

Karma glared and started grabbing her extra weapons. She studied her frightened stepbrother and then made sure to find her deck of cards. She didn't deal herself a hand. She didn't see the point. She was going to do the job, and she hoped after she was done maybe, just perhaps, she could change her luck.

Chapter 4

"Mr. MacBain." Brice, one of Rea's water base guards, caught up to him as he strode down the hallway. "Doctor Gears is here to see you."

Rea stopped walking and ran his hand through his red hair, making it stand on end. All these new guys Ken hired were idiots. He swore they were always trying to dodge work.

"Just call me Mac." Rea shook his head at the young man. "And the name's just Gears, not Doctor Gears. Go back to Ken and do something useful."

Man, it was a good thing none of these men knew his full name; otherwise, who knew what they'd end up calling him. Right now, most of them had a hard time remembering Mac. If they knew his full name was Joseph-Rea MacBain, all their heads might explode.

Gears appeared behind the lanky guard and gave him a sideways smile. He was wearing so many coats the pile of fabric made his friend's head look tiny. Gears chuckled at Rea's response. Rea didn't think the men he had on his water base were amusing.

After Gears had fallen into step next to him, Rea gave a glance to the doctor. Gears pushed his large glasses up his skinny nose.

"I'm not going to bother giving Brice orders." Rea didn't add that there was no point. The water base guards loved to agree with his directions; then later he'd find them on the opposite side of the base with no explanation of what they were doing. Their antics were enough to make him want to scream. He'd fire them all, but the idea of starting all over with a new batch of men was depressing.

Gears nodded and began to take off a pair of heavy wool gloves. His friend regarded him thoughtfully.

"Ken assures me that these are the best men for training. I know what you're going to say."

"What I was going to say involves more swear words than you'd be willing to listen to."

Gears shrugged. "I was looking for you because I wanted to talk." From one of his many coat pockets, his friend pulled out a map. "I came to tell you the building of this water base is almost done. The skylights have been added. All the major construction men have moved on to start a new base. The electricians, plumbers, and earth movers are gone."

Rea frowned. This wasn't new information. He didn't even look at the map. Why was Gears really here? Gears was the doctor for the water base and a brilliant scientist. Construction wasn't normally a subject he cared to review. When Rea didn't respond, Gears went on.

"Our facility is up against the ocean here. The building's part above ground and part below." Gears gestured with a wave of his right hand.

Rea's green eyes scanned his only friend as they passed the training hall. Up ahead of them he could vaguely hear men eating and the general horseplay in the mess hall.

He wanted to say he didn't care, but instead he held his tongue. If Gears wanted to talk about the state of his water base, then fine, he'd listen.

"This place is built solid and will be easy to defend when it's up and running." Gears tipped his head toward some of the sleeping quarters as they continued to walk. "Everything here should be ready to go by now. Setting up water bases doesn't typically take this long. If your dad was still alive…" He smoothed the corner of the map as he trailed off.

After a moment of awkward silence, Gears pulled out a stack of papers from the backpack on his shoulder. Rea had to stop while Gears struggled to free the papers from being caught in the zipper. He slapped what appeared to be a list of men's names at his chest.

Rea barely looked at the documents. Instead, he began moving again. His feet picked up his pace. He was tired. He wanted to get to his room and just sleep for a while.

"Get to the point."

"These guys can be trained. Then we can hand the base over to Miller if you like that idea. Miller is still resting after he broke his leg, but his rehabilitation is almost complete. If Ken helps him, the base could run smoothly. Then you can do whatever you want."

"I know," Rea responded as he shoved his hands again through his bright-red hair.

"Mac, I don't think you do know. Gears put his hand out and stopped him from moving forward. Rea was forced to look at his friend. "You don't have to stay here after this is built. I'm not trying to keep you here. I know you think you're responsible for me, but I'm a grown adult. I don't understand why you're dragging your feet. I thought you wanted to leave." Gears nodded his head, and his short sandy-blond hair didn't move an inch.

"I do want to leave."

"So finish the base and go if you like."

At times like now, Rea was pleased his friend was around to hound him. Right now, he was floundering. Rea wasn't struggling because he didn't know how to get a base operational. He'd done that many times when his father was alive. Hell, he'd even created two bases after his father died, but right now, he was struggling because he just didn't know what he was going to do when the building was finished. Rea was honest enough with himself to face that he didn't want to be doing this kind of work any longer. He didn't think someone like Gears could understand, so he didn't try to explain more. Gears liked his work, his home, and he wouldn't grasp wanting a different life.

"These new guys could be decent if they'd stop screwing around. I think they stay up all night." Rea exhaled.

He looked at Gears and realized talking to him did nothing to temper his frustration. Training men was so dissatisfying. One day he was going to do something else, anything else. His father was no longer alive to keep him beaten down. Soon he was going to do something with his life besides telling idiots what to do. Maybe he'd try having a room where he could unpack. That'd be a novel idea.

He thought about his sparse living quarters. He tried to picture the space with real furniture. He couldn't see it.

Rea shrugged off the thoughts and began walking again. Gears continued to trail him as he rounded the corner past a large cement column.

"These are the guys we have right now, but they'll improve. I have to go back to the lab and continue working on the new drug I told you about. I know God will help you find your way. You're a better man than your father. These men will give you loyalty. They'll improve."

"I think I liked you better when you were an atheist. You were less idiotically cheerful," Rea muttered.

"Very amusing. I don't plan on going to hell. You should pray more. God will help you when you can't find your way." Gears pulled on a skullcap over his tan hair. His bright-blue eyes narrowed. Clearly, he wasn't joking. His glasses slipped down, and he pushed them up again.

"Screw praying more. I'm looking forward to going to hell. At least it's warm there."

"Don't joke about that," Gears scolded. Rea could tell he was getting under Gears' skin when he scolded him like he were a naughty child. His sharp retort made him smile.

"You know, you're the only scientist I know who believes in God and the afterlife," Rea added.

"I don't think one cancels out the other. Besides, when you live every day with the chance of running out of food or freezing to death, it's only a matter of time before you have to have some kind of faith in something."

Rea didn't have a good response to the whole faith thing. Right now he had belief in nothing, not even in himself.

Out of the corner of his eye, Rea saw Gears shove his map back into his coat. He considered the training issues as his friend adjusted his backpack. He couldn't ask Gears to drop what he was doing to help him find better men. As their doctor, Gears had men he cared for on the base. He was also making sure everything was going to be ready in the water treatment area.

Besides, Rea really didn't need Gears' help to get the men ready. He could prepare them by himself; he simply didn't want to. Rea was usually a problem solver. He didn't typically need so much time to mull over issues. Normally, training was a quick and smooth task. Gears wasn't going to be sympathetic to his hesitation.

Rea was getting more and more pressure to finish this base, and he knew why. His friend had a woman waiting for him. Gears wanted to settle down with her. Maybe a girl was what Rea needed. He could have a home base with a woman. A home was never a thing he had. His life was to simply create the base, train men, and then move on. In the past, all he had was a dysfunctional relationship with his abusive father and continuous work.

They reached Rea's bedroom. He stopped at his door and realized Gears was putting his gloves back on. The way Gears dressed, Rea would've thought he was heading to the surface instead of back to his lab. The water base hallways weren't that cold. His lab wasn't on the other side of Canada.

"Wish me luck. Tomorrow, I'm going to the training ring to see if any of these morons know their head from their ass," Rea grumbled as Gears turned to go.

"You, Mac, need faith and a little luck. We all do." He grinned. "If you get the base up and running, then you'll get everything figured out. I know you will. You don't need your father."

Gears left on that parting sentence. He shuffled off toward the greenhouses.

As Gears departed, Rea considered what he'd said. He was grateful Gears was trying to keep the base on schedule. Some days their friendship was his rock, but Gears didn't understand. Rea's problems had nothing to do with his father dying. Hell, he'd practically jumped for joy when he watched the body getting incinerated. No, he didn't need his father and all the pain and humiliation to get him moving. What he needed right now was… he didn't know.

Rea opened the door to his room. As he entered, he glanced around his sparse efficiency kitchen and the worn wood table by the door. Right now he needed to focus on getting the base done. Then he'd have time to decide what he wanted for his life.

He scanned the list of names Gears had given him. He had to come up with a better training program for these men, or he'd never be able to open the base.

The papers were tossed haphazardly onto his table. He could put together a base with his eyes closed and both hands tied behind his back. Already, he had the greenhouses running. The goats and chickens had arrived with no difficulty. He even had some surface harvesters working on collecting household items from the ice to enhance the place. The base was only missing men to be trained as a police force. The scientists who worked in the water treatment areas wouldn't come until the base was completely safe. From his past experience, he understood most of the workers had families. The layout was the same at all the other bases. Until everything was done, he was stuck here.

Rea threw himself down on his bed near the far side of the room. He wished he had someone to talk to about his future plans. He thought about the few men he'd trained over the years. None of them he considered friends. Men that he liked and respected had moved on to other bases. They were spread out over the NEDs. They all had families now, too.

Rea stared unblinkingly at the ceiling fan spinning above him. He wanted a home to come to, and he wanted to not always be working. Always working is what his dad ended up doing. After his mom had died, his father worked himself into his grave and forced Rea to join him. His dad had only cared about the men he'd served with in the U.S. Army and his old squad. That wasn't going to be the rest of Rea's life, if he could help it.

"Can I come in? I did knock, but I don't think you heard me."

Rea sat up in surprise, and then rose to his feet.

"Holy shit, Eric. I haven't seen you in years," Rea exclaimed as his old friend passed the threshold.

As Rea stood, for a second he could see the young boy he once knew. It had been years now, and time had taken its toll, but Eric was still a large, commanding figure. Eric took a few steps into the room, and Rea studied his slightly rounded belly. Gray hair now dusted his thick black mane. Stress must have aged his friend. The world was no longer a soft place to live in.

"I'm amazed you recognized me. It's been a long time. I think the last time we saw each other was the morning your dad told you to join five of his best guys in the training ring. You threw up."

Rea smirked and reached out to shake his hand. Eric's personality was exactly like he remembered. He liked to tell it like it was.

"That's right. Your father left to join the harvesters. What happened after? Last I heard, you were living the high life on the Equator."

"My dad and I harvested for a few years. Then in a fluke accident, I hit a hidden oil reserve. The Canadian government gave both of us a cushy time after that. I have a beautiful place now, and I just got a dog."

After the word *dog* had been uttered, Eric gave a sharp whistle. A large tan fluffy-looking beast flounced into the room. It jumped on Rea's bed before skidding to a halt near the kitchen trash. Eric snapped his fingers, and the hairy mutt tipped its head sideways.

"Shelly!" he called. After initial hesitation, the animal finally came to sit next to his owner. Shelly's tongue hung out, and her tail never stopped sweeping the floor.

The mutt's antics brought a smile to Rea's face. Maybe he needed a companion. He could get a dog. He trusted a dog's judgment about people almost as much as he trusted his own gift. He held out his hand, and after a few seconds, the dog licked his fingers. He patted the soft fur.

"She's great, Eric."

"Thanks." Eric sat at the table and got the dog to lie at his feet.

"I think I heard that you'd made it big. How're your parents?" Rea sat down at his table across from his old friend. It was good to see someone who was not only making it in the world right now, but thriving.

"Mom and Dad are okay. They're retired now." Eric gave a strangely uncomfortable pause. He didn't sit long. He patted the dog's head and got up again. "I mostly meet people. I move around a lot, and…"

Eric trailed off and began to slowly walk around Rea's room. He stopped in front of his desk. Six four-inch monitors were glowing with the black-and-white camera views of the base. Eric's eyes scanned them before he headed over to the door to the bathroom.

Rea didn't talk. He just watched.

Eric wandered around as if he couldn't stay still. His eyes roamed nervously. Rea saw a look of trepidation flutter across Eric's face, but the look was gone as soon as it had appeared.

"Six feet under isn't normally a vacation. You came here of all places for a visit?" He asked to break the charged silence that was building. His gut said something deeper was going on.

"Not exactly." Eric's eyes looked older all of a sudden, and he meandered near the table. Eric's shoulders dropped, and he set his large frame on one of the wooden chairs. They regarded each other solemnly.

"I thought maybe you missed your oldest friend," Rea said to lighten the mood. A current of tension was riding the air between them.

"We are old friends," Eric exhaled. "But you're right; this isn't a vacation. I came here because I have a problem. I thought you'd help me. I've heard a lot about how you've grown up. It's vague information, of course, but I knew it was you they were talking about. People say you're made of iron. They whisper that you run the Northern Earth Dens with hostile determination."

"I think you're cleaning up the language," Rea said slowly. "They use more cuss words, but I appreciate your tact." He'd heard all that before. All the names he and his dad were called for how they chose to run the water bases. If Eric was here to tell him gossip, he was wasting his time. He waited for him to continue. When he didn't, Rea decided he was going to have to ask.

"What's the problem?"

Eric took a huge breath.

"I think the Canadian Government wants me to be the next president of the C.T.O.N.A."

Over the years, Rea had developed a gift he'd told almost no one about. He could tell if someone was lying. There was a deep feeling in his gut that was never wrong. Right now, according to his gift, Eric believed what he said. If this was true, why would Eric come to see him?

Chapter 5

Karma did a functions check on all of her weapons and checked her ammo. She crouched close to the perimeter of the water compound, and for now, only watched.

Even half a klick away, the structure appeared huge. The building was partly above ground among the ice and snow. The remainder was below ground where the temperature was stable. Everyone was being forced to build this way. Even in areas where the ground wasn't completely frozen over, the Northern Earth Dens, or NEDs as they were sometimes called, had taken over. She thought about the map she'd reviewed. She remembered the compound had some shuttles and trains that ran underneath. The tracks, she decided, weren't good access points. They'd be heavily guarded. No, coming from the ground level was the best since it was bitterly cold. Most guards couldn't be outside for longer than five or six hours before a shift change. Also, sensors didn't always work the best at negative twenty degrees Fahrenheit, which was another advantage.

Flipping her phone open, Karma checked her blueprints of the facility. She hoped she still got a signal here. She cupped her hands and willed some warmth into her fingertips. As she studied the information Fletcher had given her, she tried to commit the data to memory so when her phone quit she'd still know every pertinent detail.

What she'd learned so far was that her target, the man who worked on the compound, was from a generations-old military family. There were a lot of those around. Everyone she killed seemed to be the same.

She frowned. She couldn't trust any of the data so far, but what Fletcher had given her was all she had. Her target was currently working with a researcher named Adam, aka Gears, who had discovered how to turn even the most chemically saturated water into clean drinking water. The two men had formed a comfortable alliance. While this guy named Mac trained guards and police to protect the water treatment plants, Gears, in turn, convinced the C.T.O.N.A. to let him have water compounds where they thought suitable. If higher-ups in the government wanted the water, they could have it, but only as long as the elite protection could go along.

Gears was only in his early thirties. Something seemed off here in both the age and the alliance. She thought she'd read the leader of the water bases was an old man. She couldn't place what was wrong.

She snapped her phone closed and rubbed her hands together for warmth. There were a lot of holes in her information. She stood up stealthily and proceeded closer to the base. After ducking behind large snowdrifts, a thought struck her that all of this seemed strangely familiar. Karma recognized that her past was only trying to taunt her, so she pushed it out of her mind. She had no time to let any of her ghosts haunt her. There was no time for distractions—she was rusty as it was. Instead, as she broke into a jog, she reviewed what she'd read about Eric Bennett.

Eric Bennett, a wealthy playboy from the Equator, was indeed on the compound. Apparently, Eric had just gotten access to the base. His name seemed familiar also. Maybe she'd seen it somewhere. Someone could've put a hit out on him and it was one of those missed opportunities. The name was from somewhere. She figured it would come to her sooner or later.

When she took a moment to pause behind another snow mound, she considered the intelligence Fletcher had on him. Bennett was tied to the water bases in no way she could see, and this was as perplexing as everything else she'd learned so far.

As Karma slipped next to a chain-link fence caked over in ice, she became irritated with herself. Why care about any of this shit? She should just do the job. Once this was all over, then she'd go back to her freedom.

After pulling on white gloves, which matched her snowsuit, she began to climb quickly over the icy barbwire. The specifics of this job were nagging at her. She didn't like puzzles. This situation was strange because neither the researcher nor Bennett was her target. They both seemed vastly more killable. She simply didn't understand. No matter how many times she stared at what Fletcher had given her, it didn't change. Her target was some random guy named Mac—a man about whom she knew almost nothing. He was a teacher, a trainer. All he seemed to do was protect Adam. He was the equivalent of mindless armor. As far as Karma was concerned, Mac didn't exactly warrant killing, especially compared to the other men named.

Thinking back on all the people she'd executed reminded her there were always people she didn't think should be killed, but she'd done the job anyway.

Karma landed on the other side of the fence and gave up trying to make sense of all the facts. One thing she knew for sure, the last time she'd been on a water base, someone she cared about had died. Now it seemed fitting she return to a base to kill someone. Her dad would've said this was how the chips fell. He'd have insisted this was what she deserved.

Wrinkling her brow in concentration, Karma tried not to let all her thoughts keep distracting her. *Damn Fletcher and damn my rotten luck*, she thought. Instead of doing any more pondering she silently moved up to the first guard, who was shivering in the snow. He was a short sentinel. She easily wrapped her arm around his neck.

When he stopped struggling, he went down with a soft thud on the hard-packed snow. Once she was sure he was out, she let go. She yanked him into one of the shelters near the doorway, out of the unforgiving wind, and hoped he'd be found before he froze to death. She glanced around and then continued on.

If what little information she had was right, her target was living somewhere in the main building. Fletcher had guessed he was probably training men at this time of day. She guessed he might be showing the facility to Bennett. If he were showing the base off, as most visits went, Mac would show his guest around, and then he'd settle into his private quarters.

Ahead of her were rough brick and more snow. She paused and leaned on the wall. She considered Mac might also retire to an office to work. The map had many rooms labeled, but nothing marked as Mac's specifically. Wasting time on needless searching didn't appeal to her. Besides, she didn't have that kind of time. If he was the type of man to task out work, then someone else could be showing Bennett around, and she'd still find Mac in either his office or quarters.

Tossing out the idea of hunting for him, Karma made up her mind to just sneak into where the security cameras were. It would be easiest to get clues to where Mac was, and to come up with a plan on where to start. She didn't have a clear description of him, and that was her biggest problem, but she might get some luck once she got inside. The info she had stated that Bennett was a large six-foot-tall man with black hair peppered with gray. He was also fairly rotund from what she could see in the pictures she had of him. She would be unlikely to miss him. The researcher was a shorter man with big eyes, tiny nose, and skinny frame. So, if she found either of these two men, she had a pretty good chance of finding her target.

She needed to get moving again. Karma rushed along once more and stayed close to the facility. Her eyes studied the layout. The compound was massive, with the water treatment rooms at its heart. As she crawled along the wind shelters, she stayed out of the cameras' view. When she came to guards, she silently knocked them out, one by one.

Karma moved stealthily without stopping, keeping in mind her timeline.

As she located the main building, which she was sure housed the security cameras, she took a moment to assess this scenario. Why had Fletcher passed this to her? What was she missing? She looked for something to tip her off that this was a trap. The grounds were as peaceful as ever, and the dull gray pile of stones in front of her stood sleepily amongst the snow.

Not being able to put a finger on what was wrong, she started to climb a catwalk that wrapped all the way around the second floor. All the ventilation grates were bolted to the building with large locks on them. She figured she'd pick a vent, slip in, and make her way to the security room.

With that as her next plan of action, she moved surreptitiously along the railing and waited next to one of the larger ventilation grates until she was sure no one was around.

Using a bolt cutter and a small torch, she freed the cover. Unfortunately, she'd have to abandon her supplies. The items were too bulky to lug around. Effortlessly she wiggled her body through the large piping. The fans impeded her progress, and she had to stop for them. Once they were dismantled, she looked over the sensors.

When she stopped at the sensor boxes, she closed her eyes for a second. She recalled what her father had taught her about rewiring them. She gauged the plastic boxes as a minor problem. Again, as she moved along, it had her thinking this was so basic. What made killing this guy so difficult? Apparently getting into the building wasn't the tough part. Maybe the problem lay in the issue that no one had a description of the man. Not having an exact picture of her target would slow her down, but not stop her. She hoped she wasn't going to find him and figure out he was bulletproof. Well, she'd never met someone bulletproof before.

Karma chuckled at her musings. She then stopped at a vent directly above a set of neatly organized greenhouses on a thick dirt floor. She shimmied out of her white snow suit. After she had waited to make sure the earthen chamber was empty, she dropped out of the middle vent and landed on soft soil in a raised wooden flower bed.

Descending the large flower box, she noticed she was in a long room with only cement beams holding up the ceiling. She could tell she was now completely underground. The temperature was a pleasant sixty degrees. Ahead of her were greenhouses, all the same size and separated by the same distance across the floor. The smell of fresh earth and healthy growing plants greeted her as she ducked behind a huge bathtub that had been converted into a planter. As much as she was curious to see what they were growing, she had a strict timetable. She checked there were no other exits and then stood up.

The large wooden door at the far-right corner was the only entry into this room, other than the vents. She assumed that access point would get her into the hall. She reviewed her next plan. Find her target, kill him, come back, and then exit through the vent again. This area was empty, so she was confident she'd be in the clear if she made it this far after completing her mission. She could also escape through the train tunnels a few floors down. Near the tracks were other stored snowsuits and snowmobiles. That'd be her Plan B.

While she was getting her head clear on her strategy, she put her hand on the door handle. The cool metal knob turned in her palm. She pulled away as if her fingers had just been burnt. Cursing her rotten luck, she rushed back around the first greenhouse. Behind her, the door opened with a rusty squeak. Through the plastic walls, she tried to see who entered. She dipped her head just as she glimpsed a male.

Sweat started to trace a path down her back as she waited while holding her breath. Strange, but an odd feeling had come over her like this was her first hit. She had the same fears and anxiety as she did the first time. She didn't have any explanation for this phenomenon.

"This is our first set of greenhouses, but we have more. This is mostly an area for cross-pollinating," the man who entered spoke quickly as he strolled around the front of the dirt room like he owned the place.

Karma got lower to the floor. She wedged herself between a wooden barrel and the side of another greenhouse. From her new angle, she could see he was a short man with a skinny frame and sharp facial features. His hair was a sandy-brown color. His large tennis shoes were making imprints on the soft floor. He pushed his glasses up his face two times as he talked. Karma recognized him as the researcher. In her file, his name was Adam Shuler, but under nickname, it came up Gears.

"Gears, great tour, but I thought we were heading to food? Eric's starving, and I haven't eaten myself. We can do a full tour tomorrow. Ken wants to talk to us. I told him we'd be a minute." The words floated in from the doorway. Karma went from crouching to lying on her belly.

She slid like a snake behind another flower box made of stone. Briefly, she thanked her dad for sending some good luck. Through the door, she could see Bennett.

Laughing silently to herself that Fletcher and his men must simply be poor marksmen, she drew her 9mm Beretta from the holster on her right thigh. Karma held her breath again as she waited to see if she could get a clean shot at Mac, who she was positive was in this group.

The researcher spoke again. "I know you're hungry. I was cross-pollinating some plants. I grew tea. I've been waiting until we had a reason to drink it." Karma got her shot lined up to make sure she could hit anyone who came through the open door.

She was about to move to a better position when another man stepped forward. From where she was located, she could only catch the shine from his boots. She let out the breath she was holding to steady her weapon, and hoped the man would come further into the room. This guy might be the recluse military trainer they had no details on.

While still grumbling, the other man stepped under one of the grow lamps that hung from the metal piping along the ceiling. He was nothing like she'd pictured when reading his insufficient history earlier. If this were "Mac" she'd be very surprised.

The new addition to the room was easily six feet tall, like Bennett, but he was lean. His clothes barely covered his massive arms and broad chest. He was fit, she could tell, and his large black boots spattered mud as he walked.

Karma was struck by him. Only one time in her life had she ever seen hair as red as his, or eyes that green. As his eyes scanned the plants, she was captivated by his wild flaming hair. She was mesmerized by the freckles that dusted his nose and cheeks. For a moment, she went back in time. He was so familiar to her, but he couldn't be the man that popped into her head. That man was dead, and so was his father. Maybe she'd seen him before on another mission. That repeated nagging thought chose this moment to enter her head again. Why was this guy considered so fearsome that Fletcher had passed this job to her? Sure, she'd heard about the old man who ran these water bases, but this man was far from old. Was she given the wrong information?

Karma squeezed her eyes closed for a second and admonished herself. She was lying there staring at a man instead of doing her job. If her dad were here, he'd tell her to get her shit together. She crushed down all her emotions and stopped trying to figure out where she'd seen him before.

She carefully moved to a squat and hoped to get a clean shot. If they called this man Mac, then she could kill him and move on with her life. Luck was on her side as she inched to the other end of the greenhouse. They stayed in her view as both men unknowingly turned their backs to her.

"Do you hear something?" Red Hair said. Was this Mac? Say his name, she begged silently.

"It's nothing, Mac. Just my dog. Shelly's a puppy and gets into everything."

Just as Bennett stepped into the room and said the name, a large golden mutt barreled past him. The pet came to a stop in front of Gears and sniffed the air.

Mac swiftly stepped to the side out of the dog's path and out of her line of fire. He crouched next to the dog and scratched behind its ears.

In an instant, Karma took back all the things she'd thought about how this was such an easy job. Dogs were creatures that made plans go from smooth to insane in a heartbeat. She wished her luck had held a minute longer. She scooted around a rack of shovels. Bennett had referred to Red Hair as Mac. That was all she needed. The dog sniffed the air a second time. Its ears picked up. Damn, but that pet was going to hunt her down.

As if Mac could see what the dog knew, he stepped in front of Bennett. He pushed him back out the door. The dog began barking. Karma heard the mangy mutt dart around the corner of the first greenhouse as if beginning to seek her.

Knowing this might not end well, Karma switched her tactic. This was a good time to lie low. If she didn't make her move now, maybe she could get her target later when things settled down. She could simply spray the doorway with her MP5, but she'd risk hitting Bennett or Gears. She'd agreed to a clean hit. She didn't have a lot of time to sit around coming up with a plan, and the dog was a wild card.

"Shelly." Mac's deep voice gave a firm call. The dog ignored the summons.

Mac called a second command that had the dog turning to come back to him just before it rounded the corner. Karma thanked her lucky stars the dog responded to its name that time.

She shook her head at her close call. This was one of the reasons why she'd given all this up. Her heart wasn't in it anymore. She'd grown to hate the pulse-pounding adrenaline of close calls.

"Dogs are a handful. Maybe you should get a cat," Gears tossed out while he kept picking tea leaves.

"Shelly doesn't listen well. I got her a week ago," Bennett responded loudly from the hallway. He called the dog's name a few times. The animal ran back out of the room, but it was too late to stay hidden and hope Mac thought the pet's actions were a fluke. If this guy were even one bit of a good guard, then he'd never let this incident go. Mac wouldn't think the creature was crazy. If he were anything like her, he'd now investigate the area because she'd look into the dog's behavior too.

"Eric, stay out in the hall. Gears, go with him and call Ken. Tell him to send me the nearest security detail available."

Karma shifted behind stacked tires with vines coming out the top. She tucked herself down next to an enormous potted plant. The leaves smelled liked rosemary.

Realizing she wasn't focused, she tried to get her full concentration back on the mission. Her ears strained to pick up the sound of Mac's footfalls, and she pinpointed his location. His stalking her signified this was a now-or-never situation. The only problem she could come up with right now was that she'd have to be careful not to kill Bennett and Gears. If they stayed in the hallway, she could make the kill, and then get out before anyone even came to his aid.

As she shifted again, not even the rustling of plastic could be heard. Far off in the hallway, the dog was whining.

"We're here, Boss-Mac. What'd you need?"

Two men ambled through the doorway as if oblivious anything might be out of place. At their entrance, Karma got the chance to angle around the large pot and assess if these were new adversaries. She rolled her shoulders. Since these two young pups looked pretty tame, she scooted again around a leafy wall of tomatoes and paused.

Her eyes scanned the youths. The dog was a worse threat. She took out her second Berretta from the holder on her other thigh.

"Hey, Boss-Mac, we're here," the taller one shouted as if Mac's hearing was impaired.

"Ken said to come see you, so what'd you want?" The second man walked in the vicinity of Mac. From her angle, she saw Mac glare at the supposed *help*.

"Shit, Charlie. Can't you see the vent grate is off? There's something wrong. You both need to use gut instinct. I was listening to hear the vent fan. Someone turned it off. This is the kind of situational awareness we've talked about in training. Now, why don't you both shut the hell up and listen?"

Karma smiled. Mac was trying to use this as a training opportunity. She could imagine having breakfast with him, and he using the salt and pepper shakers to teach defense maneuvers.

"What're we trying to hear?" one of the newcomers whined.

"Maybe the fan is broken and someone moved the grate to see if it was being fixed. I mean, there's nothing around here. Who'd want to sneak into a greenhouse?" the shorter one with the bald head argued loudly, while he slapped the plastic door of the closest greenhouse.

He kicked some dirt like a petulant child. Mac clenched his teeth together, and a muscle in his cheek flexed.

She would've laughed at the look Mac gave both men if she didn't think she'd die because of the sound. She then decided she'd use these guys as a distraction. They seemed like the kind of men to lose their cool very fast. They'd be full of chaos. That's just what she needed.

Re-holstering her secondary weapon, she scanned the dirt for a rock. She was forced to angle around the plastic door of the greenhouse a little more than she wanted to, but she had success. She discovered a jagged medium-sized stone. Her fingers curled around her new little chaos device. With all her might she threw the rock at the furthest clay pot hanging from one of the water pipes. The sound of shattering clay signified a direct hit. As she expected, both men opened fire like they were killing an army of Canadians for oil rights.

While the room filled with bullets zinging in the opposite direction from her, Karma rolled to her feet. She rushed toward her exit route. Both men were yelling to the "Boss-Mac" for help. Mac was doing his best to get them to stop firing. His deep voice full of disgust was comical.

Karma turned to get back to the flowerbed under the vent. She'd just reached her destination when, to her amazement, she ran directly into Mac.

He'd come out of nowhere. Karma was so shocked she almost screamed. She really was out of practice. First, Fletcher found her, and now this guy anticipated her moves? This was some crap. She didn't even see him coming. She could've sworn she'd just heard him over by the last greenhouse. He'd moved fast. How dumb of her for underestimating him.

His large frame knocked her down. Karma got back on her feet quickly. She threw her weapon up and pulled the trigger. She didn't aim. While she scrambled to reach for her second firearm, he grunted. Blood blossomed across the right side of his stomach. Not many men could take a bullet with such relaxed disinterest. If she had time, she would've applauded him.

Mac grabbed the gun in Karma's right hand brutally. His other hand went for her secondary weapon. He stopped her from sliding it out of the holster. His hand crushed hers until she was sure her fingers were going to snap.

Karma freed her left hand by abandoning her other sidearm. She drew back and punched him in the face. It was like hitting concrete. He didn't let go of her weapon like she hoped. She would have to hit him again. She drew back a second time. This time, he caught her fist. Again, she tried to free her gun. He squeezed her trigger finger over and over again. Bullet after bullet hit the ground next to his right boot. After only a minute of struggling, she was out of ammo.

When she ran out of rounds in her first gun, she let go of her weapon. It fell to the dirt. She pried her hand away from his. He almost broke her fingers in the struggle. It didn't matter. Finally, she was free.

Karma reached for the pistol strapped to her thigh. She brought her Beretta up to aim at his heart. He slowly put his hands up in a peace-like gesture. For a heartbeat they stilled.

Then she heard a call to her left that broke the spell which had come over her. One of his peons yelled at her to put down her weapon. She didn't know where the other one had gone. His empty threat was amusing. But there was no time for hilarity right now.

"I'll save you, Boss-Mac!" the tall one called out. He squeezed the trigger to reveal no more bullets.

Karma wanted to shake her head and tell him, yes, that's what happens when you shoot your entire clip at nothing.

Karma only took a second to glance at how far away the tall kid was from her position, but in that moment Mac fearlessly tackled her. He didn't give a damn that her gun was pointed at his heart. He didn't seem to notice the blood dripping out of his side.

The whole thing happened so fast Karma was having a hard time keeping up. This was what she got for trying to retire. She was getting old and slow.

Mac got her to the ground. His fist hit her face so hard she was temporarily stunned. Before she could fight back, Mac moved his head a scant second before a large clay pot struck her in the forehead.

Pain sliced through her skull and then there was only darkness.

Chapter 6

Out of the corner of his eye, Rea saw Gears pick up a potted plant. He heaved the container toward where Rea was struggling with the hit man. The assassin pinned under him was fighting him hard. The killer didn't catch on to what Gears was doing.

Rea stunned his attacker with a punch to the face. He then moved just in time to have the pot fly past his head. It smashed into the front of the crazy guy's skull.

Rea looked over at Charlie, who was panting and looking sheepish for being of no help.

He then glanced around for Josh. Josh was hiding next to one of the greenhouses, also being useless. Rea wanted to hit him in the face as well. These two men were a waste of space. Rea should've never let them stay. They were hired by his dad before he died, and if his dad were here, they'd be gone by now.

Taking a deep breath, Rea slowly took his hands off the killer. He got up from the floor and pressed his hand to his side. As soon as he let the man go, the stranger slumped into the mud. The assassin was knocked out cold.

Rea took another calming breath. He guessed from the stabbing fire in his side that he'd been shot somewhere. For the moment, he ignored the insistent burning. He took a closer look at the man in the dirt. Something wasn't right.

With a sweep of his arm, Rea plucked the tight black hood from the man's face. A long dark ponytail tumbled out.

"That's a girl. You just punched a girl… in the face." Gears sounded horrified. He stared over his shoulder at the young woman lying on the ground. "And I threw a plant at her. Hell has a special place for men who hit women."

"Yeah, men who hit women go to hell, but that's not a woman, that's a killer."

Rea grabbed the black hood and studied the viewscreen mask. He noticed Gears staring at him.

"This has thermal vision," he stated, and tossed the cover to Gears.

Gears caught the mask. "I hit a girl with a plant. Maybe I should pray or say sorry?" He paled.

Rea ran his hand through his hair.

"This isn't a *girl*. This is an assassin." He snatched the black hood back from Gears. "She shot me. Stop saying *girl*." A brief dizzy spell hit him.

Gears put his arm out and steadied him.

"Maybe you should lie down. I should look at your side." Rea's injury appeared to have pulled Gears out of his concerns about hitting women for the moment.

Rea nodded his agreement and leaned on the doctor's arm

He saw Eric in the doorway looking confused and pale. The hand Eric was using to hold his large puppy was shaking.

"Are you okay, Eric? Gears, maybe you should look at Eric."

Eric gave him a dismissive shake of his head. "I'm doing better than you at the moment."

"Yeah." Gears accepted more of his weight. "I think Eric will be fine. Let's check you out."

While Gears steered him toward the door, he glanced back at the woman on the floor.

His friend was right. The assassin was just a girl. She looked in her early twenties maybe. She probably had a concussion. Gears would have to take a look at her, too. When she woke up, he'd have to interrogate her. That didn't sit well with him. It bothered him that he was the one who'd hit her. That didn't sit with him either. He couldn't think like that. He had to protect the base. He had to protect Gears. She wasn't a girl. She was the person who just tried to kill him. That was all there was to it.

"Gears, you and Eric and I can go back to my room." Rea swayed. He motioned to Charlie and Josh. "Charlie and Josh, take the hired gun to room one-eleven. She'll probably be out for a while, but just in case, stay armed. Don't kill her. I want to question her. Just tie her up."

Charlie and Josh came up to where the girl was lying. They awkwardly hoisted her up and started out the door. Charlie was the taller of the two, so he did most of the carrying. Josh followed along behind like a lost child, pretending to be helpful.

Rea scowled after them. He clenched his jaw. Why did he think having her go with the two of them was a terrible idea? Nothing he could do about it now. More blood was spilling out of the gunshot wound.

Lightheaded, he leaned on Gears again. He stepped out into the hallway to head over to his room. He couldn't believe he was worrying about someone who had tried to kill him, or worse, someone who'd just tried to kill his friends. Right now, he needed to focus on getting cleaned up. When he was feeling better, he'd interrogate her. Hopefully, she'd be able to answer questions with a minimal amount of problems. He didn't want to hurt her. He just needed to know why there was an assassin on his base.

As the three of them walked down the hall, Rea started to think more about what Eric had said about being the next president. He wouldn't be more than a figurehead, a puppet really, but maybe she'd come to kill Eric. Eric would be a likely target.

At first, when Eric had mentioned being president, he had a hard time believing him. He'd humored his friend when he talked about his concerns. He didn't know how to tell him the whole thing sounded ludicrous. Now he considered there might really be something going on, and it either had to do with Eric or him, or maybe even Gears. He had to come up with why someone would sneak into an earth den. Either Eric had brought this with him, or for some unknown reason, someone was trying to kill him.

Rea had made very few enemies in his life, and he had even fewer friends. Over the years, he was almost always alone. Most of the specifics about his life weren't even out in the world. He protected the fact he was the son of the man who'd built these water bases, but he only did that because he hated to be connected to such an awful person. Rea never hid his life due to the idea that someone might want him dead. That wouldn't make any sense. The only thing he'd done with his life was train men to protect the bases and Gears. The water bases could be under attack, or someone could want to take them over. There were a lot of people who'd love to kill Gears and command the primary water source for the C.T.O.N.A. People hired killers for all sorts of reasons, but why her and why now?

The doctor helped him to his room, with Eric following close behind them. Rea sat on the bed. He looked down at the blood that was making his shirt stick to his skin. As Rea took off his top, Gears began poking at him.

"This doesn't look as bad as I thought. The bullet grazed you. I can have you as good as new in no time," Gears murmured.

While Rea settled back on the mattress, he tried to figure out what exactly was going on.

"Eric, does someone want to kill you?" Rea spoke after a prolonged silence.

"I don't know."

"How about you, Gears? Have you seen anything suspicious?" Rea looked at the top of Gears' bent head.

Gears didn't look up, but kept working on Rea's torn flesh.

After a short time, the doctor finally answered. "When I first started cleaning water, I was so excited over what I'd created. It was tunnel vision. I couldn't see the bigger picture. Back then some people tried to kill me. They wanted the key to making clean water. Some people thought I shouldn't have the kind of knowledge I had. There were individuals who believed water shouldn't be free. That's when I came to your father. I asked him to train me to protect myself. Your dad said he could train a blind cow before he could train me. He called me a lost cause. After that, he introduced me to you. We've been together since then. If someone was trying to kill me, you'd know before me, right?" Gears glanced up at him and pushed his glasses. "Wait, why do you think she wasn't after you? She seemed pretty ready to kill you."

"She? As in a girl? I didn't picture a little girl," Eric asked, stunned.

Rea glared at him. "That was an adult hired killer who just happened to be female." Rea gritted his teeth to stop himself from swearing at Eric. He paused. He needed to get a better answer out of both of them. "I'd like to know if someone's trying to kill either of you. I want to know if you've done something I should be aware of."

"Why do you persist in thinking we did something?" Gears frowned.

"Yeah," Eric added. "You're the one that's bleeding."

Rea frowned. "I've been doing this for years, and I don't think there's a good reason someone would go to all this trouble to kill me. I think I was in the way in the greenhouse. This killer could be here to hunt for someone more important. You, Eric, are looking at taking a critical job with the C.T.O.N.A., right? Someone might not want that to happen. Gears, you're too smart for your own good. Someone might want to hijack the water bases. There are good reasons for someone to see you both dead."

"Yes, but if you were dead, then no one would be protecting us or the water bases. If you were gone, all facilities would be weak. Someone could steal Gears' information. Also, very few people know about the position I was offered." Eric paused and turned in a circle, thinking. "Besides, I've been lucky so far, and nothing has come my way."

"I don't believe in luck," Rea grunted as Gears stitched up his side. The doctor was daintily swabbing blood with a gauze pad, but it felt like he was digging into his skin.

"Mac doesn't believe in luck or God. I'd say he lacks faith in something."

"When I find something worth having faith in, I'll let you know."

"You do that. Now stop moving around. I have to get this wound immaculately clean. You know how I feel about dealing with infections down here. Cleanliness is next to godliness." Gears started prodding him again. Rea looked up at the ceiling fan near the vent in his room. The fan made lazy circles, and he tried to concentrate on that instead of the persistent ache.

"Is Gears a good doctor? Does he know what he's doing? You're going to live, right?" Eric showed genuine concern. Rea thought his unease might be a mixture of real worry for him and worry that Rea was the only person who'd help him.

Eric needed him alive and they both knew it. Eric would depend upon his support and the support of the water bases if he actually became a leader of the C.T.O.N.A. Breaking the NEDs away from Canada would be a giant undertaking. Taking on protection against the snow and ice on the surface would need a herculean effort as well.

"Gears is brilliant in whatever he does. I'm going to be fine." Rea paused, and then swore as Gears tugged on his skin again, "I take that back." He winced and tried not to pull away.

"Why do they call you Gears? Did your parents name you that?" Eric questioned, as if trying to act normal while Gears performed the minor surgery.

"My name's Adam, but I got the nickname when I was young. My family said my gears were always turning. I'm always inventing new things." Gears lifted his head. "There you go, Mac. All set."

"What did you do?" Rea asked, surprised his wound didn't hurt anymore. His skin looked smoothed over. Only a small bandage was left.

"I used this new cream I just invented called RCC100. The letters stand for Rapid Clot and Clean, and I got the formula figured out on my one hundredth try, give, or take. The thick cream stops bleeding and makes a new skin for healing. I sent you a sample to put away for safe keeping. All the guys nicknamed it Gears' Goo, and they laugh. I don't appreciate their teasing, but I can't get them to call my special cream the proper name."

"I'll tell them to call it RCC100," Rea said absently. "But don't say 'my special cream' around them, either."

He wrinkled his brow before swinging his feet off his double bed. He stood and swayed, still a bit dazed. His hand landed on Gears' shoulder.

While he got his equilibrium back, Rea thought about that last sentence. The scientist had an obsessive need to keep a small sample of everything he worked on in a locked room, so if he ever had to go back to his original formulas, he could get them back. It was odd he didn't get the sample of RCC100.

Rea's eyes swung with uncertainty to Gears. "I never got any of this. Are you sure you gave me some to put in the safe?"

"I gave it to Charlie. He was supposed to give you all the samples." Gently, Gears tried to guide Rea back into bed.

Rea shoved his hand off his chest.

His friend was trying not to say he should stay in bed and recover, but there was no way Rea was going to lie around while there was an assassin in the building, and now a missing drug sample.

Rea went over to his plastic dresser, which was shoved in the corner next to the bathroom door. He pulled out a clean shirt and slammed the drawer. The old plastic bent and sagged, but he ignored his pathetic furniture. While he tugged his shirt over his head, he considered what Gears said. There was a part of Gears' explanation that seemed off. What was it?

He reached under his bed to grab two small handguns. He handed one to Eric, and then put one in the waist of his pants.

"Wait. Did you say samples, as in more than one?"

"Yes, more than one. I gave him RCC100 and a drug that can immobilize you for about 24 hours." Gears paused and tipped his head to the side. "Oh, and a drug which erases your memories, mostly. I haven't named the immobilization drug yet. The memory drug I called Clean Slate 3000 or CS3000. I think it sounds like a really fast motorcycle."

"Not good." Rea grabbed his two-way radio off the desk next to his computers. He stomped past the table by the door. He didn't wait for Eric and Gears to follow him.

"You don't like the name? I think it rolls off your tongue," Gears called as he chased him into the hall.

Rea wasn't listening. His mind was putting together what he needed to do next. He headed out into the hallway hoping his battered body was up to whatever he had to deal with. His eyes shot back to his companions who were both staring at him wide-eyed.

"Gears, do you have your medical bag?"

"Yeah." Gears patted the straps on his backpack. "Why?"

"Eric, I'm calling Ken. He'll take you to your room. He'll get you dinner. You and I will talk later. Keep this gun on you, just in case." Rea gestured to the gun he'd given Eric and nodded at him. "You can update Ken on everything. He'll help you. I want you to stay until I get this worked out. Gears, let's go find Charlie."

Rea left Eric and hurried toward the interrogation room with Gears running behind him.

"What's the problem? You don't like the name? You know, I like motorcycles, but I guess you don't. There's no problem, really. Whatever I call it, the guys just rename it." Gears pushed his glasses up on his nose. He shrugged his shoulders as they walked swiftly.

Rea sighed and observed Gears' lack of worry. It was just like Gears to think nothing was wrong.

"The name isn't the problem. What's wrong is you gave a bunch of drugs to two men I wouldn't trust with a toilet seat, and now they have an assassin as well."

"The girl?"

"Call her whatever you want, but pick up the pace."

Chapter 7

Karma's eyes popped open seconds after cold water hit her in the center of her face. She coughed, sputtered, and then ran her tongue over her wet lips.

"That woke her up."

Disoriented, she heard a man's voice above her. It was the pounding in her head that brought her to full consciousness. That potted plant had given her one hell of a headache.

Karma blinked her eyes open as a knife stabbed into her right thigh. A burning pain overwhelmed her for a moment, and she bit her tongue to stop from calling out.

Male laughter assaulted her ears. She looked around the room through a blur of water and blood from the gash the pot had created.

Quickly she assessed she was in a small room tied to a chair. Her father had taught her to push everything away. She needed to concentrate. She breathed through the burning sensation. The holsters on her thighs had been cut off. Her wrists were tied tight with a thick rope around them. Not good. She tried to think around the hammering at her temples.

Without looking, she gathered that her legs were similarly tied to both legs of the metal chair. She flexed to test the strength of the rope. It was solid.

Again, not good.

The room was all old tan-colored tiles and harsh light. A deep-gray marble counter top dominated the wall to the right. If she carefully turned her head, she'd be able to see a door behind her left shoulder. There was nothing else in the room, but the two men standing in front of her, a bucket, and a metal cabinet.

As she took in her new surroundings, Karma recognized the man named Charlie, who she'd seen before in the greenhouses. Charlie was tall, with wide-set eyes. He had a mop of uncombed shaggy brown hair. The man next to him was much shorter, with a bald head and crooked lips. Both men generally didn't look like much, but in this circumstance, every warning bell went off in her body.

This wasn't going to be pretty, but she kept her head calm just like her father taught her to do.

Charlie came closer with a giddy expression on his face. It was a look that she found disturbing. His eyes shone, and his breath smelled like onions.

"What's the stuff you got there?" She heard the short bald man's question.

These two would've almost been humorous if it weren't for the fact she was in such a dire state.

"Gears gave this to me to give to Boss-Mac, and I forgot, but now I thought we'd use it. It's stuff to make someone not able to move. I was thinking if we gave her this, then we could untie her and put her on the counter while we wait."

"What for?" Shorty asked, but Karma knew the answer before he asked.

"You're dumb, Josh. If we give it to her, then we can fuck her before Boss-Mac gets here. He was shot, so I figure it'll take him awhile 'til he's fixed up." Charlie's voice was giggly.

He fished a needle out of the drawer in the cabinet. He then dug out three identical glass containers from his pocket. He set them on the counter, side by side.

"Shit," Charlie swore at the three matching bottles.

He held them up one by one, but they all looked the same.

"What's wrong now?" Josh asked as he gave her a quick appraising glance.

Karma could tell he was warming up to the idea of having sex with her. She tried to come up with some sort of plan. If only her head would cooperate.

"I don't know which one's the drug that makes you not move 'round. One of these messes with your head and…" Again Charlie held them up, but there was no point. Each bottle was darkened glass, the same size and shape. "…one of them's Gears' Goo."

"Gears' Goo," Josh snickered. "Doc gets so pissed when you call it that."

Karma ignored Josh's remark and instead looked at the floor. She saw that one of her guns was still in the holster kicked partway under her chair. If she could get out of here, then she could still accomplish her hit. She did a quick evaluation of her injuries and then considered where her target might be.

"Just give 'em all to her. Who cares what the other ones do?" Josh dropped his shoulders and regarded her. "He says I'm dumb."

"What if doing that kills her?" Charlie asked.

Josh now seemed exasperated. He snatched one of the bottles from Charlie. "Who cares if she dies? Then we shoot her and tell Boss-Mac she tried to get away." Josh filled the needle using the bottle he held. He handed it back to Charlie.

Karma's forehead hurt, and she didn't relish what she was about to do, but she didn't have a lot of options right now.

Charlie moved closer to her. She waited until she had an opening. When his head was bent directly in front of her face, she made her move. With as much power and energy as she could muster, she head-butted him. She used her forehead to slam into the side of his head with a swift hit. Her head screamed in agony.

"Shit!" Josh roared.

Charlie's cheek bounced off her lap. He rolled to the floor unconscious.

Karma was dizzy, and her stomach turned, but it worked. Well done, she congratulated herself.

Her eyes flickered over Josh. There was no time to think. She had to come up with what to do with him right now. She needed to think fast. Idiot number two was dense, but she was through with underestimating people.

Karma reviewed her options. She could hit the next guy the same way. If he bent over her, it'd be another opening. The idea of slamming her head around anymore didn't appeal to her. Well, she'd have to come up with some kind of a plan.

She tested the rope again. These guys might be stupid, but they could tie a good knot. Unfortunately, standing up to swing her chair was out of the picture. It appeared to be bolted to the floor. Plus, she didn't know if her injured thigh could take the pressure.

Josh picked up the needle from where it had fallen. His hands were shaking. His lips were pressed into a grim line.

She didn't like the way his swiftly moving eyes jumped around the room.

She was lightheaded, but she didn't have time to wait for it to pass. Her brain wasn't working. She was running out of time. Before a new plan presented itself, Josh backhanded her.

The room spun.

Karma could taste the blood in her mouth. Her right eye felt like it was going to pop out of its socket. Her whole head shrieked, and a groan escaped her lips.

"You bitch." Spittle flew out of Josh's mouth.

The needle pierced the back of her arm.

While her dizziness began to subside, she waited to see if she was going to become immobilized. Nothing yet. Everything about her seemed the same as always. Thanking her lucky stars, she moved her shoulder slightly. She wasn't paralyzed. What did he say about the other one? Her head would be messed up? Her thoughts were crystal clear, as far as she could tell. It could've been the other drug, Gears' Goo. She had no idea what Gears' Goo even was.

Waiting a few more minutes, she begged her brain to wake up and give her a way to escape. Slowly an idea took shape.

Happy her luck was changing; she slumped in her chair and closed her eyes. Now, if this guy was as brainless as she figured him to be, then he'd untie her and lay her on the counter. That would be perfect. It would give her the best chance to kill him. She hoped her luck would hold out that long.

"That's right, you bitch!" Josh screeched in celebration.

Keeping herself as calm as possible, she stayed slumped in her seat. She didn't move even when his knife scraped across the cut on her thigh. It was excruciating, but she managed to stay motionless.

Worried he might discover her deception, she held her breath. The feel of the weapon was lost on her due to the throbbing in her head. Her brain was becoming foggy. She dug deep into her willpower. She stayed still with her eyes half-closed. Just untie me, she kept thinking. He started to pull at her body suit along her legs.

The large blade started at her knee, and his hands tried to rip at the durable fabric. He sawed back and forth, struggling to slice through the sturdy material. He was pulling so hard it would've lifted her from the chair if she were not tied to her seat. She let her head relax against her shoulders. Below her belly button, the cloth finally started to give. Cool air caressed her unprotected skin. Her underwear was exposed, but he paused in his efforts and didn't cut them off.

Karma opened her eyes slightly to see Josh move the empty water bucket out of his way. The slimeball then kicked at his friend to make sure that the other man was out cold. Satisfied that Charlie wasn't going to get up, Josh freed his dick from his pants.

While he stood close to her, slowly he started to stroke his hardening cock. He was staring at her and touching himself. Karma kept as still as possible to seem completely nonthreatening. Just untie one leg, she screamed in her head. She tensed to keep herself from shifting away from his exposed groin and repulsive gestures.

"What the hell is going on, Josh?" The words came from behind her left shoulder. Karma was alarmed. She hadn't heard anyone enter the room.

"Shit, Boss-Mac. I thought you'd be gone for a while." The man next to her chair literally jumped when he heard the man behind her.

"I can see that." She heard a deep voice.

A tall, beautifully muscled male came into view a second later. He was like a hero out of a book. He walked in as if he owned everything and everyone around him. She sighed dreamily. He had red hair, the color of flames. He stepped in front of her with a quick, confident stride. She had to tip her head all the way back to take all of him in. There was a sexual allure about him that made her think of dirty fantasies.

Karma was floating. If she didn't know better, she would've said she had been up all night drinking. Her tongue passed over her suddenly dry lips. She needed water.

Trying to gather her thoughts, she realized they were becoming increasingly scattered. What was she doing here? Why was she tied up? Who was this sexy man?

Karma was thinking about Red Hair naked. Hot sex, soft sheets, and the smell of sex in the air. She needed to think about a different topic. Her eyes squeezed shut. She was supposed to do something by 1:05 a.m. The time seemed important. What did she need to do?

She'd just pry her eyes open and demand an explanation. Karma struggled to lift her eyelids all the way. Only a slit of light came through. Maybe her one eye was swelling shut. Now that she wanted to pay attention, it all seemed like too much work. Inside of her was the demand to rest. Maybe she'd been tired of all this for a long time now. Whatever *this* was, she wanted no part of it. All she wanted was a bed with Red Hair. Sleep, skin, and warm blankets.

When she finally pried her eyes open a little more, she saw another guy next to Red Hair. When had he come in? This guy was skinny, with glasses too large for his face. Red Hair and Mr. Glasses were watching the man in front of her, who was shoving his small penis into his pants. There was an uncomfortable silence in the room. She needed to get her head together. If she got untied, then she could get to the greenhouse and... was she going to plant flowers? She listed off things you did in a greenhouse. None of them seemed pressing. Why did the time keep popping up in her head? What happened at 1:05 a.m.?

"Were you planning on raping her?" Red Hair acted like this was the most boring topic ever, but on some level, Karma thought he might be seeing something no one else could see.

"No, I wasn't. Honest, Boss-Mac."

"You're lying. Was Charlie going to rape her, too?" Again Red Hair spoke like he didn't care, but in her gut, she felt that he did. There was a weird element to the way he talked that tipped her off. His voice was as cold as surface ice.

"It was all Charlie. He got some stuff to knock her out, and then he was going to fuck her, but she head-butted him and knocked him out cold. I wasn't doing nothing here. 'Sides, she's a piece of shit, so it doesn't matter what we do with her."

The Boss-Mac, as Josh called him, curled his lip in disgust. Karma could tell Red Hair didn't like what Josh had to say in defense of his actions, and she couldn't blame him. If the positions were reversed, she didn't think anyone deserved being raped. Then again, maybe she did. After all, she didn't know why she'd been tied to a chair. Maybe she was a bad person. It was becoming impossible for her to recall anything other than this moment.

Red Hair motioned to Charlie on the floor. "Gears, take a look at Charlie."

Mr. Glasses, who was apparently named Gears, did as he was asked. He knelt down, checked over Charlie, and then nodded to Red Hair.

"He's out, but alive," Gears announced as he stood.

After he'd straightened, Gears came closer to her. She thought she should make some grand action to fight him off. He was an enemy, right? The more she thought about it, the more nothing came to her. Maybe they were her friends. She sat there while he flashed a light in her eyes from a small pen light that he produced from his pocket.

"What do you think, Gears?" Red Hair asked.

"She's not unconscious and these cuts are new," Gears replied.

Red Hair turned to Josh. "I can't believe how dumb you two are. She was probably waiting for you to cut her loose so she could make her move." Red Hair paused. He ran his hand through his hair. "You know our policy on rape. You knew that when you signed on with my father. I'm sick of your shit. I'm done with both of you. You and Charlie get off my base."

"But, Boss-Mac, I didn't do nothing, really," Josh pointed at her.

"I don't trust you. You and Charlie will be escorted off the base as soon as you collect your personal items."

"But your dad said—"

"I know you were both hired by my father, but I don't care what he said. You won't live on *my* water bases." Red Hair sounded final. Karma didn't think there was any way he was going to change his mind.

"I didn't rape her," Josh argued. "She's still wearing underwear."

Karma looked to her lap. What he said was true but Red Hair seemed unconvinced. His voice was as tough as concrete.

"If you were willing to rape someone for any reason, you can't stay here, and I'll not recommend you for any other base either. Get out of my sight."

Red Hair took out a handheld device that looked like a cross between a cell phone and radio. He kept his eyes on Josh, and she could only hear parts of a muffled conversation he was having. Gears stood to her right. He kept staring at her like she might do a trick for him. She wasn't in the mood to do cartwheels.

"What do you mean Ken is coming to my location right now? I thought he was testing a new weapon."

Karma couldn't hear what the person on the other end of the radio responded, but from the look on Red Hair's face, he didn't like it.

"He doesn't know where I am," Red Hair barked into the speaker, making her start.

As she glanced around, she realized Josh was pissed. He glared at her like something was her fault. A muffled response could be heard again on the radio. Red Hair spoke again, loudly.

"When you see him, tell him to get to room one-eleven now. I have a couple of assholes I need thrown out immediately."

Karma was getting the idea that no one around her was happy with the situation. She couldn't remember why, exactly. Everything was becoming hazy. The weight of Josh's eyes on her made her squirm in her chair. Gears looked upset. He played with his glasses. Everything appeared like it was moving in slow motion. Her right eye was almost completely swollen shut. The swelling made it hard for her to see much of the room. Both of her eyes refused to open all the way.

She was about to comment on the situation when there was a loud thud behind her. It sounded exactly like a door had just been thrown open.

"There you are, Ken. I need—" Red Hair didn't get the last of his words out. Since everything seemed to be in slow motion for her, she watched through a fog as a huge man lunged at Josh. She didn't recognize the man. Because her eye was swollen shut, he was merely a blur. Red Hair and Gears rushed past her. Together they shoved Josh and the stranger apart.

Karma closed her eyes for what she thought was only a second, but when she opened them again, the scene had changed. Gears and the stranger were now out of her sight. In front of her were only Red Hair and her would-be rapist.

"Put the gun down, Ken. I handled it," Red Hair stepped to the right of her chair.

As soon as Red Hair turned his back, Karma got a clear look at Josh. He was coming up directly behind Red Hair with a knife raised. The blade was aimed at the center of his back.

"Behind you!" she called automatically. Her arms stiffened against the ropes in her response to save him. He turned just in time.

Red Hair knocked the knife out of Josh's hand. The blade hit the floor. He swung one fist forward while using his other hand to block. The crunch of bone hitting bone filled the air.

Blood spurted out of Josh's nose. A crimson stream ran down his face. He stumbled backward. Red Hair knocked the other man out, and he crumpled to the floor.

As soon as the altercation was over, Red Hair barked out orders to tie both men up.

"Ken, you need to calm the hell down. Take a walk." Red Hair quickly began removing a rope from one of the drawers in the metal cabinet. He tossed a length of it to Gears. The two of them tied up the unconscious men on the floor.

All the noise and excitement scared her. Now that the ordeal was over, she shut her eyes tight as if she could pretend the violence never happened. She wanted no part of this. No more blood. When she opened her eyes again, Gears was hovering over her. She felt like a bug under a microscope.

Gears eyes went from studying her to looking at Red Hair intently. "That was close. God was looking out for you."

When Red Hair didn't answer him, he pulled out his little flashlight again.

"Not God," Red Hair exhaled.

"Fine, not God. How about this girl was looking out for you, then?" Gears chuckled, and she could tell Red Hair didn't think his comment was funny. His expression was stony. The sharp angles of his face seemed harder somehow.

"Tied up assassins don't call out warnings to people who have captured them. What's wrong with her, Gears?" Red Hair folded his arms over his massive chest. The muscles flexed under his shirt. Karma enjoyed the way the light hit his strong features. He was menacing and lovely, all at the same time. Behind her, she could vaguely hear someone leaving and the door being shut.

Gears shook his head and shrugged. He bent over to look at the cuts on her right thigh.

"I need to clean these cuts and close them. Cleanliness is next to godliness," Gears said in an off-handed way. "Josh said 'gave her stuff,' but I don't know what they did exactly. I'm examining her."

Gears swabbed her cuts with a cotton ball. After a few minutes, he glanced up at Red Hair again. "Is Ken coming back to take care of Josh and Charlie?"

"He'll do it after we're done here. He's hot-headed, but he gets the job done. I don't know what his problem is, but he'll cool off. He never did like those two. My dad hired them long ago at a different base, so I gave them a chance. I think Ken was pissed I kept them."

Karma was momentarily distracted by the conversation. She barely noticed as Gears ran his hands down her arms. His fingers were soft as they smoothed over her flesh.

"Hey, Mac, check this out."

So, Red Hair was named Mac? Karma wanted to giggle for some reason.

"Your name is Mac? That's silly," she murmured. "Like mac and cheese? That's noodles in a box. I had them once." She slurred her words. They hung around her ears in a mist.

Mac and Gears both looked at her. She stared into Mac's eyes. They were a delightful shade of green. She thought about how she used to have a pot of grass when she was younger. His eyes were the same color. Thick green grass, back when the sun could melt the snow.

"What's going on?" Mac leaned closer to her.

"I think one of them gave her my memory drug."

"Why do you say that?"

"I looked at the bottles set on the table. One of them is RCC100. I can tell because it's a cream, not a liquid. The other one is the drug that keeps you immobilized for 24 hours; that one has a scratch on the cap. I assumed that was the 'stuff' Josh was referring to. When he said that and I saw the bottle wasn't tampered with I didn't worry about it. But look here." Gears pointed to the floor. "There's an empty bottle. The only other thing he'd have had on him is the memory drug. The container is empty. You can see where the needle entered here." Gears' finger started to tug on her arm again.

"First, why didn't you label them? Second, what does the memory drug do exactly?"

"I lost my label maker."

"I'll get you a new one." Mac took a deep breath. "And the drug?"

"It erases your memories." Gears pressed his finger to his mouth like he might vomit. His eyes widened. He looked like a guilty puppy that just crapped on his master's bed. Karma thought she should be more concerned about losing her memories, but she wasn't. Caring about anything was way too difficult right now.

"Damn it. This is a mess. We need to know why she's here." Mac started to pace. He stopped in front of her chair. "First, we'll reverse it." Mac seemed to take charge. She accepted that. He was assertive. The confidence was sexy. "What do we give her to get her memories back? I want her exactly the way she was before."

Mac ran his hands through his hair. The red locks stood up on end. She liked it.

"I don't have anything for reversing it." Gears cringed like giving up that piece of new information physically hurt him.

"Tell me you're screwing with me."

"I'm sorry, Mac." Gears frowned and studied her again.

"Why'd you create a drug like that? What the hell is it for?" Mac's hands clenched into fists.

"I invented it because I heard on the news about elderly people who were having a hard time living in the NEDs. They couldn't stand being underground because they could still remember what it was like to live on the surface. I thought it would help some people transition. Look, it's still being worked on. I haven't perfected it. It's my first sample." Gears appeared defensive. Karma wanted to agree with him. Mac should back off. Helping old people was noble.

"I'm not placing all the blame on you. I know you work on your drugs in stages. Tell me how it works."

Mac gave a sharp nod like he had a handle on things. She let some of the tension ease from her shoulders. She had the feeling that he could deal with whatever came his way. They were working this out, so she'd sit back and let him problem-solve.

"If it helps, it doesn't seem permanent. I haven't tested it on humans yet, so I don't really know, but the rats I gave it to, most appeared to get their memories back over time. Some of them forgot how to do the maze for only a few days. Some forgot for months, and some for a few hours. Some rats it didn't seem to affect at all, but then again, you can't ask rats how they feel."

"You're telling me you don't know what'll happen?"

Karma tilted her head away when both men leaned close to her. Their eyes were roving all over her. Their whole bodies were tipped over hers as if waiting for her to speak. Were these men waiting for her to answer a major question? She actually wanted to help, but she didn't know how.

She stared back.

"I don't know exactly what'll happen, but I should tell you, some rats died."

Gears eyes skidded to the floor. Karma saw waves of pity in that look, and maybe fear, before he turned away. She wanted to tell him she'd live. Gears probably didn't know her well. If he did, he'd know she was strong. She always bounced back. Her father always said she had luck to spare. Flashes of her father popped in her head, and then vanished just as quickly.

"I'm bigger than a rat... so I probably won't die." When she spoke both men stilled. Their eyes widened. One of Mac's eyebrows rose.

Stop looking at me like that. It wasn't like she had two heads. She was about to demand they let her be, but the words became jumbled in her head. Why couldn't she keep her thoughts straight?

"What's your name?" Mac asked softly. "It's okay. Just tell me."

Taking in the whole room, she realized it wasn't familiar to her. Two men lay on the floor. How did they get there?

"Karma," she answered automatically. She knew her name. What an odd question.

Gears looked at the man with red hair and raised his eyebrows. A clear, silent question passed between them.

"The answer is the truth and a lie. It must be a name people call her, but it isn't her real name."

"Like when I go by Gears instead of Adam. It's a nickname, or a code name maybe?

"Right." Mac focused on her again. "Why are you here?"

"Because..." Why was she here? It was hard to remember. Her shoulders dropped. She didn't want to talk anymore. She wanted a glass of water.

Her eyes dropped to her lap. Blood was smeared along her legs. A large gash was etched into the front of her thigh. How did that happen? The redhead in front of her snapped his fingers at her. Had she met this man before? She studied his handsome features. Maybe she should know him. She merely needed a moment to think. If everyone would just be quiet for a second.

"Why are you here?" His voice was no longer soft and coaxing. He had an urgent note in his burr. If she could just try to think hard, the answer would come to her.

"My brother's a loser." She smiled. Her amusement didn't last long. Pain radiated over her face. Running her tongue over her lips, she tasted the coppery taint of blood. For some reason, that really didn't bother her. In fact, right now, nothing bothered her. She would've been happy to sit in this chair forever. She didn't have anywhere to go.

"I don't think this is going to work." The man in front of her moved to her side, while he took off his glasses to rub them on this shirt.

"What she said is true, but I don't know what it means. It could be code." He sighed. "Gears, how long before she won't remember anything?"

"I told you, they were rats!"

"Right. Look at me, Karma," Mac spoke in a stern voice. She focused on his face. She decided she liked his strong jaw, high cheekbones, and his slightly crooked nose. Thick red eyebrows curved above his green eyes. She wanted to run her fingers through his crazy mane of hair. If she could, she'd pull his head closer and drink him in.

Thinking of his strong arms and the muscles hidden beneath his shirt, she had the urge to push up the fabric and lick his skin

"Listen," he repeated sternly. "Why are you here?"

She wanted to tell him whatever he needed to know, but the problem was she didn't know what to say. She didn't know what he was asking.

Exhausted, she said the only thing which popped into her head.

"It's just my luck?"

Chapter 8

"I don't think taking her to your bedroom is a good idea."

Gears had a valid point, but Rea wasn't going to tell him that.

"I didn't ask your advice."

Rea carried her through the doorway of his bedroom past the kitchen table. He passed his computer desk before setting her down on his bed. Gently, he placed her head on his pillow.

"What if she gets her memory back and tries to kill you again?"

Gears arranged her legs so he could look at the bleeding cut on the front of her thigh. He bent over her.

"I know this isn't a thing I'd normally do, but I don't have a lot of options. All the men on this base are new. Ken does most of the hiring, so I have more time to train. I can't leave her to be raped in the interrogation room. If she wakes up alone, she could free herself and kill me or you or Eric, or she could leave. If she goes, I still won't have any answers as to what's going on." Rea ran his hands through his hair in frustration. "Gears, help me take the rest of these clothes off. I'll find something to put on her. You can close any other cuts."

Rea lifted her carefully into his arms and started to unzip, unbutton, and unsnap the elaborate front of her body suit. He found a sack sewn on her back. He pulled out an H&K MP5.

He'd felt a rigid metal item along her spine earlier. Now he knew what kind of weapon she'd been hiding.

While Rea pulled out smoke grenades and throwing knives from her pack, Gears washed his hands.

"Mac, I don't get you. Why do you care if some killer gets, well, taken advantage of by your men? Why are you protecting her? Because she saved your life when Josh tried to stab you?" Gears came over to the bed. He set his medical supplies down before helping Rea.

"Stop being dramatic; she didn't save my life."

"Why are you doing it, then?"

Rea didn't answer. Instead, he bent Karma's fragile frame forward. He tugged her arm out of her sleeve and realized he couldn't explain what it was about this woman. Over the years, Gears was one of the only people he'd ever told about his gift to know if someone was lying to him. Gears never judged him as a freak or tried to figure him out. Rea appreciated that. However, he didn't have the words to explain the fact he couldn't let this woman get hurt. He didn't know why, but she reminded him of someone. Letting her get hurt just wasn't in him.

As he removed pieces of bloody fabric that were stuck to her skin, he thought looking after her might be because this was the last base where he was going to work his ass off. Perhaps, now that his dad was dead, he was just trying out doing whatever he wanted.

Well, it didn't matter why he was looking after her. All he knew was he couldn't be so heartless as to allow her to be unprotected. In the end, he couldn't let her fend for herself with strange men, most of who rarely seemed to follow his orders. Gears could understand his having a gift, but he didn't think he could understand this unexplainable need to safeguard her.

After Gears and Rea had removed her suit, Rea sat back and studied the material. He also looked at the cell phone he pulled from one of the many pockets. Other than the weapons, the only other thing he noted was an old deck of playing cards.

Gears patched up her leg and all the other little cuts he could find with his healing cream. When he was finished, he gave her a drug he insisted would ease the pounding in her head.

As Rea noticed the tattoos that covered her arms, he scratched his head. Tattooing was expensive and rare nowadays. He read the words out loud, looking at the bold cursive lettering.

"What goes around," he read on her right arm, "comes around." He finished as he glanced up at her still face.

What goes around comes around was what karma was all about. Rea actually believed in that. He considered the type of person who would tattoo those words on her body. In the dark hours when his father was beating him, he had clung to the belief that one day his father would get what he deserved.

Wrinkling his brow, he picked up her body suit, pushing the unsettling reflections out of his mind. He thought instead about the workmanship of her outfit. He considered all the places where she could've gotten it. The cloth around her core was reinforced with a material similar to chain mail. The arms and legs were comprised of a thick breathable material. This suit was made to stand up to the harsh snowy elements and gunfire. The fabric was fantastic. He'd never seen anything even resembling it. This woman was no off-the-street killer hired to do a job. This woman was a professional who probably had money. No ordinary person would have a suit like this. No off-the-street hired gun would have a tattoo, either.

"She's all patched up. I even put something over her eye. After a few hours, she'll have less swelling and bruising." Gears paused. "Why do you look so upset now?"

"This fabric is incredible. This body suit has some serious design to it. She isn't some randomly hired gun. This woman's a professional and probably has money. Who'd hire someone like this to kill me? I can't come up with a reason someone would want me dead."

"I can."

"Thanks, *friend*."

Gears glanced up at him. "I'm sorry. That's not what I mean. I just meant that without you, I don't think the water bases would be the kind of safe places they are. Really, these bases are underground cities, and you're the mayor. That's a reason. You're our leader now that your father is gone."

"I think you're the mayor. Besides, all the water bases have someone left in charge of them. Those guys would be as much a target as me. My father would've been a target, too, but I never saw anyone trying to kill him."

That was too bad, and I'd have helped, Rea added in his mind.

"Yes, but now that your father is dead, everyone answers to you." Gears pushed up his glasses. "Maybe you never saw anyone try to kill your dad, but it doesn't mean no one ever tried. It wasn't like your dad would've told you about it. You were not close."

Rea didn't respond.

Actually, what Gears was talking about wasn't even helpful. Rea had more questions rolling about in his head than answers.

"Did you get anything off the phone?" Gears asked after silence fell between them. His friend picked up the body suit.

Rea opened the only message window blinking on the phone. "It says '1:05 Karma.'"

"It'd seem she had a timetable; either that or it could be code for who she was supposed to kill."

"A killer with a timetable isn't unique, and the Karma name could be 'coz of the tattoo." Rea ran his fingers over her arm and stared into her face. "I've a lot of questions for her when she wakes up. Is she awake? I'm having a hard time being able to tell."

Gears shrugged. "I don't know. Her eyes are open, but she hasn't talked for an hour now. She didn't even flinch while I was cleaning that deep wound on her thigh. I don't know what's going on with her. My rats didn't do anything like this that I can remember."

"Don't mention the damn rats again. It makes me want to punch you." Rea smirked so Gears would know he was joking, but really he *was* tired of the reference.

Rea was about to tell Gears he could go and that he'd call him on the intercom system later, when she groaned. Both men went to her side.

When Rea stood by the bedside, he took the opportunity to really study her as she lay there unmoving.

Karma was slight, but he could see her well-defined muscles. She had lush, full waves of dark hair. It was the kind of hair which, left free, would be everywhere. Her eyes were a rich brown, and a black fan of eyelashes surrounded them. If it were not for the circumstances, Rea would've said she was gorgeous. He'd never seen a woman like her. She had perfectly proportioned features and a small sharp nose above a soft-looking sensual mouth. Her lips were plump. The only thing which marred their perfection was the bruising on the right side.

Standing there feeling dumbstruck, he let his eyes wander slowly lower. He looked first to the swell of her breasts, which rose and fell, and then he gazed at her smooth belly.

He found himself staring at the junction of her legs where he pictured lying. He realized where his eyes were traveling, and he quickly pulled them back to her face. They betrayed him, and he glanced again at her rounded breasts encased in a light-pink lace bra. Her underwear matched with the same pink lace design covering the dark hair he could see slightly. The sheer lace was flimsy and utterly feminine. Tiny flowers were sewn into the elastic at the top. Rea thought it ridiculous that under hardened fabric designed to shield her from bullets she chose to wear this. He wished she was wearing more unattractive undergarments instead. If she were wearing ugly panties, then maybe he'd feel differently. Who was he kidding? She could be dressed in a brown-paper sack, and he'd still feel completely captivated by her.

"What kind of woman puts on pink lace underwear to go kill people?" Gears voiced Rea's thoughts. Rea was instantly annoyed that Gears was seeing her practically naked.

He grabbed the corner of his old blanket and threw it over her body.

"She looks sexy in it, too." Gears grinned at him as if he knew what he was thinking. Rea felt his neck heat up. He was acting possessive. It was not a good idea to think of her as anything other than the assassin who tried to kill him. She wasn't his… anything.

"You've a girlfriend. Keep your eyes to yourself." Rea knew he sounded jealous. He silently dared Gears to comment on it.

"I can look at the menu; I just can't order," Gears muttered back at him.

"May I have some water?" Karma's weak whisper pulled both Gears and Rea away from the awkward staring contest.

Both of them looked down at her and stood there mutely. She looked slight and pale. She seemed like the last person on Earth Rea could picture hurting anyone.

"Water, I can get water." Gears rushed to the kitchen. He threw open one of the cabinet doors and fumbled for a glass. A plastic cup fell to the counter and then bounced to the floor. Gears still had his eyes on Karma, and he didn't pick the lost cup up. Instead, he filled the glass clutched in his hand. Water splashed over his fingers.

He hurried back to the bed. His friend's hands were shaking, and his eyes jumped to Karma, then to him. As if the whole thing was too much for Gears to deal with, he shoved the glass into Rea's hand. Water splashed on Rea's wrist.

The doctor turned away from Karma. He went to sit in front of Rea's computer monitors at the desk. The squeak of the chair was a clear sign Gears didn't know what to do. He was effectively passing this whole mess into Rea's lap. He'd thank his friend for that later.

Rea handed her the water, making sure their fingers didn't touch. She struggled to sit up enough to hold the glass. He stopped himself from helping her and rested his hands on his biceps.

In a strange show of modesty, she held his blanket close to her chest. Karma held the glass with one hand and the blanket with her other. She drank the whole glass before giving it back to him.

Once she handed the glass back to him, her hand flew up to the bandage over her eye. The other eye, which wasn't covered, ran all over his face. He could see the question there. He fought the urge to reach out to comfort her. His fingers squeezed the water glass until he was afraid it might break.

"You have to keep the patch on so the swelling goes down. Do you know where you are?" Rea asked instead of soothing her. Touching her wasn't a good idea. He needed to keep his distance. He needed to think interrogation and killer.

"Yes, of course I do. I'm..." She faltered. Her perfectly sculpted eyebrows came together in confusion. Some black-and-blue bruises darkened her brow.

"Do you know what your name is?" Rea was going to be as stern as possible. It fell flat.

Again she half smiled and nodded, but when she opened her mouth nothing came out.

Panic filled her eyes, and they bounced around the room. Tears gathered. Rea hoped she wouldn't cry.

"Your name is Karma. Check your arms if you don't believe me." Rea ran his hands through his hair.

What the hell would he do if she cried? Professional killers didn't cry. He couldn't question her like this. He'd have to start after she was feeling better. Maybe he'd wait and see if her memories came back.

She lifted her arms. Her fingers traced the words tattooed on her flesh. The tears didn't fall. Instead, she smiled at the black cursive. Rea heaved a sigh of relief, and then turned to Gears.

"I guess that answers the question of what she knows. This is great, Gears. *Great*." Rea spat out that last word.

He couldn't stand there and watch her with that half-mystified expression on her face. He turned away to walk back to his kitchen area when her voice stopped him.

"But you didn't ask me if I knew what your name was."

Rea tossed a quick glance at Gears, who shrugged. He then turned around and braced his hip against his desk. Crossing his arms over his chest, he lifted one of his eyebrows at her.

"You got my attention. I'll play along. Do you know what my name is?"

"Absolutely. Your name is Joseph-Rea, Joseph-Rea MacBain, but you let me call you Rea."

The glass in Rea's hand slipped. The crash of it hitting the cement pierced the charged silence. As the glass shards sprinkled across the floor, he tried to get his shock under control.

Gears shot up from his chair. His eyes went wide.

"What's wrong?" Gears asked, but Rea couldn't speak. He just stood there trying to process. How the hell did she know his real name? His father had only ever called him MacBain in training. Gears called him Mac. The men who worked for him called him Boss-Mac. Who could possibly know his real name?

"What is it?" Gears insisted.

"That's my name." He barely got the words out. They came out in a strangled whisper.

"No, it's not; it's..." Gears frowned "It's... I thought it was... something MacBain..." Gears paused again. "I never realized I didn't know your full name. I guess I never asked." His friend chuckled, but when Rea didn't laugh, he sobered. "Mac, are you feeling well?"

"Yes, it is. Joseph-Rea MacBain. MacBain is my last name. How could she know that? She knows my full name."

"It's no big deal. Maybe she has some type of gift like you do. It's a nice name, I guess. Don't worry about it. I don't think less of you because your name is Joseph-Rea." Gears paused. "And no one else will either."

Gears was nodding like the gift thing was the answer. Rea hid his irritation. Sometimes Gears could be the dumbest smart person he'd ever met.

Still reeling, Rea looked around Gears at Karma. She was settling herself in his bed. Her blanket kept falling down as she moved. She kept trying to fix it to cover her chest. Her shyness was almost endearing, almost. This was a killer, Rea reminded himself. Killers were known to be conniving.

As soon as she noticed him looking at her, she stopped moving and smiled sweetly at him. The way she looked at him was odd, like she recognized him. Like they were friends. They weren't friends. He didn't have friends. He only had Gears, work, and more work.

She gave him an inviting grin and patted the bed like he should join her.

"How do you know that?" Rea demanded to combat the warm feeling growing inside of him.

"Your father named you. He named you Joseph-Rea because he got the name from an Irish boxer he heard of who was young and healthy. It's a strong Irish name, your dad claimed. He liked the toughness of it. Your mom didn't want to call you that. She hated it. But your father made a big deal out of it because she got to name your two older brothers. Your father insisted it was his turn. That's what he picked. He wanted you to be a real Irish fighter like him.

The only problem was he thought you didn't live up to his grand fighting name."

Rea shook his head. No one knew that. No one. He needed to think. Gears was standing like a statue. No help there. He stepped around the doctor and towered over the bed. When she tipped her head up and smiled at him again, Rea threw his body forward. He put his face inches from Karma. He tried in vain to read her expression. He wanted to uncover how she knew so much. He tried to see into her mind, to where she'd gotten that information.

To Rea's surprise, Karma didn't see the movement as an act of aggression. She didn't tip back or try to move away from his crowding posture. Her lips twitched into another slight smile. She seemed amused by him. He didn't know what to make of her reaction.

Karma's eyes studied him intently. They bounced over his face. Flecks of gold danced in her dark, enchanting depths. She reached up with her hand and slowly moved one lock of red hair away from his brow. His breathing became ragged as she dragged a finger across his cheek before letting her hand fall to her lap. Karma looked understanding and much too adorable. Who was this woman? How could she know all about him? It was strange to feel like he knew her, yet not know her.

"Who told you that?" Rea's voice came out hypnotic. She'd have to answer him. She'd feel compelled. His gift would force the truth from her just like it had forced the truth from so many men before her.

"You did, silly." Her smile turned broad. A dimple appeared on her left cheek.

When her smile disrupted her lips, she winced. Her tongue darted out and ran over the swollen area.

As they faced each other, he started to feel uneasy. He didn't like that she was staring at him like they were the best of friends. He dropped his gaze from her face, and instead concentrated on the thin blanket covering her body.

"Is what she said true?" Gears moved to sit in the office chair. Rea heard it roll across the cement.

"She thinks it's true."

"But is it really true? I mean, does your gift say she's telling the truth?"

Rea thought about how to answer his question. His gift was more of an unnamed gut instinct. Her answer was true to her, and her guess on his name was accurate, but it was hard to explain all that to Gears. The doctor part of him would never let this go. It wasn't like him to have an unsolved mystery. He wished he had the right words so Gears could understand.

"Yes, my gut says it's true, but this doesn't make sense. I was named after some boxer my dad was impressed with, but Mom used to call me Jo-Jo." Rea thought about how much it hurt when his mother died. He cleared his throat and swallowed. "Dad said Jo-Jo was not manly, so he called me MacBain. Dad said Mom ruined my name. No one called me Joseph or Rea, ever. Dad said those two names were too friendly. He also made sure I always protected my name and my identity. We moved to build new bases, and I never got to know anyone long enough to tell them my real name. After a while, I didn't give a shit anymore."

Rea leaned further away from Karma, drained after talking about his father. He'd worked hard to bury as many memories of his father as he could. As for Karma, he didn't know what to make of her or the electricity between them. The warmth of her skin called to his.

He shoved away from her and turned to face Gears. His hand gestured to Gears to get up. Gears frowned at him and took a deep breath. They had known each other for so long he didn't have to speak a word. Gears got up and stepped to the side. Rea sat down with a hard flop and folded his arms. The chair made a squeak as it rolled back.

"My turn is it, Jo-Jo?" Gears' eyes danced with amusement that Rea didn't appreciate.

"You're on thin ice, Mr. The-rat's-didn't-do-this-kind-of-thing."

Gears chuckled as he sat on the corner of the bed. He reached out for Karma's arm and turned her wrist in his hand. She let him turn her palm up. He put two fingers on her pulse. Gears cleared his throat a few times. He took his time crossing his legs, like he was getting ready for a long chat.

After this had gone on much longer than it should, Rea decided he wanted to kick him.

"Karma, it's nice to meet you. I'm Adam, but you can call me Gears." He readjusted his legs and crossed them at the ankles. "I was wondering how you know so much about Mac. Would you like to share with us?" Gears' smile was a little too solicitous. Rea could see Karma wasn't enthusiastic about his condescending tone. She snatched her hand away.

"You don't need to treat me like a child. I know Mac, as you call him. Rea and I've been friends for… well, I don't know how long, but…" She hesitated. "He and I were… or we are…" She trailed off and looked befuddled again.

She picked up her blanket and looked down at her underwear.

"What's wrong?" Rea tilted forward in the chair.

He didn't like the troubled look on her face. Some part of him wanted her safe and content here with him. That was insane, but he couldn't shake the thought. Maybe if she didn't look so cute and disoriented. He wished she was trying to kill him again, so this wouldn't be so damn confusing.

"It's only… just that… we were sleeping together, and I guess we must still be together, because I've no other reason why I'd be in Rea's bed with no clothes on. I don't have sex with just anyone. I have morals."

The word "morals" coming out of an assassin's mouth made him almost smile. He stopped himself from commenting.

"Wait, how do you know it's Mac's bed? Maybe it's my bed, or this is your room." Gears squinted. He tipped his head to the side. Rea recognized that look. Gears got that look when he was trying to assess a problem that was baffling him.

"I know where I am. Really, this is where Rea lives. It smells like him, like his soap. Plus, the setup of the room is the same. When we were younger, Rea, I mean, Mac or whatever you call him, he used to put his dining table there so if his dad came in to beat him the door would hit the wood. When the door hit, that'd give Rea time to get up and sometimes run away. Sometimes he didn't get away, though. I remember a few times you fell face-first into that table."

"My heavens, is that right?" Gears sounded horrified. His eyes held pity. "You said that your dad only beat you in the training ring. I didn't think he'd do that to you alone. Do you want to talk about it?"

Rea didn't want pity. He speared Karma with a hot glare and rubbed his palms on his jeans. How could she possibly know that about him? He tried to remember telling anyone about his past, but nothing came to mind. Over the years, he had known very few females. He'd moved to so many different bases. He'd remember a woman like this, wouldn't he?

"No."

"Okay." Gears tipped his head again. He seemed to be considering his next question.

"Karma, how about if you tell me how you met Mac. I mean, Rea."

Frustrated at both the lunatics in his room, Rea ran his hands back and forth through his hair.

"How I met Rea? That's a great story, if you don't mind me telling it. As I recall, you didn't like it when I told people." Karma shot him a quick sidewise glance. A dazzling smile crossed her face. Her one uncovered eye shone as she giggled at him. It was evident she was warming up to this new topic. She looked stunning when she smiled at him. Rea decided he hated it.

"Go ahead." He frowned at her. He crossed his arms back over his chest.

He didn't care what she had to say. He didn't care about her bright smile or her lovely eyes or her hot body. He reclined in his chair, waiting to see what insane nonsense she'd utter next. It was one thing to know his name and guess about his room, but she'd better tell a story he could remember. Otherwise, he was going to tell Gears the drug he'd made had the ability to make people delusional.

"My mom and step-dad had just died," she began. "My stepbrother took all our money and ran off. I was on my own. And I'd just moved here with my uncle, who was a big, tough harvester. Uncle worked on the surface collecting things from the snow. He brought things back and lived at the water base. He was the only family I was in contact with, and he wasn't around much. I was sixteen when I came to live with him. I think he didn't really know what to do with a teenage girl. So one day he asked Meghan, that's Rea's mom, he asked her to watch me.

"Meghan and I worked in the greenhouses at first, and then one day I was lonely so I asked Meghan if I could have dinner with her and—"

Rea held up his hand, and the action stopped her from continuing. The memory started to come to him vaguely. Slowly, the more he thought about it, that one happy year he had in his youth came back to him. As he recalled it, the more vivid it became. Long ago, he'd pushed it all out of his head, but now he remembered parts. Little instances flashed in his brain.

"And you came in all muddy. Mom said you could use our shower. I heard the water turn on and I snuck in."

"And you watched me shower." Karma's laugh was like tinkling bells. Chills ran down his spine. Her voice was so full of joy he could feel it all the way down in his toes. He remembered that sound.

Now, staring at her, he could see just a tiny bit of the girl he knew a long time ago. She was no longer a young girl, sure, but the color of her eyes became heartbreakingly familiar. The Karmen-Marie he had known had a larger nose. She also had a sharper chin and chubby cheeks. Her form was soft, plump, and short. This woman didn't look anything like her, yet it was her. All the pieces started to fall into place.

"You caught me." He looked up at the ceiling for a second before scanning her again. This whole situation was starting to feel surreal.

"And I gave you hell. I told you I was going to tell your mom. I called you a pervert, I think," Karma spoke again. She giggled, and her eyes danced.

"But you didn't tell Mom. I begged for you to not say anything. We became friends."

"I forgave you, but I nicknamed you Peeping Tom. But, yeah, you became the best friend I ever had." Karma gave another one of her joyful laughs. Rea scooted forward in his chair, and the sound of her laughter seemed to melt his soul.

He placed his forearms on his thighs. Every memory of the one year they spent together filled his mind. Back then he'd been completely captivated by her.

"You didn't forgive me. I never worked so hard for a girl in my entire life," Rea chuckled. He found her laughter contagious. A broad smile forced its way onto his face when he thought about all the things she'd had him do to earn her forgiveness. "You made me brush out that messy hair of yours." He scooted closer to the bed. Her hand squeezed his knee.

"It wasn't that bad," she hooted and tossed her still incredibly long hair over her shoulder.

"I did it for a month." Rea stopped his hand from reaching out to those soft strands.

They'd had so much fun back then. When he'd been with her, it didn't matter what they did together; it had been fantastic. Karma made brushing her hair as fun as one of those old amusement park rides he'd read about. It was an essence that was a part of her.

"I forgave you for looking at me in the shower, but after you just wanted to lose your virginity. I'm pretty sure you did all that work to get into my pants."

"You gave in, but it took a lot of brushing," Rea snorted.

"Once I slept with you, I recall you used to whisper to me every night that you loved me. Remember you named me Kitten? You were so cute. You were so devoted you'd follow me around everywhere."

"I did not." A short laugh escaped his lips.

He remembered she was completely right about how hard he'd worked for her. He'd said whatever he could think of to keep her in his bed. Back then, she was the only thing that had made the water base bearable. Back then she'd been the only thing that had kept him together after his mother died.

"As I recall, you promised to never be with anyone else as long as you lived. I think you even promised to go up to the surface for me. All I had to do was ask." Karma glanced at Gears and added, "It was all very romantical."

"Romantical? That's not a word," Gears said with a scowl on his face. He looked so austere that someone might've thought that they were discussing Canada's current rule over the C.T.O.N.A.

"Romantical is Karma's word for romantic and magical," Rea answered automatically. He couldn't believe he remembered her made-up word for their relationship.

Rea and Karma burst out laughing when Gears gave them both a look of irritation. Rea remembered how much laughter the two of them had shared. That half a year when his mom was still alive and he was with Karmen-Marie, he'd been truly happy. She was right when she said he'd have done anything to sleep with her.

He remembered them losing their virginity to each other. It had been just before his mom had died. She'd been, as she always was with everything, fearless. Karmen made everything look easy. After one taste of her, he'd become obsessed. She'd been incredible in bed and out of it, and she honestly cared for him. Karma had been the only person in his life other than his mom who had ever actually known him and loved him. She was smart, sweet, and plucky.

Late at night, after his mom had died and things got horrible, he'd snuck out continually to be with her. Sometimes he'd gotten beaten for it, but it didn't matter. Karmen-Marie had been worth every hit. Then one day, she was gone. She didn't even say goodbye. Rea had been so heartbroken he'd pushed her out of his mind for good. He never let his mind think of her.

After all these years, it was strange to have the memories come back to him.

Rea put his hands out and pushed himself away from the bed. The chair groaned as it rolled back. He sobered when he thought about how she'd left him. It had been cruel. One day she was wrapped around him like a purring kitten. Next, it was like she'd never existed.

Staring at her now, he couldn't believe how she still had beautiful eyes and that same abundant mane of dark hair. She still had a dazzling smile and a laugh that made him feel like he could conquer the world.

She was all that, and she'd tried to kill him.

"Where did you go?" The words fell from his lips as he realized they were not friends reminiscing. She was a killer. She wasn't his girlfriend anymore. They were no longer sixteen. Karma had come here to kill him, and he didn't even know why.

"I didn't go anywhere, silly. I'm right here."

Chapter 9

"I'm sorry if I don't remember you, Doctor Gears. I guess this bump on my head is worse than I thought." Karma smiled shyly and settled against the pillow.

She was so happy to be laughing and talking with Rea, without him looking upset like he was earlier. She was so pleased that she didn't care her head still pounded or that she didn't have all her memories. Soon it would all come back to her.

"It's fine that you don't remember me," Gears mumbled in an almost sarcastic tone. "My name's just Gears. Like I said, I'm the doctor on this water base, so I'm aware of your memory issues."

Gears sat at the end of the bed. He smiled a wobbly smile at her. The smile wasn't sincere. Karma could tell. She didn't know why she thought he sounded irritated, but she was sure he was annoyed at her for something. She'd have to ask Rea about her relationship with Gears once they were alone together.

When she didn't respond to his second introduction, Gears stood up, pushing his glasses up his nose. He gave Rea a pointed look.

"I think I'm interrupting your catching-up session. I feel like a third wheel. I'm going. I'm tired. It's late."

"Gears, don't go. You gotta help me." Rea quickly rose. He put his hand out to stop the doctor from exiting.

Rea's voice had a demanding edge to it. Was he still worried about her health? Maybe he didn't want the doctor to go because he didn't think she was healing. When she took stock of her whole body, she felt not *that* bad. She didn't know how she'd gotten hurt in the first place, but after some rest, it would come back to her. She wasn't going to worry about her memory loss right now.

Karma ran her hands under the blanket and over the bandage that covered the front of her leg. Her thigh didn't hurt, and even her headache was abating. Whatever had happened must have been minor. Other than the patch covering her eye and the cut in her mouth, she was relaxed. The muscles in her shoulders unwound like she had been stressed for a decade and was finally getting a vacation.

As soon as Gears pushed past Rea, both men went to what must be the exit into the hall. Karma spotted the bathroom. She decided to get out of bed while Rea and Gears talked. She looked down at the chilly concrete to see if she had any shoes. Her feet ached from the cold, and she almost abandoned the idea of leaving the warm blanket. She wrapped the thin fabric around her body tightly, knotting it between her breasts.

Distracted by the chill, she located Rea's enormous green slippers near the front of the bed. She reached down to slip them on.

She had just grasped them when she was jerked abruptly by her arm.

"What the hell are you doing?" Rea looked at her like she was a thief about to steal his most precious possession.

His hold was brutal. His entire hand was wrapped around her upper arm.

As his body crowded hers, his chest pressed against her breasts. Her nipples hardened at the contact, and she reacted to him like she always did. Their sexual chemistry hadn't changed. It didn't matter how much time had passed.

She tried to twist away from him. His grip felt like it would turn her bones to dust. Rea was so aggressive, so angry. Even with his harsh movements, her body yearned for him and her blood heated. Why was it, no matter the situation, she always wanted him? Some things didn't change, even if they were older.

"I was going to put on your slippers. I have to use the bathroom… maybe clean up?" Her voice quivered, and her eyebrows made a deep "v" above her eyes.

She wished she didn't have this bump on her head and that she could put together what was wrong between them. She'd always cared for Rea. That hadn't changed no matter how old she was. Maybe he didn't like her the same way any longer? What would she do if she found out they were no longer together?

That couldn't be the case. They had to still be together because she wasn't the kind of girl to be naked in a man's bed unless they had some type of commitment to each other. She could also tell Rea was still attracted to her. He'd never been able to hide the way his eyes hungrily roamed over her.

"Oh." He let go.

Clutching the blanket tighter, she moved around him toward the bathroom.

"I've weapons under my bed. I thought she was going to reach for those," Rea muttered to Gears, who was near the door.

Her back to Rea, she paused with her hand on the bathroom door. She frowned. She didn't even know how to shoot a gun, so why would he think that?

She decided to push all of her worries out of her head for now. She could figure out everything once she was feeling clean and refreshed.

Karma entered the dingy bathroom. Once there, she went around the room in a trance as she used the toilet and brushed her teeth with his toothbrush. She hunted for a hairbrush through the shabby cabinets, and she browsed some of the things on the shelves. He had the same toothpaste, the same deodorant, and the same soap. His bathroom was clean but tattered. This room had the same cement floor in front of a rusted sink she remembered from her youth.

Things here were so identical that, if it weren't for the fact she was taller, she'd have thought no time had passed since the last night she could remember being with him. She remembered the last time they had sex, but then it was all blank. She tried in vain to remember how she'd hurt her head, but after a short period, she gave up.

Karma found a mirror in the last cabinet she opened. Slowly she eased the patch off her eye. While looking at the purple-and-blue bruises on the side of her face, she squinted at her reflection. Her eyes scanned her face. She realized she wasn't as old as she had originally thought. She felt eighty, but she guessed that she was in her twenties. Holding the mirror closer, she studied her nose, chin, and some faded scars on her neck. It was evident she'd had work done to her face, but she couldn't come up with why.

She couldn't let go of the mirror. She was positive she had a different nose. It was smaller. She turned her head first one way, then the other, and knew her chin was different as well. Because she'd never been vain, plastic surgery seemed out of character.

Maybe it was best she put the mirror away. None of this really mattered. Who cared if she'd had some plastic surgery and lost weight. She was still her. She'd have to ask Rea why she made all these changes later. When she was feeling better.

Once she put the mirror back, she expected some panic to envelop her. When it didn't come, she considered how odd that was. A huge part of her kept saying that even if she knew nothing about her life right now, it was all fine as long as she was with Rea. As she started to loosen her ponytail, she reminded herself that Rea had always cared for her. He loved her. He'd help her until she healed. No reason to freak out.

After slowly brushing all the tangles out of her hair, Karma made up her mind that the one thing that would make her feel better would be a shower. First a shower, then she could talk to Rea about her memory loss. When they were younger, they always talked and figured things out as a pair. If she could get cleaned up and spend some time with him, everything would feel normal again.

Her fingers unknotted the threadbare blanket. Karma stripped herself of her bra and underwear next. She stepped into the small tiled area next to the toilet, over the cement blocks that divided it from the rest of the room. Carefully, she pulled the brittle, short white shower curtain as far as the plastic rings would go.

The plastic divider barely covered the space to separate the shower from the rest of the bathroom. She adjusted the curtain as best she could. Bending over slightly, being careful of her injuries and the bandage on her thigh, she turned the water lever to hot.

She stepped in front of the water, but then jumped out of the spray coming at her with ice-cold velocity. She fiddled with the handles until the water turned to a tepid cascade.

Wetting her hair, she groped for some soap and began to gently wash her scalp.

"What're you doing?" Rea's deep baritone voice made her jump. She screamed and clutched the curtain she had just painstakingly straightened.

"You scared me." Karma laughed.

It was a silly question to ask her what she was doing. Wasn't it obvious? She giggled. Did Rea come in to check if she was feeling well? The idea he would worry about her made her heart do a funny flip-flop in her chest. It was wonderful to have someone care about her like he did.

"I'm showering, silly. Do you want to join me?" Smiling carefully so as to not disrupt the cut in her mouth, Karma pushed the shower divider away from her body. She saw his eyes widen, and a slight exhale slipped past his lips.

Whatever the state of their relationship, she could tell his attraction to her hadn't changed, and she thanked God for that. She stood still and let him drink in the sight of her naked wet flesh.

"I don't think…" Rea stammered, but he didn't look away or move. He stood frozen in front of her. She could see some sort of internal war take over his thoughts. She didn't want him thinking or worrying about her right now. Right now, she wanted to feel him, touch him, and connect with him. If they could have some time together, she'd be able to tell if they were going strong.

"That's right, don't think, silly." Karma reached out to grab his shirt in the center of his chest. Her wet hand left dark drops of water spreading across the green fabric.

She used only one swift tug, and it had him stumbling into her embrace. Once in the shower, their lips locked instantly. Her resolve to have him intensified.

Kissing Rea was like being doused in flames, and every part of her body wanted to dance in that fire. His lips were firm and insistent. She liked that once he started he didn't hesitate. His mouth took over hers with a powerful aggressiveness. He kissed her as if he was a dying man and she was the only thing that could keep him alive.

Rea reached around and cupped her ass. His other hand in the middle of her back, held her even closer, with no regard to his clothes getting doused. This was what it had always been like for the two of them, and she wanted it to never end. Karma immediately sensed the passion in her rise like music hitting a crescendo. His hand lifted her ass. Water ran down her front and drops caressed her already wet pussy. Her wet slit squeezed in anticipation, and she let all the sensations of having him thunder through her.

His cock was straining against his jeans. A primal need in her wanted him naked right this second. Her body was heavy, aching, and yearning. Rea moved from Karma's lips to her neck, while he nibbled in between each heart-throbbing kiss. Karma tipped her head to the side to give him better access. Rea got a mouthful of her wet, wild hair. He took a small step back as if to escape her. She wouldn't accept his retreat and tore his shirt right down the middle, exposing his damp chest hair. Karma didn't know where the strength came from, but she couldn't stop herself from letting her hands run over his exposed skin.

"What the hell? That was my favorite shirt." The smile that tugged on his lips made her think he really didn't care. He looked down at her and brushed his hand over her cheek.

Karma wanted him naked and inside of her... no waiting. She wanted him wild and rough as always. In her memories, Rea was the aggressor. When she had asked him why, Rea told her it was because sex with her was the only time he was in charge. Karma had thought that funny; now, however, she wanted him in charge and unrelenting.

"It's your fault. You shouldn't be in the shower with your clothes on," Karma responded quickly, with a mischievous smile playing on her lips. She dipped her head to lick the water dripping off one of his nipples.

As Rea shoved out of his torn shirt, Karma latched her nails onto his back and held on. She started to kiss his chest and lick his nipples again. Warm water rolled down her back, and she could feel the water slide along her anus. Her pussy was rubbing against him, and her ass was begging to be touched as well.

When he finally ran his hand over her backside to dip between her cheeks, she sighed. Everything about him was as she remembered, and she moved in the way he liked. She wanted this desire to be mutual and to chase away all his worries.

He groaned in her ear. Good. She could still make him frantic. Rea was about to kiss her again when Karma held out a hand to stop him.

"I'd suggest you take off your favorite pants before I do."

Rea laughed and splashed some water on her face, making her sputter and giggle.

"They're not my favorites."

He ran his hands down her slippery back, and she could tell he was going to give in to her. Knowing she'd won made her inwardly cheer.

"Good." She latched onto his belt. Rea quickly pushed her hands away and started undoing his wet pants on his own. How long had it been since they had been together like this? Karma had the distinct feeling this urgency, which was taking over, was because it had been a while for them both.

"I'll get this one." Rea bent his head and was now trying to stay centered while taking off his pants.

Karma continued to touch and taste his skin as the water, and her pussy, slowly started to heat up. She was giddy with the idea that soon he'd be naked before her, and she tugged him closer to capture his mouth once more. With his head bent and his flame-colored hair turning a deep, dark red, Karma half-heartedly watched him keep his balance while kissing her.

Before he got his last leg out of the clinging fabric, Karma's hands found his swollen, hard cock. She gripped the thick shaft, overwhelmed to have the hard flesh rubbing against her palms. His prick was long, and the moist tip dripped into her hands. His dick was much bigger than she remembered. She heard his breath come out in a whoosh as she stroked him.

"I don't think…" Rea began a second time. She saw the inner battle return, but she kept touching him and trying to keep his thoughts from returning to concerns. She wanted him with her now and not thinking about the past or the future. That's how it had been when they had sex before. She didn't want anything less.

"That's right, don't think," Karma whispered to the hot damp skin of his neck.

Rea lost control, tried to kiss her, shove off his pants, and touch her, all at the same time.

With all his pent-up passion and erratic movements, he fell over.

Karma looked down at him lying at her feet. A burst of laughter tumbled out of her mouth. When he glanced up at her, she bent down to see if he was injured and if he could get up again. With suppressed giggles, she offered him her hand.

"Are you hurt?"

"Only my pride," he responded, as he began to push himself up on his elbows.

"Silly," Karma grabbed at the thick muscles of his arms as she helped him to his feet.

She quickly distracted him by gently grabbing his rod and stroking the head, hoping she could get back to where they were only moments ago.

The feel of him under her fingertips was so intense. It seemed as though Rea was thrusting himself into her hand. She liked how his eyes turn drowsy and sexy as they slid shut.

His head dropped back. Rea wrapped his arms around her again and pulled her chest to his face so he could fondle her breasts. In one quick move, he had one nipple between his searching fingers and the other drawn into his hot mouth. Karma stopped moving her hands and enjoyed the attention as her head fell against his shoulder. She inhaled his scent while she pushed them both out of the spray of the now-hot water.

When her hand slowed its movements over his body, Rea stopped and looked at her.

"I didn't tell you to stop moving your hand," Rea growled at her. His voice was ragged and demanding.

Karma smiled at his insistent tone. She excitedly started pumping his hardness again as he bent his head toward her breasts. Rea was pinching one nipple and being extremely gentle with the other. It wasn't long before she stopped moving her hand again while moaning with pleasure. She saw Rea glance up into her eyes. She hoped he could see the ecstasy he gave to her. He could always read her so well. She could feel her pussy clenching as if seeking his dick, and she wanted to beg for him to end the torment of being empty inside.

Without warning, he spun her around, bending her against the shower wall. He pressed her against the tiles, letting his hands roam freely over her back.

"Beg me." Rea's deep baritone was thick with desire. There was an unyielding order hovering in the air.

He took a firm position behind her this time, probably so he wouldn't fall. She felt his erection nudge her ass.

"Please, I'm begging," she gasped while she pressed harder against the wall.

Both of his hands reached around her, and he put one hand on her wet pussy lips as the other continued up to tease her nipples. With his fingers, he spread her lips wide for his eager pole and rubbed slightly in a slow teasing gesture. Moan after moan escaped her as Rea slipped in effortlessly from all of her moisture and the pre-cum dripping from him.

Karma let out a garbled cry of euphoria as her channel clamped down on his prick and she thrust back against him. This is what she would always want. She wanted him inside of her forever. If they had ever broken up before, none of that mattered. From now on she was never leaving his side. Karma had her hands braced up against the wall to push back into Rea, but she started to slip, and she grabbed onto the shower head above her. Rea began to pump into her vigorously, and she heard his breathing becoming rapid.

He didn't seem to notice her legs shaking as she tried to hold the position. It didn't take long before Karma's body exploded under the touch of his seeking fingers and thrusting cock.

Rea's fingers were dancing over her clit, and her body was in tune with his shaft swelling inside of her. He would ejaculate soon, she was positive. That's what she wanted. His rod moving inside of her was calling to another orgasm that was just out of reach.

Her body twitched with a barely contained frenzy. As she got close to coming a second time, she gasped his name and snapped the shower head off the wall. The spray of water was brutal. Rea reached over to turn off the water before the rough spray sliced through both their skins.

"No!" Karma cried with her body strung tight like a bow.

Rea only laughed as Karma spun around and threw her wet willing body at him.

Chapter 10

"What's wrong?" Rea asked playfully as he reached over and turned off the gushing water. He turned to watch Karma with wide, unblinking eyes and pretended ignorance.

He knew exactly how she felt right now because he was energized with all the pent-up sexual tension as well.

Rea didn't let it show in his expression as he stared down into her alluring eyes. His dick was still painfully hard, and it throbbed between their bodies. He wanted to explode more than breathing right now.

He grinned when she squirmed against him in a brazenly shameless gesture. Her belly was rubbing lightly over his engorged tip, and he had to grit his teeth to stop from entering her again. How long had it been since a woman had wanted him like this? Hell, he would've said the last woman he could remember being eager for him would've been Karmen-Marie when they were young. There was something powerful in knowing he was making her wait; having the upper hand was a potent aphrodisiac. He loved making her lust rise.

"You know what's wrong," she pouted, and she reached between their bodies to grip his overly sensitive shaft. Her tongue passed over her bottom lip, and she fluttered her eyelashes. He wanted to bite her mouth and then lick the sting away.

When the hot spray blasted his skin, he thought he had a moment of clarity about what he was doing. He shouldn't be having sex with her. What they were doing was a bad idea, considering she didn't even know who she was. At any moment her memories could return. But as soon as he was near her, all his good intensions vanished. When he tasted her, he found himself wanting to be with her like in the old days.

As he smiled down at her upturned face, he gloried in the fact she thirsted for him so badly. He clamped down on his own lust for a second and scooped her up into his arms. She always made him feel desired and wanted. He ignored all other thoughts and left the shower.

Karma quickly wrapped her arms around his neck and lifted her legs around his waist. Her face brightened in eager anticipation and triumph. Rea carried her to the door of the bathroom and pressed her back against the smooth wood surface. He loved it when she looked at him like there was some sort of victory in getting him to have sex with her.

"Do you remember this, Kitten?" he whispered into her ear. He kissed her neck as he slowly started to lower her body onto his still-hard cock. "Do you remember all the things we used to do?"

She shivered in his arms and moaned his name as he slowly penetrated her. Some animalistic part of him felt he'd captured her. It was so right to have her trapped in his arms. Short of an avalanche, nothing was going to stop him this time.

Karma gripped his dick like a hot, wet glove. She'd always made him feel like the dominant man when he was with her. That hadn't changed. Having sex with her had been an eraser. It had the power to delete everything dark that had happened to him all day long. When he was inside of her, he was in charge, and no one told him what to do. He didn't have to be anyone but her lover. He had no responsibility other than to make her scream his name.

"I remember when you used to tease me. Don't tease, Rea," Karma pleaded.

Rea settled her all the way down on his penis until he was buried to his balls in her tight folds. She gripped him with such force it took him a second to keep from falling apart.

Gasping, he struggled not to come as Karma leaned forward and ran her tongue leisurely up his neck to nibble on his earlobe. He thrust forward, no longer with any control over his hips. When she touched him with such knowing hands, he became like clay for her to mold into whatever she wanted.

Slowly at first, while he savored the feel of her tight, wet channel gripping him, he thrust into her with one long, deep drive. She rocked her hips to meet his seeking flesh, and her movements spurred him to press her harder against the door. Nonsense words followed by her begging sputtered out of her mouth. He couldn't stop himself from picking up speed. He shoved her almost savagely against the wooden door of the bathroom, and she pleaded with him as he pinned her. He forgot everything as she urged him on, tugging and pulling at his hair.

All thoughts about going slow or taking his time departed. All he had was his basic carnal needs. Her hands eagerly roamed, and her nails dug into his back. She tightened her legs around his waist until he was sure he wouldn't be able to breathe.

"Yeah, Kitten. That's right, want me," Rea demanded against her seeking mouth. His fingers gripped her ass as his seed began to spurt out of his body.

Some sane part of him thought he should pull out, but the feel of her clamping down on his quivering flesh was just too good. As soon as he started to climax, it triggered her orgasm, and her inner muscles began to milk his cock in a pulsating rhythm. The feel of her was exactly like he recalled from long ago. Everything about Karma was as he remembered, including their chemistry. Right now, holding her was as close to heaven as he was sure he'd ever get.

Out of breath, he dropped his head down, and she placed her cheek on his shoulder. Vainly trying to still his shaking body, he paused as all the problems he'd been trying to banish out of his head began to intrude. He wanted to hold on to the feeling of power and strength that she always inspired in him, but it began to wane as soon as his concerns returned. This was a huge mistake, an inner voice of reason whispered to him. What was he going to say when all her memories came back? He thought about how horrible the conversation was going to be. He wished he didn't feel this connection to her. A part of him held her tightly, hoping her memories would never return. The problem was that he needed to know what was going on in her head. Her brain contained the answers to who'd want him dead. He needed to know.

"Thanks for checking on me," Karma purred into his shoulder, and he couldn't help the answering smile that spread on his lips.

"Karma, you have a bad bump on your head. We shouldn't be doing this until you're better. When all your memories are back things will be different."

Rea chose his words carefully and slowly let her feet go down to the floor as his now-limp penis slipped from the warmth of her body. Damn, but just the thought of being back inside her made him start to get hard all over again. No, he thought angrily, he had discipline. From now on he was going to use it. He shoved the sexual hunger and odd protective feelings aside and tried to get his head on straight. He had to make sure they never did that again. For all he knew, in a few days they'd be trying to kill each other again. Maybe if they were trying to kill each other, they wouldn't care that they'd had sex. Even if she didn't care, he would.

Staring down at her large, dark eyes, he couldn't imagine ever hurting her. She looked like the kind of woman you should champion. She looked like *his* woman.

"I know I have a few injuries. It's only… I wanted you so much. You know I've no power to stay away from you. I never did, really. From the moment I met you, you always had a way to charm me. I can't help myself when I'm with you. I'm sure I'll love you for the rest of my life."

"God, Kitten, don't say that to me."

"Why? It's the truth. You could pull the truth out of me if you wanted to, so why bother hiding my feelings? I wanted you from the first second I caught you watching me in the shower. No matter how old I get or whatever has happened between us, I know my love for you will never change. You make me feel special, and I love you. I always will."

Rea shook his head as if hoping he could dispel the warm feeling that spread across his soul, but it didn't work. He still felt loved, cared for, and actually respected by her.

She had always looked up to him and always looked at him with her heart shining in her eyes. Intellectually, he knew that as long as this drug was ruling her, he wasn't going to be able to fight the spell that he'd fall under with her around.

"Kiss me, Rea, or Mac or whatever you want me to call you; just kiss me." She gave him her same pout and tugged on his hair.

He scooped her up into his arms, and cradling her close to him, he left the bathroom. He carried her to the side of the bed and lowered her onto the sheets. He didn't want to let her go, but reluctantly he did. Before he pulled away, he kissed her with all the feelings he had inside. He couldn't tell her he loved her. He didn't know her anymore, but still the feeling was so strong it almost pulled the words from his mouth.

This was it, he thought angrily. He'd kiss her one last time and then he'd go. He'd lock her in. He would tell Gears to make an antidote first thing. If he couldn't cure her, then he wouldn't come back until the drug was out of her system. He couldn't let her confuse him any longer. He felt her tongue timidly explore his teeth, and her arms stole up around his neck to hold him tight.

"There, I kissed you. Goodnight." He lifted his head and gulped some air. "I'm leaving."

"You can't leave. I'm afraid of the dark. Stay and hold me."

She didn't let go of his neck like he hoped she would, and he found himself being pulled down until he was lying beside her. Their still damp skin sealed them together, and it was almost as if the water was conspiring against him.

"Karma, you can see in the dark. When we were younger, and I found out I could make people tell me the truth, you confessed to me you had a gift too. Remember how you made me put on my dad's night vision goggles and then you juggled in the dark to prove it?"

"I know, and you got beaten for stealing those goggles. Don't remind me." Karma paused and gave him an exasperated sigh. "Fine, you got me, what a shock that you know I'm lying." She sighed at him dramatically, and her antics made him want to laugh. "I don't want you to leave, and besides, just because I can see in the dark doesn't mean I can't be afraid of what I'm looking at. Please stay, Rea. You make me feel safe. I'm lonely without you."

She curled her body around him like a well-fed kitten, and he could almost hear her purring. It was a struggle to want to care for her. He shouldn't feel like this. Where was his self-preservation? Where was his good sense? She was a stranger and an assassin.

"I should go, Karma." He used her name again to appear unyielding. He used the word *should*. He grinned when she snuggled closer and let out a yawn. This was why he had nicknamed her Kitten shortly after they met. Karma didn't move once she was satisfied. She would sleep hard once he was finished feeding her or fucking her.

"Why did you nickname me Karma?" she asked drowsily. "I like Kitten better."

Rea looked down at her and realized he could do two things. He could tell her the truth and go, or he could stay. The decision was a hard one. Go, and not come back until she knew who she was, or stay with her breasts plastered up against his side. He didn't move. Her leg intertwined around his thigh, and it made the choice for him. Damn.

"It's just a name you picked up instead of Karmen-Marie," he faltered.

Fine, he'd sleep with her for this one night. Come tomorrow, he was going to tell her the truth, and he wasn't having sex with her ever again. They would go back to being enemies first thing in the morning.

Chapter 11

Karma rolled out of bed and landed lightly on her feet. She grabbed one of Rea's button-up shirts out of the plastic drawers and slipped the garment over her head. Without making a sound, she crept into the bathroom and used the facility before returning to the bedroom again.

She came out to check on Rea, who was snoring. He looked handsome even while he slept. A lock of red hair covered one eye. His face seemed serene, and worry was no longer evident. She resisted the urge to crawl back in bed and wake him in a very naughty way. He looked so calm she didn't have the heart to wake him, even if it would be fun. It made sense why he was sleeping so hard. They had both been up most of the night. Not that she was complaining.

Last night, she'd been awakened by him twice, and both times were everything she had missed about him.

The first time he woke her, he was sweet and loving. He carefully pulled her to him and touched every inch of her as if trying to memorize her skin. She could tell by his murmurs of approval that he missed her screams of pleasure and her declarations of love.

The second time was when she'd stroked him until out of pure frustration, he flipped her over and took her from behind. She thought she should be more tired after a night like that, but for some reason, she was refreshed.

Instead of getting back into bed she meandered over to the computer and clicked on a few of the buttons that showed different areas of the water bases. Strange, but snooping around the computer seemed natural. Nothing looked familiar on the screen like she'd hoped, so she roamed into the kitchen space. She figured she could make Rea food, and she ambled past the dark wood cabinets and tan counter. She opened some broken drawers and the fridge, but she didn't know what he would want to eat.

Frustration flooded her that she couldn't remember even the most basic item of what he ate for breakfast. Giving up on food, she glanced at the clock on the microwave in the kitchen. The time blinked 7:11. Her body had summoned her awake fairly early. She thought about that. She was restless and fidgety. Did she normally get up this early? She used to love to sleep in and snuggle all day in bed with Rea.

As she glanced around the room, a few other thoughts struck her as well. From what she gathered, this was an entirely different water base than the one they grew up on. If that was the case, everything looked exactly like she remembered. The broken plastic drawers that held his clothes were in the corner. The blanket on his bed was the same thin rag with the blue diamond pattern. The few plates and cups in the cabinets were adorned with the same green flowers, and even the bathroom layout was identical to what she remembered. If she and Rea were so much older, why was their home the same? Why had the two of them not cleaned his room and decorated together? Did Rea's father still hate her? She remembered how bad life got right after Rea's mom died. Was he still being beaten? Too many unanswered questions nagged at her, and she resolved to get some answers today. When Rea awoke, she'd ask him then.

Karma started to head back to the computer, not bothering to turn on any of the lights since her eyes had adjusted to the dark perfectly. As she moved silently, so as to not wake Rea, she passed by the kitchen table. When she reached one of the pushed-in chairs, her ears picked up the sound of footsteps outside the door. She moved around the table and checked to see if Rea had awoken.

Curious about who'd be here this early, she opened the door. Gears was standing just outside the door with his fist raised in a position ready to knock. A look of surprise was written on his face when she appeared. He cleared his throat uncomfortably.

"Good morning," she whispered with a slight nod.

She didn't know why, but around the doctor she was edgy, like there was a secret he wasn't telling her. Gears looked at her with apparent distrust, and she considered all the actions she could've done to warrant that look.

"Good morning, Karma." Gears gave a solemn smile. He looked around the hall nervously. He then tried to lean past the doorframe. "Is Rea here?"

"He's sleeping," Karma answered. She kept her voice low so as to not wake Rea. Why did everyone keep asking stupid questions? Of course, Rea was here, where else would he be? She waited for Gears to say more. Did he regularly show up this early? That seemed odd to her also.

"He's sleeping, really?" Gears' eyes went wide with astonishment, but Karma couldn't think of what could possibly be so shocking about that. People had to sleep, didn't they?

As a snore cut into the brief pause in the conversation, Gears began looking her up and down. She could tell he was assessing her and drawing conclusions as to what they'd been doing during the night. She tugged at the bottom of Rea's shirt and wished the fabric was longer. She also awkwardly brushed some of her wild hair so the tendrils didn't look like she had just been rolling around in bed.

"He had intercourse with you?" Gears voice went high on the last word. He cleared his throat and pushed his glasses up his nose in an almost nervous gesture. Karma thought she was either getting used to that particular move, or his action was familiar.

"We're grown adults. I don't think you should be concerned. People do sleep, and they have sex, and they eat too. It's all really boring, actually. I thought you were a doctor."

There was something about how Gears reacted to her that bothered her. She had the impression that when she was talking to him, he was silently interrogating her. Maybe she had caused some type of rift between Rea and Gears. It was also possible Rea's father could favor the doctor over Rea. There was a chance Gears worked for Rea's dad and was reporting back. If they'd just tell her what was wrong, she was sure she could make amends.

Gears seemed to recover and collect his reaction. She noticed a tiny smile play on his lips.

"That came out all wrong. You're right. I'm a doctor. I was making sure you were healing. I didn't want you to engage in any activity that might not be good for your health. I know you're an adult. I was concerned as your doctor only. Just keep your wounds clean. That's important. I always say cleanliness is next to godliness." Gears paused awkwardly, like he wasn't sure what he should say next. "I brought you some clothes my girlfriend left at my place. I thought you might need them."

Karma looked down at the pile of fabric in his arms and relaxed. Maybe she'd gotten Gears all wrong. She offered him a small smile. She shouldn't be so quick to judge him. He was the doctor here, and she should give him the benefit of the doubt.

"Thanks for the clothes. I didn't know I didn't have any here. Where are my clothes normally?"

Gears looked uneasy and glanced past her again. Was he hoping Rea would answer her question? Another awkward silence filled the air between them.

"Maybe you should wake Rea and tell him what time it is. You can ask him your questions. This is a friendly doctor's suggestion." With that curious sentence, the doctor quickly departed.

Karma was left standing in the doorway, and as Gears left she mulled over what to do next.

She supposed the first thing she should do *is* get dressed. She closed the door and went into the bathroom to try on the clothes he'd brought.

One by one, she tried them on, only to find nothing fitted properly. If this clothing was Gears' girlfriend's, then the other girl was a lot shorter than she was, Karma concluded.

Finally, she discovered a pair of black stretchy pants that had enough fabric to cover her legs down to her knees. She then chose the largest shirt she could find. The shirt was royal blue, and the garment covered her breasts but clung to her like a second skin. Since she couldn't find anything else that looked like it might fit, she dressed. She then brushed out her hair with a hairbrush she found on a shelf.

As soon as she got back into the bedroom, she decided it was probably a good idea to take Gears' advice and wake Rea. A part of her didn't want to wake him, but if he had somewhere to be, she'd hate if he slept all day and missed his appointments.

From what she gathered, Rea was somewhat of a busy man. If his father were still around, he wouldn't be happy if Rea wasn't doing whatever he was supposed to be doing. The idea of meeting an irate Rea's father was a frightening thought. She remembered how he used to bust into Rea's room. She hoped he didn't still do that.

Karma lay down on her side and cushioned her head next to Rea's face. She softly kissed him and waited to see if he'd wake up. He mumbled incoherent words in his sleep and moved closer to her, as if seeking her out. When his hand found her breast, he brushed his fingers over her shirt and then gave a lazy smile. She loved when he did that, and she scooted closer so he could wrap his arm all the way around her.

"Hey, handsome," Karma purred as his eyes leisurely lifted open.

"What's going on, Kitten?" he mumbled sleepily, still caressing her.

"It's past seven, so I thought maybe I should wake you. We could have breakfast or…"

The word "seven" brought out the strangest reaction in Rea. One moment he was snuggled next to her making lazy circles on her back, and the next second he'd thrown himself out of bed like he'd been laying on razor blades.

"After seven? Shit!"

Karma scooted to the edge of the bed as Rea started to wildly throw on clothes. She was amazed at the speed with which he could get fully clothed. When he was dressed, he shoved his feet into boots that lay next to the bed.

"What's wrong with seven?"

"I'm late for training. I haven't been late since—" Rea looked like he was going to say more, but he stopped himself and ran his hand through his rumpled hair.

Frowning, he crossed to the door of the bathroom and disappeared. Karma sat on the side of the bed and waited for him to come back. How was she supposed to know what time he had training? She didn't even know where her clothes were.

Rea rushed out of the bathroom and headed straight for the exit. He paused at the door with his hand on the knob. For a moment, she thought he was going to exit without saying anything more to her. He spun around and looked at her like he'd completely forgotten she was there. Karma was mildly annoyed.

"Damn it. What am I supposed to do with you?" He swore two more times and then swiveled his head back to the door.

Karma stood up and went to stand next to him. She could tell he was worried, and she could see the war within him starting.

Ignoring his frantic state, she wrapped her arms around his shoulders and brought his mouth down to hers. She kissed him with barely leashed passion, not letting him go for a second. She swept her tongue inside his mouth to taste the toothpaste he used. She clutched at his muscled upper arms. She didn't let go until he wrapped his arms around her body and crushed her to him. When he finally surfaced from the kiss, he looked at her with a bemused expression on his face.

"What was that for?"

"I wanted to say good morning before you left, and tell you I had a great time last night. I can wait here for you. I can sit around and try to get my memory back while you're out. You don't need to worry about me."

Rea's expression turned grim. He ran his hands through his hair again. Her words had the opposite effect on him than what she'd intended. He looked more worried now than before.

"No, you can't stay here alone. Your boots are over by the chair. Put them on and come with me."

"You want me to go with you... to training?" Karma was truly astounded.

Once she'd snuck in to watch his training with his dad. After his father had humiliated him in front of everyone, he then pitted Rea against two men who were better trained.

Karma remembered keenly watching Rea get slammed into the mud repetitively. When Rea found out she'd seen it, he had made her promise to never come to training again. She'd honored his request because she couldn't watch his sadistic father in action ever again. Watching the love of her life get crushed had been a hell like none other.

"Hurry up." He pulled a pair of socks from a drawer and tossed them at her.

Karma was still stunned he invited her. She fumbled with the socks as she put them on. She grabbed the soft black leather boots he pointed to and sat in a chair by the table. They felt like they were made for her, and she zipped them up over her calf. These boots gave her a measure of comfort because out of everything, these were familiar. A memory of her zipping up these boots popped into her head, and the thought was comforting.

Rea didn't spare her another glance as they hurried out into the hallway. As Karma trotted along after Rea, she glanced at the empty rooms to the right and left. The plain cement walls were smooth on either side of the large walkway. Bright round lights hung every few feet above them. Each room they passed had the door open, and empty beds and sparse furniture came into view.

"Why are all the rooms around here empty? Are we antisocial?"

"It's 'coz once I leave to build a new base my room and all the rooms in this area go to the scientists and their families. Once the men are trained, they'll be the police and the safety of this water base. Scientists, women, and children can't move onto the base until it is safe. It's my father's rule."

"I didn't know this was a new base. Thank you for bringing me along while you build it. I heard you're not supposed to do that." Karma mulled what they'd been discussing. Was having no one around him hard, or did he want it that way? Maybe he liked that his life was just her, him, and his dad. Karma shuddered at the thought of Rea's father. She was glad she hadn't run into him so far.

After a few seconds of silence while they walked, she started to wonder if they were going to stay on this base or if they were going to move on to build another one.

"After this base is fully operational and people move in, will a family or a couple live in your room? After the scientists and workers move here and this base is safe, where do we go?"

They turned a sharp corner and headed down similar hallways of cold cement with large fat columns. The walls were sterile, like they were waiting for someone to decorate them. She thought that adding finishing touches to a base might be fun.

"My room and the others around me are for single people and sometimes for couples. Down further, there are rooms for larger families. This way is past the greenhouses that grow some of the food. Spouses and children are responsible for the underground farms that get added after

I leave." Rea sounded resigned to this, like he was a tour guide educating her. "All the best shit gets added after I leave."

Rea hurried Karma along over the rock flooring, past the different areas of the water base. They rushed past large equipment rooms where the scientists would clean water from the surface and put it into huge tanks. They passed barracks for the single men and an enormous empty cafeteria.

Something about the greenhouses was familiar to her. The time 1:05 a.m. leaped into her mind. As soon as she tried to catch the memory, it was gone again.

"Until the families get here, who takes care of the greenhouses?" she asked to chase away the perturbed feeling seeping into her. She was practically running to keep up, and she was irked she had no memories.

"All the men have to spend time in the greenhouses. It's partly 'coz we have to grow our food, but mostly it's mandatory that we all have to be under the sun lamps. Gears gets after us if our vitamin D drops too low. He checks our health once a month."

"That makes sense, but you didn't really answer my other question. Where do we go after this water base is built? What do we do when we don't have Gears with us? Does he come with us, or is there another doctor?"

"We?" Rea gave her a quick side glance and kept up his jog.

"Yes, we. Are we going to a new base to train others, or are we going back to an already established base? Do we stay here? Where does your father go? Does he come with us? Does Gears move with us? I thought he was a close friend of yours."

Rea abruptly stopped. They came to a large metal door and paused. His hand reached out and grasped a long metal handle.

"That's a lot of questions, Kitten. We're going to work it out." He spoke meticulously. He stopped and turned around to look at her. A fierce frown wrinkled his brow as his eyes slashed over her. "What are you wearing?" he added after studying her.

"Clothes."

"That's not clothes. That's a second skin, only in color."

Karma looked down at herself and shrugged. The boots came up to where the black stretch pants left off, and the blue shirt covered her torso even though the top was snug. The clothes did fit, but he was right about the fabric not hiding much. It seemed tight, but she could move easily.

"Gears gave the clothes to me this morning." She smoothed her hand over the bottom of her shirt. "He also told me to wake you. I think he was surprised you slept in."

"I bet he was," Rea grumbled. He then mumbled under his breath a few more words about how Gears was trying to make his life miserable. With a frown now permanently plastered on his face, he put his hand on the doorknob and swung the door wide. The entrance was a large double door, but the opposite one stayed firmly shut.

"I would've worn my clothes if you'd told me where they are," Karma commented to his back. What did he expect her to do, run around the base naked? This was better than nothing.

"We can work that out too," he grumbled, preoccupied.

It was apparent he was now dismissing her from his thoughts.

Rea's stride was swift. He entered the room with head held high and back straight. Karma followed him, and she recognized the huge training room. The massive room had only a mud floor, but the ceiling was cement and at least twelve feet high.

She looked up at the columns, which held up the giant chamber, and she let her eyes pass over the different things going on around her. On her left side, near where they entered, two shirtless men were fighting with jagged looking knives. On the opposite side, a large group of men was practicing with some type of club and shield. The center of the room was only a big ring, which wasn't occupied, but all the way around the circle, men were standing as if waiting for someone to enter it. The ring in the center was familiar. She remembered Rea in the center, being beaten to the floor while everyone stood by watching. A part of her knew this wasn't the exact same ring, but the area was so recognizable a feeling of helplessness swamped her.

To banish the raw memory, she looked at all the different sizes and shapes of the men around her. Every male was fit, but they were as different as light and dark. Some were black, some Hispanic, and some maybe Asian or Indian. Tall, short, and medium, the room was a collage of sturdy warriors, and all of them were intimidating and well built.

"I want you to stay close to me. Don't talk or draw attention to yourself. You already look too damn sexy. These men haven't been around a woman for a few months. Dad says women are a distraction and shouldn't be around during training. Especially, not a hot woman like you."

"You think I'm sexy?" she purred.

"I said *don't* talk," Rea groused, but Karma couldn't help but smile anyway.

"If women aren't allowed on the base because they're not safe, then why did you let me come?"

Karma knew she shouldn't ask, but she couldn't help herself. She hated that she still didn't have the ability to recall even the simplest information.

"We'll talk about it later."

He was brushing her off again. Karma wanted to be offended, but she wasn't. She could tell Rea wasn't happy about bringing her near a bunch of men while they were in training mode. If Rea hated doing this so much, he must have an excellent reason to have asked her along. He wasn't the kind of man to jeopardize her safety or cause problems for his men.

Even though he told her not to say a word, it didn't matter. Her presence caused enough of a stir that she might've shouted at all of them instead of meekly walking behind Rea.

"Boss-Mac got a piece of ass?" someone in the back called out.

"I thought he was gay!" another man remarked loudly.

"I heard that, Essie," Rea yelled over his shoulder as he kept striding forward.

A few other men gave out hoots and whistles behind her.

"Now we know why he slept in." A man to her left gave out a sharp bark of laughter at his own comment.

"Did you bring us a prize to fight for? I heard your dad used to do that. If we get to do her when we win, then I'm first up to fight." A large Asian man to her right spoke, as his eyes raked her body like she wasn't wearing a stitch of clothing.

He adjusted the small pistol on his belt so he could grab his balls and wink at her.

The vulgar way he looked at her made Karma's blood run cold with rage she didn't even know she had inside of her. She thought she wasn't a violent person, but the idea of grabbing his gun off of his belt and beating him over the head with it filled her head.

"I'm up for fighting this morning if she's the prize," a shorter blond with a big nose called out from the back of the crowd. "Hell, I'd even marry her."

Karma felt like a piece of meat thrown to dogs. She quickly assessed what other weapons were around the room and which ones would be easiest to steal.

"Hey, Boss-Mac," a brawny brunet man standing next to her side spoke up. "You said if we're late for training then we have to be in the ring first thing to fight you, so who do you fight if you're late?"

Karma studied Rea. His face looked like it could've been carved in granite. He seemed like he didn't care if anyone had sex with her or if he had to fight in the ring with all of them. He took bored to a whole new level. Karma couldn't believe this was the man she'd had sex with last night. When he was with her, he was so expressive and caring. Now he looked like an icy stranger.

"First off, I'm the Water Base Boss. I get the women around here. If you guys want to get laid, then become better fighters. Learn the rules to make this base secure. After it's safe, you can chase as much trim as you want. You can also bring your girlfriends and wives here once this is fully operational.

"Second, as boss, I can be late. However, to honor the rule, I'll step into the pit. Who is first up for me to beat?"

Rea strolled into the center of the ring without even looking back at her. Karma found her hands going up to her hair. She began swiftly pulling the strands into a tight ponytail. She didn't know why she was doing it, but the action was as if it was ingrained in her to have her hair out of the way right at this time.

From behind her, she heard some of the men grumbling about fighting Rea. She could tell from his overpowering confidence he wasn't worried about sparring with any of them. She recalled a bandage near his rib cage that she'd seen last night. She couldn't believe he'd fight with an injury. He didn't appear concerned about any of it, injury or men.

As he stood casually in the center of the mud, he waited like he had all the time in the world. His body was hard and muscular, with strength radiating off of him. Karma's body felt like her insides were winding up. As if someone was twisting her internal organs. She could feel the heat of the men around her pressing in, and a deeply rooted battle cry was trapped in her throat. She wanted to fight all these men. She wanted to defend Rea even though he was standing so mighty before her. She didn't want him to stand alone.

"I'll take you on, Boss-Mac," a Hispanic-looking man, with a thick accent, called from behind her.

Karma turned slightly to look at the tall, husky, curly-haired man casually striding toward the ring. He stopped when he came to her, and something about him seemed recognizable. He smiled at her, but the flash of teeth wasn't friendly.

"How about you watch a real fighter?" Curly spoke as he walked up to her. He was talking loudly enough for Rea to hear from where he was standing.

She glanced to Rea to gauge what he wanted her to do. Once Curly had Rea's attention, he wrapped an arm around her waist and pulled her to him.

"Playing a damsel in distress, Karma?" he whispered to her before he nuzzled her neck. No one seemed to hear what he said, and she had no idea what that meant.

Disgust filled her at his smell and touch. She tugged away from him. He only laughed at her squirming, but he let her go and slapped her ass. She restrained herself from striking him, but her muscles tensed to do so.

The slap seemed loud in the space. Although it only took seconds for him to touch her, it was as if time had slowed down. She saw Rea's eyes darken only slightly, but he kept his face as an unreadable mask.

"Quit fucking around," Rea barked out.

When Curly entered the ring, Karma could tell he was slightly shorter than Rea but just as fit. The two of them looked evenly matched. Karma's heart dropped to her stomach. Curly was a good fighter. He was dangerous. She didn't know how she knew that, but she did, and she trusted her knowledge.

As soon as the two men faced each other, Rea's eyes narrowed. Karma started to study Curly as if she was going to enter the bout with him herself.

"Who are you?" Rea asked as they eyed each other.

"My name's Nash," Nash spoke with a slow drawl. "I'm new."

"I don't remember seeing your name on the roster." Rea's voice was flat.

"I transferred here from another base. I showed up yesterday, around the time you kicked out Charlie and Josh. I heard about what went down. Guess I can't blame you. If I were fucking an ass as fine as that bitch, I wouldn't be sharing either."

Rea's anger swelled noticeably. He threw the first punch.

Nash blocked Rea's fist. He landed his elbow straight into Rea's gut. Rea bent over with the hit. The crowd of men cheered. The room filled with noise all the way up to the ceiling. Rea got back up quickly, and his eyes flashed with rage. He threw his entire body at Nash, wrapping his arms around the other man's waist. They wrestled to the floor. More cheering followed.

Karma moved closer to the ring. Rea's eyes caught hers for a moment. She shifted slightly through the men, who were now captivated by the spectacle before them. They cheered and shouted. None of them even noticed her any longer.

As Karma moved through the crowd, she had the urge to call out the command for Rea to focus on what he was doing. He needed to stop looking for her.

Biting her tongue, she moved until she was standing on the opposite side of the ring. She was following Nash's movements. She didn't know why. As she moved, the two men exchanged hit after hit. Nash was pounding at Rea's injured side. Blood could be seen smearing across his shirt.

She thought she should be appalled at the blood, which splattered on the dirt, or at the crack of bone hitting bone, but she found the fighting dull. She was resigned, bored even. An odd jaded feeling was filling her. She shifted her weight to the balls of her feet. She was waiting for something. Even though she was waiting, she didn't know what she was looking for.

The air crackled with unexplained discord. What was she expecting to happen? It was the way Nash moved, the way he glanced at her. His actions were speaking silently to her. She trusted her instincts.

Everything happened so fast Karma wasn't sure why she did what she did.

As she saw Nash pull a sleek steel dagger from the side of his boot, she turned and grabbed a handle-heavy throwing knife off the belt of the man shoved next to her. For some reason, she wasn't happy with his knife selection, but that idea came like a quick bolt of lightning. She balanced the rusted blade on her palm. The action was as if she'd done this a thousand times.

With ease, she threw the cumbersome knife with practiced grace. The throwing knife lodged in Nash's hand. Swiftly, she moved again between two more men. Nash hollered with pain and surprise. His eyes shot to her for a second. Her actions startled the man next to her, but she slinked away from him around the circle. None of the men moved quickly enough to stop her.

Stepping to the edge of the circle, Karma assessed what other weapons were within arm's reach. The dagger Nash had held now lay on the ground, forgotten. The knife was stained with mud and splattered blood. The blade had never reached its intended destination.

Nash swore at her in fury.

Rea stumbled backward. Shock etched into his features as he rotated his head toward her.

Nash brought his hand, with her knife stuck between the bones, down to his middle. With a concentrated effort, he pulled the oxidized blade from his skin. Dark, rich blood spurted in all directions.

Now that he had the old throwing knife clutched in his good hand, Nash turned to her. His eyes were ablaze in outrage.

"Fuck you, Karma. I knew you switched sides, you sneaky bitch."

The entire room stilled collectively as if they were holding their breath.

Nash charged her. In a flash, she felt the swipe of the knife at her belly. Karma jumped back before the next swing of Nash's weapon. Warm blood and ripped cloth fell to the ground. Her body reacted even as her mind went blank.

Karma crouched low, sweeping her leg under Nash. She knocked him backward to the dirt. As her hand reached for the gun hung on the belt of the man behind her, her mind rejected her actions. She fought to focus on what was happening. This was starting to feel like a dream… or a nightmare.

Rea threw his body over Nash. He kept him pinned to the ground. They grappled for the knife Nash still held. Rea's hands forced Nash to stab himself in the neck.

The sound of a single shot being fired reverberated around the room. Scared, she glanced around to see who'd fired a gun.

Finally, there was only an eerie silence in the training room.

Blood flowed freely from the huge gash that had been cut into Nash's throat. As the dirt around him turned red, she spun away. She was lightheaded and trying valiantly to not vomit. What had she done? She looked around the room. The weight of every man's eyes was on her. This time, they weren't assessing her figure; they were afraid of her. Every man, including Rea, looked tense and alert.

Rea stood unsteadily. He stepped between her and the lifeless body. He didn't speak but merely stared at her like all the other men. Her eyes jumped to him. She wanted to beg him to hold her, to chase away what had happened. She wanted Rea to comfort her, to tell her he was there for her.

"Karma?" Rea said her name slowly.

His voice wasn't more than a whisper of sound, but she felt it in her heart. She could feel the persistent connection that said he'd be there, no matter what. Rea would be there for her. He loved her.

"Kitten?" Again he spoke slowly, like he was trying to soothe a wild animal.

He took one tiny step forward, then another, until he was only a few inches from her. Carefully, with his hands steady, he reached out to her.

Karma looked down at her hands when he reached for them. She realized she was tightly gripping a gun. Where had she gotten it? When?

Wildly, she spun around. She let her eyes return to the dead man on the floor. A perfect bullet hole was in the center of his forehead. What had she done? Tears welled up at the corners of her eyes, but she couldn't seem to let them fall. Everyone was waiting for her to give up the weapon she still clutched. This was evident without the words being spoken. She didn't want to let the gun go. That idea frightened her more than anything that had happened so far.

She released the small pistol into Rea's hand and waited to see what would happen. She had killed a man who worked for Rea. What would Rea's father say when he found out? What would Rea do?

"Gears," Rea called to the doctor, who appeared at his side. Karma was stunned to see him. She didn't even know he'd shown up in the training room. "Take Karma back to my room and check her injuries. Check her memories." Rea linked his fingers through hers. They rushed through the men who moved out of their way like they were an avalanche.

They got to the far side of the room with Gears following them. Rea opened the door. The hallway looked like a welcoming sanctuary that would let her escape this madness. She turned to Gears, who was now standing next to her. Gears and Rea exchanged a look. The men were silent, which made the training room seem abnormal.

"Gears, I'll stay here and handle the body. I have to speak to Ken. Take Karma home. I'll be there soon." Rea pressed the gun she'd had moments ago into Gears' hand. Gears looked at the weapon and wagged his head back and forth.

"Back to your room again? Really? Don't you think you should reconsider that?" Gears pushed the weapon back at Rea. Rea pushed it back again.

"Take her to my room. Do what you have to do to look after her. I'll tell Ken what happened and have him handle it. I'll be there soon."

"I don't think so." Gears shoved the gun back again into Rea's hand. "What if this triggers all her memories? Does Ken know what's going on? Maybe I should talk to him instead. You go with Karma. I'll stay."

Gears' hands were shaking. He looked like he was scared of going with her. She hated that. He took a step away from her and moved closer to the training room door.

Rea was not to be swayed. He stepped in front of Gears, handing the gun to him one final time.

"I'll only be a minute. Ken will help me remove the body and talk to the men. He's efficient." Rea started to push him out into the hallway. Karma meekly followed, feeling dejected.

"What if she…" Gears trailed off.

"She'll be fine," Rea insisted.

Rea returned to the crowd of men around the body. At this point, she didn't believe him. She thought she'd never be fine again.

Chapter 12

Rea returned to his room after dealing with the men. As he came back, he expected Karma to be waiting to meet him. An unusual warm feeling was flowing through his body at the thought of her waiting for him.

He silently opened his bedroom door, and instead of Karma, Gears was waiting for him. The doctor paced, looking far too concerned for Rea's peace of mind.

"Where's Karma?" The thought that she'd run off scared him. He was honest enough to admit that he secretly didn't want her memories to return. He hadn't pushed Gears for an antidote. He wanted her to stay exactly as she was, but he didn't want to examine that too much.

"I'm fine. Thank you for asking," Gears snapped at him.

"Where's Karma?" Rea repeated, ignoring the barb.

"She's sleeping on your bed. I was so scared she might kill me I knocked her out. I was afraid her memories had returned when she shot Nash. If you don't mind my saying, this is getting out of hand."

"I do mind you saying." Rea paused. "Wait, you knocked her out? How?"

Rea pushed past his friend and found Karma on the bed. She was under his blanket sleeping peacefully. As far as Rea could tell, she looked unhurt. He let out the breath that was becoming painful in his lungs. She was safe. That's all he wanted right now.

"I gave her a drug that's basically a low-dose sleeping pill. The medication will knock a person out for about an hour unless there's more put into their system. While she slept, I cleaned the new injury and washed away all the blood. It was a small scratch from Nash's knife. RCC100 closed it up. All her cuts are healing well."

"Thank you, Gears." Rea spoke with more calm than he felt. He reached down and lovingly moved a lock of hair away from her face.

"You're not welcome."

Gears' outburst surprised Rea because his friend was rarely upset at him about anything. They almost never fought.

"You can't keep doing whatever it is you're doing. You know that, don't you? She isn't an old friend, and she isn't here for a visit. She might kill you or me or Eric, or she could leave. Don't you remember saying that? You have to do something with her. You have to lock her up or tell her the truth, something other than this." Gears swept his hand across the room, encompassing the whole thing.

"I'm not locking her up. Don't be dramatic."

"Dramatic? What you're doing is straight-up lying. I can't stand watching this anymore. When all her memories come back, what then? What're you going to do then?" The look Gears threw at him was pointed. Apparently, he wanted a precise answer.

"I don't know. Okay? I don't have any idea what I'm doing. And don't act so damn superior to me, either. The only helpful thing you've said has been 'some of the rats died.'"

Gears didn't respond. Instead, he snatched his bag off the table and headed to the door. Rea wanted to stop him, but he truly didn't have any answers that would placate either of them.

When Gears reached the exit, he finally spoke, "I'm leaving. When you do figure out what you're going to do, you tell me. My advice is to stop lying to her. She's going to be even more pissed when she figures all this out. Hopefully, you'll come to your senses before she kills you."

Gears threw open the door and didn't bother to look back. He marched out into the hall, sweeping his bag onto his shoulder. The door slammed behind him. Rea was left alone with Karma.

His friend was right. He was playing a dangerous game. Sooner or later this was all going to fall apart. He couldn't blame Gears for not wanting to be there when she remembered who she was.

He took a settling breath and then returned to Karma's bedside. He sat down next to where she was sleeping. She looked sweet, lying there with her arms holding the blanket. Karma looked like the women he's always fantasized about having in his life. He couldn't help but want to keep her with him.

As he studied her, he lifted the quilt and looked at Karma's upper body. He tried to see if she had any more bruises and cuts, but as he glanced at her scantily clad frame, his body stirred to life.

She was down to her bra again. The sheer fabric made his blood heat up. He let his eyes look over her pants, which molded to her long shapely legs. He could feel his pulse quicken.

As he moved the blanket, Karma's eyes fluttered open to meet his. She looked tired and much too pale. Gently, he lifted the quilt partway and tucked the corners around her waist.

Once he had a clear view of her body, he studied the small bandage across her stomach. He kept his head bent so she wouldn't be able to see his eyes. He didn't want her to read his anger at himself and this whole dilemma.

He focused on the white medical tape right under her bra instead. He acted as if he was going to adjust it. The cut was covered, and Gears had done a good job of cleaning the skin, but he didn't really feel better knowing her wounds were healing.

His mind reviewed the entire event over and over again. He remembered the tip of the blade just missing her. At that moment, time had stopped. His rage at not being able to be there in an instant had made the idea of losing her sink deep into his brain.

He was happy the cut wasn't deep. It could have been worse. Gears said the wound was closed already. That should've been comforting, but it wasn't. In his head, he thought of all the close calls she must've had in her life. Those thoughts were alarming.

Rea ran his hand along the bandage. "What're you thinking, Kitten?" he asked quietly. He could feel her eyes drilling into him.

"I don't know."

"Yes, you do." Rea waited. She didn't say anything, but he could see questions rolling across her face. She closed her eyes slowly and then opened them again. He hoped her brain wasn't filling with her memories. Rea wanted to kick himself for even taking her to training.

He adjusted the covers over her exposed flesh and got up from the bed. He couldn't take being near to her while trying to figure out what was going on in her head. On top of his piling guilt, he also realized his body wasn't accepting that she was injured.

"Rea, why did you bring me here?" Her words were hesitant, like maybe she really didn't want to know.

"I couldn't leave you alone." That was the truth as close as he could get. His heart pounded a little too hard whenever he thought about her discovering their real relationship. He hated lying, but he couldn't give her up.

He couldn't keep up this charade. He needed to tell her the truth. She might never get her memories back if he never told her who she was.

He should make a solid decision. Just be honest and deal.

"Do I train with you?" she asked as she bent her head, running her hand over her bandages.

Rea frowned as he considered how he was going to answer. *Don't lie.*

"I don't think you need any training from me, Karma. I wouldn't want to teach you those kinds of things anyway."

She chewed on her bottom lip and appeared to be mulling over what he said. Rea was surprised at how true the statement was. He didn't want Karma as a sparring partner. He didn't want to train with her and have her on this base as a killer or a guard. Rea wanted her in the most elemental way. He wanted her as a companion to talk to— someone to come home to at night. He wanted Karma to hold and to love, and he wanted her love in return.

Everything he wanted from Karma, he couldn't have. She'd leave one day. He was resigned to that fact. He accepted that like he might agree to a sword going through his heart.

"Rea, kiss me and chase away what happened today." Karma reached out her hand and clasped his wrist. She wasn't going to let go until he gave in. He could see that in the soft reflection of her eyes.

Some stupid part of him soared when she said those words. He wanted to kiss her more than anything right now. He didn't even care that what he was doing might have dire consequences.

"Do you think that's how it works?"

"I'm sure that's how it works." Her smile was broad as she tugged on his arm.

Rea let the relief spread through his body. She was still his, and everything was still where he wanted it to be. He didn't care that he'd have to explain his choices one day. He had this moment with her, and he wasn't going to tell her the truth. He was going to keep her.

Rea dropped to the bed and settled himself next to her. He liked the look in her eye right now. She looked adorable and kissable. He wanted to kiss away today and forget they'd ever gotten out of bed.

He settled alongside her, careful not to disrupt her body, and leaned in to capture her waiting mouth. She wrapped her arms around his neck and pulled his head lower to feast on his tongue. Her lips tugged at his mouth, and her tongue dove past his teeth. He let her take over his every thought, and he sank into the feelings she drew from him. Everything they were doing was absolute insanity, but he understood what she meant about being able to kiss it all away. When he was in her arms, the whole world fell away, and for a brief tick of time, life didn't suck.

That's how it had always been with the two of them.

He pushed down the blanket that he'd recently rearranged. Her injury slipped from his mind. Once the blanket was no longer a barrier, he pressed closer to her body. His mouth was still attached to her wet lips. He growled out an incoherent word as he dug his hands into her thick hair. He held her to him and rode on the wave of passion that swept through him. Rea heard a moan escape her mouth, and he pulled back slightly when he realized his body was probably crushing her.

"Kitten, you're too hurt right now to have me climbing all over you." He wasn't a hundred percent sure if Gears had taken care of all her injuries. He lifted his body away from hers. Gears said she was well, but he really didn't want to hurt her. He should get up and leave. He *should* be a good person.

"Don't go, Rea," she murmured his name dreamily and scooted closer to him once more. "I'm okay when I'm with you."

Her chest was pressed to his shirt, and she successfully closed the gap he'd created between them. Rea looked down at the pebbled nipples he could see through the sheer fabric of her bra. She was rubbing her breasts back and forth against his shirt, and he reached behind her to unclasp her bra.

She let the bra slide from her arms, and the article fell between them. As his gaze dropped lower still to the blanket, which was lying loosely around her waist, he noted she was still wearing pants. Rea wanted them both naked. Having her under him was becoming urgent.

Rea sat back until he was kneeling on the bed. He stripped off his shirt. She laughed a lighthearted sound. Briefly, he closed his eyes when she reached up and feathered her hand over his chest. The combination of her sensual laughter and inviting touch had his body begging to be inside of her.

"Let's stay in bed for a week," she giggled.

"No clothes or interruptions," he added, as he tossed the blanket aside. When it was gone, he hooked his thumbs into the waistline of her pants. She raised her hips to give him better access. She shifted, and he pulled both her pants and her underwear down to her ankles before sliding them all the way off. He dumped them on the floor without giving them a second thought. He returned to touching her creamy skin.

As soon as she was naked, he stood and his hands went to his waist. They hovered there. The cold air of the room on his heated skin made him pause. His fingers were on the buttons of his jeans, but he couldn't bring himself to unsnap them. His head was clearing, and his lust subsided. She was still wounded, both physically and mentally. He was lying to her every time they did this. Her eyes bore into him, and a question danced in their depths.

"Karma, you've got some injuries. You don't have your memories, and you just got cut in the ring. I don't know if we should be doing this." That was an understatement. Definitively they should not be doing this.

"I can do it by myself, but it's not as much fun." Karma laughed and reached over and unsnapped his jeans.

Rea grinned when he thought about how Karma never was one to take no for an answer. When she wanted him, she always made that abundantly clear. Actually, when she wanted anything, she made it abundantly clear.

With one sure movement, Rea shoved his pants down and stepped away from them. He returned to her side naked and resumed kneeling on the bed. As soon as he was close to her, she reached out. Using steady strength, she wrapped her arms around him and yanked.

"You're freakishly strong. Has anyone ever told you that?" He landed down hard on top of her and inhaled her irresistible scent. Her left hand went straight for his cock.

She gripped his dick with a smooth stroke like she was on a mission.

"How would I know? I can't remember anything, silly."

Her other hand tipped his head down to meet her hot, insistent mouth as he accepted her urgent actions. She ground her lips on his, and he sucked on her tongue, wishing this would never end.

"Slow down, Kitten, or you'll hurt yourself." He tried to breathe out the words between passionate kisses, but Karma seemed insatiable.

"I only have turned on or turned off. I don't have slow down as an option." Karma gripped him again tighter. She began to rub his prick until a sigh was drawn from deep within his soul.

Only Karma, with her unrelenting desire, could make him forget the world outside this room.

"What am I going to do with you?" he mumbled into her shoulder before returning to her mouth. That was a dumb question. He knew exactly what he was going to do. His body longed for Karma. There never seemed a way to deny the lust. Rea would've said he didn't even understand the term need, but with Karma, need was the only word he'd use for this never-ending ache which permeated his entire being.

He pressed her back as he rained kisses down her breasts, stopping to suck each of her nipples in turn. After lavishing attention to her chest, he skimmed over her bandages as he moved lower. He figured he was going too fast, but as Karma had said, slowing down wasn't an option.

Rea paused when he settled his shoulders between her legs, putting both hands under her smooth ass. His fingers stroked her cheeks as he lifted her up toward his waiting mouth. He kissed his way up first her right thigh, and then her left, before gently lowering his mouth to her clit.

Karma gasped and lifted her ass higher as she offered herself up to him. His eyes stayed on her flushed skin as he licked deeply, wanting to absorb her essence. He hadn't remembered how magnificent she tasted, but now he was sure he'd never be able to forget.

As he delivered passionate open-mouthed kisses to her pink folds, the world dropped away. This was what he wanted, and not just now, but forever. The thought was a frightening one, but he didn't dwell on it. Her smell and taste were causing everything to seem unimportant. His only concern at this second was making her scream in ecstasy.

Heat pooled in his shaft until even the slightest accidental brush against the sheets made him want to explode. Karma's head thrashed against the pillow. He wanted to see how hot and sexy she'd become as he licked her. He loved to see her rising need and sizzling arousal.

Focusing on what he was doing, he clamped down on his own raging wants. Instead, he concentrated on sucking her engorged clit as he rigidly forced himself to not climb up her body and slide inside of her. He wasn't going to stop or speed up this time. This time, he was going to savor this because it would have to be the last. After this, he'd tell her the truth.

Lost in a mixture of lust and regret, he heard her moans grow louder and more desperate. He was captivated by the noises she uttered, and he predicted she was close to orgasm.

She exploded into his mouth just as he guessed she would. She sobbed his name.

His mouth covered in her wet cream made his prick ache to a fevered pitch. As soon as she climaxed for him, he couldn't wait a second longer.

He rose up onto his forearms and shifted until his thighs were between her parted legs. His erection was poised at her slick entrance.

She didn't let him hesitate, but put her arms around his neck while she drew his mouth down to hers. She wrapped her legs around his waist and continued adding pressure. Her heels dug into his ass as he shoved forward harder than he intended. His cock buried deep inside her as she pushed her tongue into his mouth to lick away her own cream.

A rhythm he couldn't halt started from a primal place inside of him. He began to pump mindlessly into her wet welcoming warmth. His body hummed. Digging his fingers into her ass to keep her tight against him, he felt her nipples rub along his chest hair. His damp skin seemed to seal them together.

She yanked her lips away from his mouth harshly and threw her head back as her body started to squeeze his pole. She was exploding again, and she whimpered his name.

"That's right, Kitten."

He closed his eyes as he felt her moist channel hug him tightly. The incredible friction caused his body to fall apart. Thoughts vanished and time stopped as ecstasy spiraled down from his head to his toes. His dick poured into her as if his sperm had a mind of its own. He called out her name as he pumped vivaciously. His hot seed spurted straight into her body with such force Rea was sure she'd be able to taste it. Never had sex been as amazing as this.

Exhausted, Rea dropped his head to her shoulder and inhaled the smell of sex and her sweat from the air around them. The cold room cooled his burning skin, and with a lethargy that was unprecedented, he grabbed his blanket.

He tossed the blanket over the two of them and let his penis slip from her body. She shivered, and he tucked her closer to him as miniature aftershocks radiated up his spine. Karma snuggled against his side, and he let the weariness of the morning finally crack his hard exterior.

"You wore me out," he whispered in her ear, as he settled next to her warm body.

A sexual stupor had come over him, and he didn't want to fight it. He wanted to sleep here with Karma and let her welcoming body make him forget his predicament.

"Rea, I love you."

Rea moved his head into her hair and squeezed her tightly. He thought his heart would break. He didn't want her to see his face, so he buried his head closer to her temple.

"You just think that right now. Go to sleep. I promise I'll be here when you get up."

Rea closed his eyes and tugged her as close as he could get her. He couldn't say he loved her. He didn't really know her, but damn, why couldn't this be different?

"Rea?"

"Mmmm?"

"You don't have to say you love me too. I know you do. You take good care of me. You've always been my best friend. I'm truly lucky to have you."

Karma's hand ran slowly up his back, and as good as that felt on the outside, on the inside, he felt horrible. How could she make his whole world fantastic one minute, and in the next second say things that made him feel like a snake? He hated himself and the position he was in.

Rea pretended to sleep until she grew limp in his arms. He arranged her around him and closed his eyes. Gears was right. He needed to tell her the truth and face whatever might happened next.

"Ah, Kitten, you're not lucky to have me," he whispered into the darkness. When she didn't speak, he guessed she was asleep. "I don't believe in luck."

Chapter 13

Karma woke sleepily and looked at the clock on the desk next to the computer. It was 1:05 in the early morning. The time was bothering her, and she couldn't fall back to sleep. The numbers cast an eerie green glow to the room, and the only other light was from the computers near the bed.

Restless, Karma sat up slowly and stretched. Rea rolled over toward her and cushioned his face on her pillow. He looked relaxed while he slept, and for a long time, Karma simply watched him.

It had been awhile since she and Rea had left the room. Now, as she looked at his eyelids flutter in sleep, she decided she needed to talk to him about his demand that they stay here. In the morning, she'd tell him it was time to return to his work on the base. He really couldn't ignore all his responsibilities and lie around. He had duties to perform. It was nice for the two of them to be together, but it was time for both of them to get back to whatever work they did. They honestly couldn't spend all their time in his room lounging. Gears would soon start complaining they needed some sun. She realized they should both hit the greenhouses.

Besides that, she was going to ask Rea why he wouldn't have sex with her. He'd made love to her right after the incident with Nash, but then abruptly stopped. He refused to touch her. She was recovered, and the cut on her stomach had healed almost completely. It was only a faint red line now. Whatever Gears had used for the slight wound had done wonders. The cut on her thigh was still rough, but overall she was feeling well. It was time they got back into a routine. It was also time Rea stopped treating her like a glass doll. He claimed it was for her health, but they both knew that was a lie.

Two things she was sure of. First, if they got back to their regular routines, then she'd probably get her memory back faster. Everyone would be happier if her memories were back.

Second, she was positive that if she were perfectly healthy Rea would stop turning her down in bed. If they could go back to being close again, that'd make them both happier.

Karma rolled over onto her tummy and slipped closer to Rea. She ran her hand over his chest and let her fingers travel down until they danced close to his cock. A sigh passed his lips. He was rock hard like he always was around her, but if he were fully awake, he would bat her hand away. Why did he fight their attraction?

A mischievous smile kicked up her lips. She peeled the blanket back so she could scoot down and place her face near his engorged member. Her lips pressed together to stamp down on her urge to giggle. Instead of laughing, she let her tongue snake out to slowly run over the swollen purple tip. She wet her fingers next so she could let them run down around his balls toward his ass.

When Rea had been younger, the two of them had done a broad variety of sexual acts, and Karma was bewildered at his current prudish behavior. She could recall every naughty thing they'd done together before. It didn't make sense why he was keeping her at arm's length.

In the past, Rea had shown her exactly what he liked and what he wanted her to do to him. Now all he ever said was no. She smiled as she kept touching him in an unhurried way. He might say no to her when he was awake, but sleeping, he lifted his hips to seek her touch.

Karma had to lean over him so she could get a better grip on his erection. She held him firmly and started to squeeze. He thrust into her hand willingly and moaned in a half-asleep, half-awake balance. She closed her mouth over the head of his rod, stretching her lips over the massive tip. She fed his prick down her throat to make him even wetter. Her other hand started to make figure-eights on his balls. Her fingers would drop to his asshole and ring the puckered flesh before heading back up to smooth the skin out at the top of his sack.

A simple rhythm started effortlessly. Soon he was bucking his hips forward. He was fully awake when he sputtered some nonsense words.

"Oh God, stop." Rea's hands went to her hair. Both hands then dropped gently to her shoulders.

Karma slipped his cock from her mouth, but she didn't fully let go of him. "Do you mean that?" She slipped a finger over his anus again.

"No."

She tried to smile as she settled his shaft back into her mouth.

Rea jerked against her wet tongue, shoving his shaft further between her damp lips. His rough actions secretly pleased her. She loved when he became swept away by something she was doing to him. He didn't pull away or stop her; instead, he mindlessly moved with her.

Soon he became even more swollen at her touch. His balls were tucking themselves closer to his body. His hands slid up until both were on the back of her head again. He shoved his fingers into her thick hair and encouraged her to keep sucking.

As he got close to climaxing, she took her wet finger and slipped the wet digit smoothly into his ass. It was all it took to push him over the edge.

He grabbed her hair. His cock shoved further down her throat while he barked out a configuration of nonsense words. He came hard. Shuddering, he let go of her hair and the back of her head. She let the hot cum shoot into her mouth and didn't let go completely until every drop was drained ruthlessly from his body. Drips of cum and saliva dribbled down both sides of his pole, and he lay back on the bed panting.

"Hi, handsome," she whispered as she returned to her spot next to him on their shared pillow.

His eyes were open, and he was staring at the ceiling fan that was spinning below the vent grate above him. He didn't speak but kept staring at the lazy circles the fan blades made. He looked sexually satisfied and upset with her, all at the same time. Only Rea could look happy and sad simultaneously.

"Damn, Kitten."

"What's wrong?" she asked after the silence headed to uncomfortable.

"You shouldn't have done that. I told you, no more sex. Not until your memories—"

"Boring." Karma cut him off and crinkled her nose. She summed up her best look of irritation, which wasn't too hard. She was irritated.

"When did you get such a stick up your ass? We used to have fun, you and me. Remember the time you tied me to the—"

"No, Karma." Rea cut her off sharply. His retort brought a grin to her face. He didn't fool her. She could see it in his eyes. He did remember.

"What about when I put that toy you got up my—"

"No, Karma." He cut her off again. "No sex. It's my rule. I'm doing the right thing."

Karma burst out laughing. He scowled at her. She was sure he hated this damn rule as much as she did. Why was he doing it?

"That's a stupid rule," she sulked.

"Stupid or not, it's the rule. I can't keep doing this." Rea paused. "We can't keep doing this."

Karma got up, snatching the blanket off of him. She wrapped the cover around her body with a big sweep of her arms. He was left lying naked on the bed looking baffled.

Rea stared at her like she'd lost her mind. She stuck her tongue out at him and made a knot in the fabric at the center of her chest. A smile was playing on his lips, but he wouldn't let it out all the way. That bothered her too. He was probably trying to show her he wasn't backing down. Instead of thinking him cute, she found him frustrating. How dare he tell her she couldn't have him? The two of them were made for each other. They had the kind of chemistry people looked for their entire lives. He was idiotic to waste even one second of their time together. He, of all people, knew how time on this planet could be short. They should make the most of it.

"I remember you once told me I could have you forever. I'm holding you to that."

Rea shook his head, and Karma became livid.

"Fine, I'm going to take a shower now that it's fixed. Then I'm going to get dressed. After I'm dressed, I'm going to the greenhouses." Karma spat the words out as she headed to the bathroom. She stuck her nose in the air, refusing to look at him again.

"Oh, no, you're not. It's the middle of the night!" He dove for her off the bed and tried to grab the edge of her blanket.

Happy she'd finally gotten his attention, she shrieked with laughter. She moved too fast for him and made it to the bathroom door mere inches ahead of him. She had the door almost closed when he put his hand on the wood to stop it from shutting. She was always awed at how strong he was.

"We're staying in bed, Karma. I mean it." He looked inflexible, but Karma didn't care.

"I'll stay in bed when you start giving me a reason to be in it."

With that, she slammed the door in his face and propped herself against the wooden panel.

One of two things were about to happen here. One, either he'd take her back to bed and give her what she wanted, or two, he'd take her to the greenhouses so they could have a chance to talk about their schedules. They needed to settle into a routine. She could explain that to him at the greenhouses. Either way, she figured it was a win-win for her. She wanted him to return to his work, and she wanted to go back to her regular life as well. She must do something around here other than screw and sleep.

At the thought of doing anything that might restart her brain, Karma grinned. She used the bathroom, showered, and combed out her hair. As soon as her teeth were brushed, she located the pile of clothes which Gears had given her before. She found a pair of pants that were again too short for her, but she found a T-shirt that sort of fit. She stuffed her breasts into the fabric holster before glancing at the mirror. After hunting for her boots, she put those on as well. She felt more like herself today. She was more settled about how she and Rea were getting along. She was sure it would be even better once all her memories came back.

"Your luck's running high, Karma." She glanced down at the tattoos on her arms and ran her hand over them. She'd ask Rea about the tattoos today and some other specifics once she got him in the mood to talk.

Karma turned to the door. She planned to return to Rea, but as soon as the door opened slightly, she heard Gears' distinct voice.

"I was staying up to make a bird's nest out of twigs and human hair."

Gears' sentence caught her attention. She stopped for a second, not wanting to interrupt. His words struck her. He was up in the middle of the night due to a bird's nest?

She waited, and Gears' voice turned grave.

"This picture appeared on the phone a little after 1 a.m. Around 1:05, to be specific. I came over as soon as I saw it. I don't know what it means. It's revolting, but we have to show it to her."

"No. I'm not showing it to her." Rea's voice was as unbending as iron.

"This man could be someone important. Maybe it's who she was supposed to kill. What if this is all a mistake? Did you think of that? We have to show the picture to her because it might get all her memories back. What if this is someone she killed? What about that?"

"I said no." Rea sounded even fiercer this time. A trickle of fear twisted down her spine.

"I know you're in charge here, Mac, but I can smell the sex in the air. I don't think you're making healthy choices for the water bases. You've men who depend on you, and here you are, thinking with your downstairs parts."

"Back off." Rea's voice was like steel. His tone didn't invite argument, but Karma didn't think Gears was going to give up. Whatever the picture was, Gears believed she should see it, and Rea was trying to protect her from the ugliness of life. This was more of him treating her like a glass doll.

She wasn't fragile. She'd prove that to him.

Karma heard a sharp clap when Gears turned and violently slapped an item down on the kitchen table. It looked like a small black cell phone. He turned on his heel and cast a look of disgust at Rea. That look spoke volumes. It was clear he wasn't accepting Rea's decree.

She stepped out of the bathroom. Gears' eyes blasted into hers. The scowl on his face made him look sinister. Karma felt like she had stepped into a book where she was the villain.

As she advanced on Rea, she came to stand next to the table. Rea reached out his hand to her. She slipped her right hand into his, marveling at how problems disappeared as soon as she touched him.

"What's wrong?" Her words were barely audible, but Rea heard her.

When no one spoke, she let go of Rea's hand and reached over to snatch up the phone before either one of them could stop her.

Karma only had a second to glance down at the man in the photo before Rea plucked the cell out of her hand. He whipped it at the wall behind him. The phone shattered into a hundred pieces, with plastic and metal littering the floor. He glared at Gears as if daring him to speak.

Again, Rea put out his hand and reached for her arm.

"The cell is nothing, Kitten."

Karma stepped back. The image of the dead man in the photo wouldn't budge. How did she know that man?

"Gears, get out." Rea heatedly threw the words at his friend.

The doctor's eyes widened and flipped from her to Rea. Shock washed over Gears' face. Maybe Rea had never spoken to his friend like that before. The tense feeling circling the room made her decide not to ask.

Karma took another hesitant step back from Rea. She replayed the image over and over in her head. She wrinkled her brow in concentration. The man was young, with a bullet hole in his forehead. His face was so swollen and bruised she'd hardly made out what it was at first glance.

She closed her eyes and every thought she had except for the photo dropped away. The picture was stuck in her brain on repeat. Who would kill someone like that? Her mind swirled as images of dead men popped up to make her sick. Her stomach rolled. She opened her eyes slowly.

"Kitten?" Rea was looking at her like she was an untamed horse about to bolt.

She looked to Gears to make sense of it all, but he was of no help. Gears stood still as if frozen in place. Something was wrong. All her happiness and wellbeing vanished. The picture stayed firmly planted in her head no matter how hard she tried to banish the image.

Her eyes closed again. Tad's smile appeared in her mind's eye. Tad had begged her to help him. Her loser stepbrother had brought his problems to her doorstep. It was like a floodgate opened. So many memories filled her head all at once. Karma staggered. She could barely take them all in.

For the briefest moment, she was happy it was all coming back to her. She stood in the silence of the room and let her thoughts flow over her. When she opened her eyes again, she was looking down the barrel of Rea's Colt .45. She blinked only twice before she reached for the .357 Magnum Rea had mounted under his kitchen table.

The silence of the room was deafening.

She could hear Gears' sharp intake of breath when she lifted her gun and aimed the weapon steadily at Rea's head.

They stood there for what seemed like years, but it was probably only a minute.

"Put it down, Karma," Rea said evenly.

Gone was the man she'd slept with, and in his place was a stranger. Just as in the training ring, not one single emotion showed on his face.

"Please, Karma, you can't kill us. I healed you. We cared for you." Gears sounded distraught, but Karma didn't spare him a look. She kept her eyes on Rea. At rapid speed, she put together a plan.

If her father were here, he'd have been proud of her. Right now, her world was shaky, and she'd admit her heart was breaking just like it did all those years ago, but she was keeping her head together. She wasn't falling apart, and that was the only thing that mattered.

Karma didn't say a word but shrugged her shoulders as if what happened next wasn't important. She plastered a look on her face that conveyed they could be standing here enjoying a mild conversation.

She lifted her gun slowly so as to not cause Rea any alarm. She pointed her weapon at the ceiling and put her other hand up in a peace gesture. Both hands were raised as if she'd go quietly without a fight. Her breathing became neutral, her expression bland.

She heard Rea exhale as his shoulders slacked. From that one movement, he believed she was no longer a threat.

As soon as she saw his shoulders relax slightly, she squeezed her trigger. The bullet struck the lamp above them. Glass rained down on her shoulders.

Karma dived out of the way just as Rea fired in her direction. She climbed onto the bed as soon as the bullets stopped. Rea was serious this time. If she didn't leave now, she wasn't sure she'd have a second chance.

In the dark, she could see perfectly. She reached up and stopped the ceiling fan. She hoisted herself up into the ventilation shaft with a sharp kick of her legs. For a second, she paused, and she saw Rea rush to the bathroom. Gears cowered under the kitchen table.

She pushed the grate back over the ventilation tunnel and put on some speed. She didn't have time right now to nurse a broken heart or to revisit the past. She didn't have the time to be interrogated by her ex-lover, or to be held prisoner either. Even if she could convince Rea she loved him and meant him no harm, she didn't have the luxury of that kind of time. It would take her forever to convince Rea she cared for him.

Ignoring her frustration, she shimmied through the ventilation tunnel as fast as she could move. She was going to find Fletcher and kill him. She might've never had a good relationship with her stepbrother, but he was family. Fletcher would pay.

Right now, all she needed was luck, and with luck, maybe she could get out of the water base.

Chapter 14

The stones which made up the hallway looked like broken cement pieced back together. The edges were jagged, and Rea felt like the floor. His life felt split apart with Karma gone. In the week since she left, he'd felt shattered somehow.

He walked down the hallway weary after the training today. Even though he'd promised himself he wasn't going to do it, he was thinking about her anyway.

He stopped at Gears' door. Rea had filled his life with every conceivable project he could think of. He had taken extra guard duty, helped in the mess hall, cleaned animal stalls, and polished weapons. He was running out of work to keep his mind off of her leaving him again.

While staring at Gears' door, he silently wished he could ask his friend for advice. If only the doctor could give him a drug that'd make him forget her. Maybe Gears could erase all his memories of Karma.

Rea raised his hand and knocked on the metal door with a loud rap. The sharp tap bounced off the cold stones of the large hallway. The base doctor opened the door.

"What is it, Mac?" His friend planted his shoulder against the door frame and touched the center of his glasses.

"I was hurt at training. I need you to fix it up. It's on the back of my leg. I can't see it very well. Cleanliness is next to godliness, right?"

"Fine, I'll be there in ten minutes." Gears started to close the door, but then he paused. "Is there anything else you want to say?"

"No," Rea stubbornly lied.

After what had happened with Karma, there was a separation between them. He couldn't forgive himself for what had happened, and he didn't expect Gears to either. Damn it, but he hated her. He hated her for making him feel this way. She'd ruined his once peaceful world. He had plans to move on with his life. He had plans to leave this base and start on a different path. Her showing up changed that somehow. Her intrusion into his life had him asking all sorts of questions about what he really wanted. The worst of it was he'd discovered that maybe what he really wanted was her.

It was all Karma's fault that Gears and he couldn't get along anymore. It was all her fault he was now unhappy with his life, and he was doing a piss-poor job of training the men. Well, none of it was actually her fault, but he was going to blame her anyway. What he needed was to be able to boot her out of his life like she'd done to him. They'd never really had anything but teenage puppy love. He should've listened to Gears from the beginning.

"Hey, Mac, did they ever find the missing equipment?" Gears asked before Rea could leave.

"No. She took the extra guns, Brice's winter clothes, and the new snowmobile with the heated cover you just perfected. She's long gone. I want to blame the men for leaving those items unsecured, but I should've tied her up or kept her in interrogation. I should've killed her in the greenhouse. I could've killed her a hundred times."

He waited for Gears to say "I told you so." It never came.

"I got to thinking about it, and if it had been my girlfriend, I'd have done what you did." Gears pushed up his glasses. "I had no right to judge you. Besides, I'll say this, you were happier with her here than I've ever seen you before."

Rea didn't want to hear that. He wanted everything to go back to the way it used to be.

Soon the training would be over, and then he was going to go far away. Some place he wouldn't be able to remember Karma's name. Since she'd left, he'd talked briefly to Ken about the whole situation, and the gap that existed with Gears. In the end, Ken didn't have answers for him, and he was still stuck on this water base. She haunted him in a way he couldn't explain.

Rea gave Gears a curt nod and didn't say goodbye. He couldn't trust himself to talk. He wanted to yell and punch something. Instead he spun on his heel and started to walk back to his room. He was so strung out. His body ached with the tension to hold it all in. His mind begged for sleep, and that was part of the problem.

As he walked along the corridor, Rea reviewed the events of his day. He'd been preoccupied at training, and one of the men had knifed him in the back of his leg. Ken had suggested he get some rest. He pointed out how absent he'd become at training.

After Gears looked at his injury, Rea was going to crash. Maybe Gears could give him a sleeping pill to knock him out until tomorrow. Sleep that didn't have him dreaming about Karma seemed like heaven. It'd been a hellish week, and a part of him screamed that she wasn't coming back. He asked himself if he wanted her to. No, he couldn't have her back in his life. She would make him love her. She'd fill his life with her energy and spirit, and then she'd leave again. He couldn't go through that a second time. It hurt. He didn't want her to come back. That's what he insisted when he talked to Gears, Ken, and himself.

Rea stopped in front of his door. He dropped his forehead against the entrance instead of going inside his room. His hands refused to twist the knob. He couldn't stand looking at his bed and remembering how he'd held her. When he was all alone, he speculated on whether she was alive or dead. She was a killer. She was probably dead or killing people. Both were dark thoughts.

He wished he could go back in time and figure out a way to keep her. He wanted to know who had turned her into an assassin. Who'd made her do this kind of work? Did she want to do this?

Rea glanced up when he heard some of his men walking down the hall. He quickly opened his door and clicked the light switch for his overhead light. He frowned when the room stayed dark. He punched the switch again. The light above the bed flickered but didn't come on.

He'd tried to fix it by himself last night, but the lamp was still busted.

His mud-soaked shirt fought with him as he struggled to remove it. Finally, he tossed the garment to the floor. He walked to the bathroom and flipped on the small light above the sink. He paused at the threshold of the bathroom.

Something was wrong. He spun around to assess what was making him feel uneasy.

As he turned, he found Karma staring at him.

She stood next to his table by the front door. Her hand was holding a compact handgun. It was a different one than what she'd taken from him. The firearm she held was aimed at the floor. He didn't move, just in case she changed her mind and decided to point it at him. To be fair, the last time he'd seen her, he had shot at her. It had been more of a gut reaction, but still, he wouldn't be surprised if she aimed at his head again.

She was studying him. Her eyes were tired, and she was dirty. The body suit she was wearing was utterly filthy, and her dark hair looked matted to her head.

The stillness between them stretched almost to a breaking point. A bead of sweat traveled down Karma's forehead. It fell to her cheek, leaving a path through the grime on her face. He couldn't see her well due to the insufficient light, but this was no dream. She was really here.

"You've come to kill me?" His voice remained steady, but inside an inner turmoil had begun. He didn't want her here. But he did want her here. He was furious with her— furious and happy she was alive, and furious that he was happy.

He did a mental calculation of the location of his closest weapon. Last time, she'd grabbed the one under his table. She probably knew where all the weapons were in this room. He wished he was wearing a shirt. He felt vulnerable standing in the bathroom doorway half-dressed. He felt exposed and he hated how she could probably tell he was happy to see her. His body was more alive merely looking at her.

"I came because…" Karma wobbled slightly and trailed off.

When her pause became longer than normal, he noticed a bead of liquid dripping from the pistol clutched in her hand. Was she wet? He squinted at her, trying to see better.

"Are you okay?" Rea took a small step toward her and watched her slowly blink at him. The minor flutter of her eyes was telling. There was definitely something wrong with her. Even without his gift, he'd be able to see it.

She raised her hand up and wiped at her forehead. Black smudges made a trail on her skin.

"I'm fine. I only came here to warn you that you're a mark. And I..."

"You're not fine." He exhaled his exasperation that she'd bother to lie to him. He frowned when she didn't have a ready rebuttal. Her eyes remained unblinking and glazed over.

"Look, maybe I'd be willing to talk to you if you'd put down the gun."

Her eyes flared. She glanced down at her sidearm.

With a slow, jerky movement, she turned slightly to set the weapon on the table. A smattering of blood dripped onto the wooden top.

"Rea, I came to warn you, and I wanted to..." She faltered. Before she started to explain again, her eyes fluttered once more. Then she collapsed.

The faint was so unexpected Rea didn't react at first. She crumpled to the floor like a pile of heavy snow.

Rea shook his head, expelling his momentary paralysis. He didn't consider the risks and instead rushed to her side.

He sank to the floor next to her. His hands ran along her cheeks. Karma's skin was fire under his fingertips. Her face was pale and lines of strain were carved around her mouth. She looked really ill.

His mind started to problem-solve. While he reviewed all the things he could do to save her, he cradled her to his chest.

He didn't know if he should take her to Gears or put her on his bed. He tapped her cheek, hoping she might wake. Why was every second with her so insane? One minute she was trying to kill him, the next she was the love of his life, and then she left him. She broke his heart again. He rocked her body gently. He couldn't keep this up.

Rea stared down at her beautiful face. He wouldn't let her die. She couldn't *not* be alive in the world. He'd do whatever it took to help her. When she was healthy again, he'd lie to himself and say he saved her so that he could finally find out why she was here. Right now, with her sick in his arms, the truth was staring him in the face. He loved her, and he wanted her whole. He wanted her better, no matter what life she chose to live. It wasn't like him to think this way, but there it was.

The knock startled him. Rea stood up with Karma in his arms. He glanced at the door camera on his computer to see Gears holding his medical bag. Rea opened the door with the hand under Karma's knee. Relief was written across his features. Gears would fix her.

Gears took one look at him and then gaped at Karma.

"Yeah, I know, it's Karma again. And, yeah, I know she's passed out. Come in and help me." Rea stepped aside and Gears nodded dumbly.

"Did you shoot her?" Gears shut the door and set his bag on the table. He started rummaging through the pockets.

"No. Why'd you think that?"

"I thought, you know, she's always trying to kill you. I thought maybe you beat her to it."

"Hilarious, Gears."

"I wasn't joking. You did shoot at her when she got all her memories back. Remember?" Gears gestured for Rea to put her on the bed.

"I knew that was going to come back to bite me in the ass." Rea bent over and laid her on his blanket.

"Did she hurt you?" Gears pointed at Karma's blood, which was streaked along his chest. Rea shook his head.

"What's wrong with her?" Gears asked.

"You're the doctor. You tell me. A second ago, I came in here after talking to you, and she was here."

"How did she get in?"

Rea shot Gears a look that could freeze a snowman. He began to take off her body suit.

"I get it, enough questions. You take off her body suit, and I'll do a quick exam of her and—" Gears paused. "She's filthy. What was she doing?"

Again, Rea didn't bother to answer. He wanted to know the exact same thing, but until she woke up, they weren't going to get any answers. Right now, just healing her was the only thing he was concerned with.

"Why don't you help her, and when she wakes up, you can ask her all of these questions instead of me."

Rea got the top of her body suit off quickly. Gears looked intently at her arm, which had a long, deep wound. The gash was bleeding heavily. As Gears adjusted her, blood smeared along the bedding.

"She was shot in the arm. That explains the blood." Gears turned to dig in his bag once more. "The bullet went through the soft part of her muscle and missed the bone. I can fix it. She might've passed out because of steady blood loss."

"She needs a shower." Rea tugged off the bottom part of her body suit. The smell was overwhelming. He gagged as he continued to strip her. After this, he'd have to get a new blanket, if not a whole new mattress.

Gears was reacting to the smell as well. He scrunched his face into a grimace.

Once the body suit was removed, his friend swore. In all the years Gears had been on the water bases, Rea had only heard him swear once. That was a long time ago.

Rea's eyes shot to the doctor, and he studied his grave expression. He tried to figure out what was wrong.

"Rea, here's what you have to do. I need you to really get her clean. Go wash her. I have to run to my room to get more supplies. I can't work on her with this smell, and this is bad."

"What's wrong with her? Is she going to be okay?"

"I think she has blood poisoning or sepsis. I'd figure, off the top of my head, it's some type of infection. This kind of thing can be dangerous. We need to handle it immediately. The cut on the top of her thigh from when she was almost raped is infected. It looks like she tried to keep the wound clean and closed, but whatever made her so grimy took care of that. I have to check her out to be sure, but for now, you need to get her sterile so I can get started. Also, we don't want this area of her arm to get worse." Gears turned, and when Rea didn't look up, he added, "This is really gross."

Rea's eyes jumped to Gears. He didn't respond. His mind was on the one task he had right now. Get Karma clean.

"Gross... that's a fancy medical term." Gears gave him a small smile. "She'll be okay, Rea."

Normally, when things were bad, Gears and he joked to make light of the seriousness of life. They'd been doing it since the first time they met, but this time, Rea wasn't in the mood to joke.

When Rea didn't speak, Gears turned to leave. Fear was stealing the air from Rea's lungs. He reached out to hold Karma's hand. It was so slight in his.

Consumed with watching an unconscious Karma, Rea pulled her into his arms as tightly as he dared and headed to the bathroom. Get Karma clean, that was the first step in solving the problem.

Chapter 15

Karma rode on a sea of confusion and pain. Some part of her knew she had a fever, but if she could just clear her head, she'd be able to move. She needed to get up, but her body refused her commands.

Straining, she tried to pick up her head, but nothing happened. Vaguely, she felt someone touching her arm. Was that a needle or someone's hand? She tensed to fight the unknown person, but her limbs were too heavy. She opened her mouth and tried to form words. Only a whisper of air escaped from her.

Time became unimportant as she slipped in and out of consciousness. When sleep claimed her, it was the only time that she was free from the throbbing in her body.

When she woke again, she could hear someone in the room with her.

Muffled voices were floating around her. She struggled to make out what they were saying, and she tried to place who was with her. Where was her gun? And more importantly, where was she?

"I came to tell you I've decided not to leave yet. I have to do some more thinking on this president offer. Ken said

I shouldn't rush into moving on until you had everything worked out here. He's concerned for my safety."

Karma heard the deep voice of a male who was only a few feet away from her. She tried to gauge where he was standing. She reached automatically for the pistol on her thigh. Pain shot through her arm. She groaned.

So much for reaching for her weapon. She was left here unarmed with strangers. Even her eyes wouldn't obey right now. She wished for the first time since her father died that he was here to help her.

"Who's that?" she heard the voice say.

"That's Karmen-Marie. I don't know if you remember her. She lived on one of the bases with us for about a year. She's visiting, but isn't feeling well."

Karma knew the voice that responded. It was Rea. Thank God, he was safe.

"I remember her. I left with her, you know, on the shuttle out."

The other voice relaxed, like he was adding a tidbit of information that really didn't matter. Left with her? Karma searched her memory for a name. Nothing came through the fog. She became determined to pry her eyes open.

When she finally succeeded in forcing her eyelids apart, she could see Rea's back. She was so tired of trying, but not trying wasn't an option. She simply must get up, and she could do it if she gathered all her strength. She concentrated. She had to protect Rea.

Panic rose within her when all her attempts left her exhausted and no closer to action.

"Wait, Eric. What do you mean?" Rea called to… Eric Bennett! The Eric Bennett that Fletcher had mentioned. But what shuttle was he talking about? She needed to dig deep into memories she'd buried years ago.

Karma had a moment of elation when she managed to shift slightly to the right. She looked past Rea, who'd taken a protective stance in front of the bed. Beyond him was Bennett. He was standing near the door, with a fluffy mutt at his side. She recognized him from the picture in his file. Unfortunately, she didn't remember him from her past.

"What?" She heard Bennett's reply.

"What do you mean you left with her? That was a long time ago. You're probably mistaken."

"You don't remember it because that was when you were unconscious. You got that bad head injury. I'm surprised you even remember me." Bennett chuckled and then went on. "You were out with a concussion, and your dad announced to everyone on the base that women were a nuisance to the men training. He told the men all the women had to go. My dad was pissed. That's probably why I remember it so well. Your dad told my mom to get out, and my dad went with her and of course took me. We left. Karmen rode with us on the shuttle."

"That's not what happened." Rea sounded adamant.

Karma wished she could get up and calm him. The dog whined.

"I don't know what you were told, but didn't you think it was weird every woman was gone over night? I get that maybe you thought your dad was great, but he was kind of an ass."

"Karmen didn't leave the same time as you. I'm sure of it. It was…" Rea's words fell from his lips. She saw Rea bend down and pat the dog's head.

Karma could do nothing but listen. The throbbing in her arm and leg intensified with the beating of her heart.

"When we left, Karmen-Marie cried for the entire shuttle ride off base. My shirt was soaked. She was bawling because your dad told her you died in that last training accident because of her. He told her it was her fault. She said she'd killed you by being a distraction. I knew you were hurt, so I wasn't sure if it was true. I didn't say anything, but I remember it. The train ride was awful. I hate it when women cry. I never know what to do."

"Why didn't you tell her I wasn't dead?"

Rea's voice had a hard edge to it. Memories of that long-ago train ride passed into her brain. Back then she really thought she'd let Rea down. She thought he'd died that day. If she thought he was alive, she'd have connected the dots much sooner. Mac was his last name.

"I didn't know if it was true. You looked like hell," Eric said.

Now that she knew who Bennett was, Karma decided she should explain her actions from back then. She'd tell Rea why she'd believed his father. If she could lean over, then maybe she could move her lips. Her tongue moved. It felt like sand was coating the cavern of her mouth. Water would be good right now.

The dog appeared in her line of sight. He licked her cheek. Not the moisture she wanted.

Karma pushed thoughts of refreshing liquids out of her mind. Her pride demanded she explain to him that she didn't cry. That was humiliating. She hadn't cried for a man since Rea, and after losing him, she promised herself she'd never be that miserable again. Up to a week ago, she'd held onto that promise.

"You have this wrong." Rea wasn't backing down.

His stubbornness made Karma want to laugh. If she had the energy, she would have. Rea knew when people were lying, and Bennett was telling the truth.

"No, I don't. You were out of it. You have your timing off. Trust me when I say she cried an ocean of tears. I could've drowned. After I'd got to a new base, I found out you hadn't died, because my father was working with another harvester who'd heard you were both still training at the bases. I never saw Karmen after that, though, so I couldn't tell her. I never saw you after that either, as you know. It was a long time ago. We were teenagers. I'm surprised it matters to you so much."

Stark silence enveloped the room. Karma waited for Rea to respond. He looked like a statue.

After a few seconds, Rea finally moved. It was a slight shrug of his shoulders.

"Sorry, you're right. It doesn't matter. It was a long time ago. I'm glad you stopped by to tell me you're staying. I told Ken I hoped you'd stay. The men training under me are getting better. It's safer for you to stay."

"It's been a while since that assassin tried to kill you. I bet everything is fine. Gears thinks God is looking out for you and this base."

"I don't believe in God."

"Right, I forgot, you don't believe in luck, or God, or anything like that. It's a shame, you know. Everyone should believe in something."

"I know." Rea shifted like he was uncomfortable.

Rea muttered some goodbyes, and the two of them walked to the door. She closed her eyes for a second before looking up at the ceiling. Hearing the heavy fall of footsteps, she was forced to be motionless by her pain-racked body. Doors opened and then closed, and above her, the ceiling fan spun.

Her eyes were becoming impossible to keep open. Just as they closed, she heard Rea return to her side. She could feel him bending over her. She could smell him. He smelled like soap and sweat, and a scent that was distinctly his. She heard him sigh as he adjusted her arm. The action was excruciating.

"You cried an ocean of tears for me, huh?"

He spoke to the silent room. Karma wanted to answer, but talking was next to impossible right now. Rea spoke absently, like maybe he was having a conversation with himself.

"Stop fighting it, Karma." He adjusted a pillow near the headboard. "What Gears gave you will keep you still and keep you sleepy. You need to sleep for your body to heal. Relax into it, and I'll be here when you wake up."

No. She couldn't sleep. Didn't he understand? She had to tell him to not eat anything he didn't cook for himself. She had to go over weak places on the base. There was so much to do. She opened her eyes to slits.

There was so much to say about… everything.

Her eyes slipped closed again. She prayed her luck would hold a little longer. If she could at least tell him one thing…

Words formed.

"I didn't cry an ocean of tears," she croaked out.

Rea had a smile lingering in his voice. "Not an ocean? How about a lake?"

Chapter 16

The knock was loud, one hard rap on the door. Rea lifted his head off the blanket.

He blinked away the sleep and the blurriness as he glanced around.

He'd fallen asleep at Karma's side and was sitting on a chair next to where he'd placed her on his bed. He'd slept with his head next to her hand for the last three nights.

His eyes scanned Karma. It amazed him that she was here in his bed again. She was so still and pale. She looked like she might be dead. He reached out and put two fingers on her pulse. Her skin was cool. The steady rhythm of her heart reassured him. The antibiotics, IVs, and constant care had done wonders for her. He placed his palm on her forehead and realized her fever had finally broken.

A sigh of relief blew past his lips.

Another somber tap at the door and Rea jumped up. He hated that he was still treating her like his fragile girlfriend. He didn't want to worry about her, but he couldn't stop himself.

Stiff from sleeping awkwardly, he stretched as he headed to the door. He checked the cameras at his computer and saw Gears waiting for him to open up.

Rea swung the door open and blinked at the bright lights of the hallway.

"Gee, Mac, took you long enough. What were you doing?" Gears lifted one eyebrow at him.

"Nothing," Rea mumbled. He let his hand fall away from the doorknob.

He spun on his heel and headed toward the bathroom. He didn't want to talk to Gears about Karma right now. Rea didn't want another diatribe about how they shouldn't care for her. Right now, whenever he saw Gears, it made him uneasy. A part of him nagged that his friend might be right.

Rea took his time in the bathroom and hoped Gears would be finished up with Karma before he came out again. He brushed his teeth and killed time wiping down his sink. After he'd wasted about as much time as he could, Rea opened the bathroom door and popped his head out. When his friend was nowhere to be found, he relaxed and came out to resume his spot next to Karma's side.

"Before I go, I want to talk to you."

Rea ran his hands back and forth through his hair. He sighed and turned to Gears. The doctor was standing in his kitchen alcove stirring a hot liquid in a green bowl. Steam was rising out of the container. A lamp, clean bandages, and a few small bottles were spread out on his dining table.

"I've been up for days, and I feel like shit. Can we skip the lecture for today?"

"I don't lecture."

"Yeah, right," Rea scoffed and got up to see what Gears was doing in his kitchen.

"I brought you a sun lamp. It's on the table. You've been in here with her for days, and you didn't hit the greenhouses much before. I built this light for both of you. You can put it at the head of your bed and set it so you get a few hours of sun every day. I also have these vitamins for you both, and I took her off the sleeping drug today. She'll be awake soon, and once she is, you must keep that wound on her arm closed and clean. The one on her leg is closed. You need to take care of that too. No re-tearing. No infection. Lots of rest." Gears used his firm, no-nonsense doctor's voice, the one that Rea knew he couldn't argue with. The voice, Rea swore, Gears was born with.

Rea glanced back at Karma and nodded. He didn't want to argue about her care. In fact, even if it meant she might try to kill him again, he wanted her healthy and awake.

"That's it?" Rea looked skeptical when Gears didn't continue.

"No, I made you some vegetable soup from the garden. I thought you might be hungry. I put eggs in the fridge from the chickens. Those you might want later. Ken told me to tell you the pigs and goats came, and he took care of the pens. They made the trip safely, and some of the guys volunteered to help with the barn stalls for now.

"Ken also made sure training was taken over by one of your more seasoned men. He's overseeing it."

Rea wrinkled his brow. He'd forgotten about the animals and the training as well. His only focus had been on Karma.

"Tell Ken thank you, and tell the guys too."

Rea waited and expected Gears to launch into a speech on his responsibilities and how he was shirking them. The doctor would mention how the base still wasn't ready.

His friend cleared his throat and started for the door. Rea didn't know if he should say more. The gap between them was still there.

Gears stopped right before he would've turned the doorknob. He glanced at Karma still lying on the bed as stagnant as death.

"I thought about how I'm not your father, Rea. For years, you've been told what to do and when to do it. I don't want you to treat me like an evil taskmaster who replaced your father. I'm your friend and sometimes your doctor. If you like this woman, then the only thing I can do is help you. Over the years, you've helped me in many ways."

When Rea would've spoken, Gears held up his hand.

"No, listen, if it was my girlfriend on that bed, and all of the positions were reversed, I wouldn't appreciate my friend not understanding."

"She's not my girlfriend." Rea tried to convince his friend, but even he wasn't swayed.

"You don't have to explain any of it to me, but yes, she is. In fact, she's the closest thing to a girlfriend I've ever seen you have."

"That's sad," Rea said with a smile playing on his lips.

"Yes, it is." Gears smiled back.

"Are you telling me I should help her or not help her?"

"That's just it. I'm not telling you to do anything."

Gears slipped into the hallway and left without another word. Rea stood alone next to his table with too many thoughts swirling in his head.

In the last few days, he'd thought about Karma thinking him dead. She'd cried for him. The more he tried to piece together that particular time in his life, the more he realized Eric had been right. He'd gotten hurt in that training accident, and after he'd healed, it was a totally different water base. It was an entirely different world. He'd thought Karma had abandoned him. His father made it seem like she had. He'd figured she had dumped him when he needed her most. It was horrible to know he'd been holding it against her, and this whole time she thought he was dead.

Shortly after he had come to terms with her leaving, he'd left to build a new base with his dad. From that moment on, life was make a base and move, and on and on it went. There was no looking back, and there were never any women around. His father had lost his mind after his mother died, and he must've hated seeing Rea happy with Karma. It would've been exactly like his dad to destroy anything that was making him happy. To top it all off, his father did it in a way that made Rea think he'd been deserted by the only woman he'd ever loved. His father must've enjoyed being the only one Rea could rely on.

Rea realized he couldn't stand around trying to solve past problems. He picked up the sun lamp and went to the bed. He knelt next to Karma's shoulder and plugged it in. A deep hum and soft light filled the space around him. It was tranquil.

After the lamp was working, he headed back to the kitchen to check out the soup Gears had concocted.

Rea had only begun to stir the hot vegetable soup when he felt Karma's eyes boring into him. She had awakened frightened, but he knew this not because of his gift. He could feel the bond they shared. Their connection was so incredibly powerful he couldn't free himself from it. He didn't know why he felt this way about her, but he did, and he couldn't shake it. He loved her against his will.

"No gun, Karma," he announced as he turned with the green bowl in his hand.

He let her eyes drink him in, and he studied her like he'd never seen her before. She seemed different to him. She looked vulnerable and sturdy, all at the same time.

"I was wondering which way my luck was running," she whispered.

She ran her hand over her bandaged arm and pushed the blanket down. He got a healthy view of her exposed breasts. She didn't seem to mind being naked in front of him, and her stomach flexed as she took a deep breath. Her hand ran over her bandaged thigh.

Rea could see that she was assessing her physical condition. Was she coming up with an escape plan? Her eyes scanned the room. He'd strangle her if she tried to shoot out the lamp and leave again. First, she wasn't well enough to travel. Second, they were going to talk.

He kept an eye on her as he took his chair next to the bed. She was so beautiful. His body didn't care what kind of life she'd led before showing up here. He liked the incline of her head and her sharp, intelligent eyes. He remembered showering with her and washing her body when she first showed up here. She was such a mix of supple skin and obstinate will. Everything he was thinking about her was probably wrong. Karma wasn't even his to have, but it didn't matter. At this point, she might have a boyfriend or a husband. Deep inside of him, those things didn't matter. He wanted to ignore the world outside. Why couldn't it just be the two of them?

Rea scowled at her delicate fingers as they moved over her skin. He banished all the carnal thoughts in his head. The only thing he should be thinking about her is who hired her to kill him. The outside world *did* matter, and it wasn't just the two of them.

He cleared his throat when he realized he'd let his mind wander. He had to stop thinking about her in ways he shouldn't. When she looked up at him, a tiny smile played on her lips. It jumbled his thoughts. The way she looked at him told him she knew he was picturing a future with her. He hated the idea that she would know his feelings for her. Hell, he couldn't like her. He didn't even know her.

"Did you come to kill me?" He had to stay on topic this time. He stirred the hot soup and kept his voice neutral.

"If I had, you'd be dead."

Rea glared at her and tipped back in his chair. She took the soup out of his hand and began eating it casually.

He snatched the bowl out of her hands and stood up.

"That's all you've got to say?" Her nonchalant attitude made something inside him snap. How dare she return to him like this? She didn't get to show up here, tie him in knots, and then eat his soup. "I patch you up and take care of you for days, and all you've got to say is you'd kill me if you got the chance? What is it? You didn't get paid enough this time? Damn you, Karma, get out. Just leave."

"I didn't mean..." Karma trailed off. Her incomplete sentence didn't pacify him.

"You think I'm stupid, don't you? I should've tied you to a chair, and instead of closing those cuts, I should've dug my knife into them deeper. At least torturing you would give me straight answers. Maybe that's who you are now. Maybe you only respond to violence. Who the hell are you?"

Karma pushed away some of her hair from her shoulders and reached for him. Her fingers brushed his hand. He pulled it away before she could wrap those delicate fingers around him and make him forget who they were.

"I fucking hate this. I can't do this with you again. You should've never come back," Rea said the words but instantly regretted them. He did want her to come back. The problem was, he didn't want her back if all this was going to be was another heartbreak. Was it so bad to want someone who cared about him? Someone who stayed?

In all these years, he'd never been so in over his head as he was with her staring at him right now. Even at the worst times with his dad, he still knew where he stood.

"Please, let me talk. Please, give me a chance to explain." Karma reached out for him again. This time, she captured his hand. He looked down at the bruises on her skin.

Karma took the soup from him and pulled him toward the chair next to the mattress.

"You always did like it when I begged." She smiled slightly.

Some of the tension inside of him released. He stared at the scrapes going up her arm, and the scars. He'd be a fool to listen to her, but he wanted to believe in her. He wanted to have faith in her more than anything. He wanted back what he had when she showed up here and lost her memories. Rea loved it when she was in his life and in his bed. He was no longer going to lie to himself about that, even if he wanted to.

He let her tug him into the chair. She looked at him with those wide, imploring eyes. She handed him back his soup like the bowl was some kind of peace offering. Damn, but he felt lost. He shouldn't let her talk to him. He should remember she was a stranger, and their shared past meant nothing. Except that wasn't true. Their past did mean something to him.

He pictured her crying for him and his father getting rid of her. One last time, he told himself. One final time, he'd hear her out. He hoped she wouldn't let him down again.

"Please, let me speak. I'll tell you anything you want to know. Anything you ask, I'll tell you with no lies or half-truths. I won't make a move from this bed without your permission. I'll stay here and protect you the best I can. I'll even stay unarmed." She looked so earnest.

"The unarmed part? Is that the hardest part for you? Are you uncomfortable?"

"Very."

"Good." Rea smiled. He grabbed his bowl of soup back from her and set it on the bed in front of him. He tried to come up with what he wanted to know first. She bent toward the bowl and reached for the spoon. She noisily slurped from the utensil.

"Who hired you to kill me?"

"It's complicated." She smiled sadly and licked her lips.

Rea shook his head and started to get up, but again her hand snaked out and stopped him.

"I only meant I'll have to go back to the beginning. It's a long story."

"I like long stories." He picked up the soup and handed it to her. He then crossed his arms over his chest.

"I was afraid you'd say that." Karma drank out of the large bowl. He could tell she was putting her story together in her head. If she lied to him, he'd know, so he prepared himself to throw her out the second she tried to bullshit him. She stopped eating and wrapped her hands around the warm bowl. She settled herself back against the pillows and stared at the swirls of heat coming off the liquid.

"After I left here all those years ago, I went to live with my father. I won't go into how I found him or any of that. I'll save it for another time. I only wanted to tell you my dad was sort of unique."

"He was a killer?"

He didn't need to ask. Who else would've taught her this?

"Actually, he was an underground builder. And he was good at creating homes in the NEDs. He made decent money, but when he first started his business, he didn't make enough to survive, or for his team to survive. So, in the beginning, he did odd jobs, like take occasional contracts or move a product that wasn't meant to be moved."

"So, your dad was a killer and a thief. We could get him a Father of the Year award." Rea's eyes rolled up to the ceiling.

"Better that than the controlling satanic child abuser your father was, but look, do you want me to get to who hired me, or do you want to trade insults on who had a worse father?"

Rea wished he had held his tongue.

"Fine, go on. So, your dad built underground houses in the NEDs and did other *tasks* on the side."

"Yes. My father was mostly a builder, but over time people still came to him for jobs. When I showed up, I was pretty distraught over you. I begged him to make me resilient. I wanted to forget you, my previous life, and everything that happened. I was an impetuous teenager. I wanted to never feel or care for anyone ever again. My dad did what he thought was best, which was train me to be a hardened killer and a good thief. I got plastic surgery and a tattoo. He was trying to make me tough. I embraced it all."

"You asked to be this? You wanted to be an assassin?"

"When I thought you'd died, I fell apart. You were my world, and I figured I had nothing left to lose. Ultimately, hurting people and stealing wasn't really what I wanted for my future, but I needed something to cling to after losing you. My dad liked the idea. He liked teaching me. It made us close. We bonded."

Rea swallowed away the horrible feeling that rose within him as he pictured his father telling her he was dead. At first, he couldn't imagine how she could make these choices, but at the same time, it was easy to understand. He did know how she felt because he'd felt total isolation and nothing but despair when she left. It had been more than just someone you cared about moving away. It was as if a piece of him had been ripped out. He wasn't really able to judge her because he'd embraced his father's will just to take the heartache away.

"So, you started to kill people, and you took the assignment to kill me," Rea spoke slowly as these unhappy thoughts sloshed in his head.

"I would've never done that. If I'd figured it was you, I would've made different choices. Let me explain. My father had a sort of family within the builders, and some of us, like I said, did other work. He called our family The Seemyah. Seemyah was the word he used for 'family.' One of the men I sort of grew up with was named Fletcher. I grew up with him as an assassin. Fletcher wasn't good at much else." Karma gave a little laugh and then cleared her throat. "After my father died, I knew I didn't want to control the family or the business. I knew I didn't want to kill people or do basically anything I'd been doing up to that point. So I quit."

"You quit just like that?" Rea found that hard to believe. Maybe it seemed foreign to him because he'd never imagined leaving his father even at the most difficult of times. Then again, when his dad died, the idea of walking away had been very seductive. Only Gears had actually kept him bound to the water base—Gears and his responsibilities to make the bases safe.

"Yes, just like that. I made up my mind, and I just did it. My father wouldn't have liked it if I quit, but he was dead, so I decided it was time I lived a better life. I started to rethink everything I'd been doing. My dad never gave me many choices. For once, I had all the freedom I wanted. I never wanted the responsibility of the family."

Rea considered that he might be a little jealous of that kind of freedom. She didn't want to be tied down, so she left. He could never do that.

"What did you want to do? After you left The Seemyah?" he asked after a momentary pause.

"I didn't know. I still don't know, but I left anyway. I put the whole business behind me. I went to live on the Equator. I picked a safe place where the water was questionable."

Karma paused and drank more of the soup. He could tell she was collecting pieces of her story, and he let her.

A thought crept into his head when the silence encircled them. Had she loved this guy Fletcher? He didn't want to think about that. The idea of her having lovers made rage wash through his gut. Thinking about this wasn't getting him answers. He tried to remember what he wanted to know. This conversation was about who wanted to kill him, not about who might've taken her to bed.

So far, she wasn't lying to him. She had indeed quit and left her life behind. If that was the case, he was curious as to what had brought her to his doorstep.

"You were on the Equator? And?"

Finally, she put down the bowl and broke the silence.

"I was in a broken-down house in a disgusting area of the ocean when Fletcher found me. My stepbrother Tad was staying with me at the time. Fletcher took Tad. Fletcher forced me to take the job of killing you if I wanted my stepbrother back. It would be a trade. You'd have to be dead, and my brother Tad could then be alive. I didn't ask about the job. I just took it."

"For the love of your brother, Tad, you came here to kill me."

"Stepbrother," she corrected.

It all started to make more sense now. All the pieces were falling into place. Karma would've had no choice, really, and he'd have done the same thing for Gears. Hell, if he were good at killing people, he'd have shot a stranger to save someone he knew even remotely.

"I didn't love my stepbrother. I barely liked him, but I thought I should help him. Besides, I took the job to kill some random guy named Mac. I didn't know it was you. You were dead already, and everything about you was buried deep in my memory. As you know, I didn't succeed, and when I failed to kill you, Fletcher murdered my stepbrother."

"That was the picture on the phone." Rea remembered the broken man with his brains blown out.

"Yes, the picture was of Tad. Fletcher didn't waste any time. When I saw the picture, I knew I had to go after Fletcher. I had to retaliate against him. I couldn't stay here with you and explain all this." Karma's shoulders sagged.

"That's when you left, again," Rea sighed. Keeping Karma was like trying to keep the wind.

"I left, but this time, I came back to make things right. In the beginning, if I'd thought you were alive, I'd have never left you in the first place. I wish there were some way for you to see I care about you. Like if you had a gift to see if I'm lying…"

Rea shook his head. "We both changed, Karma. This is more than using my gift, and you know it."

"What I know is that, yes, we've both changed, but I came back here because I want to be with you."

Rea couldn't comment on that or face his feelings for her at this moment. He needed to figure out what was best for the men and the water bases. His life wasn't what he needed to focus on. His relationships had to take a backseat to the water base. That's what he'd been taught.

What was best right now was to figure out him and Karma later, when everything was safe again. After the bases, Gears, and Eric were all secure.

"Who hired you to come and kill me? Why me?"

"Fletcher hired me to kill you, but I honestly don't know who hired Fletcher before this all started. I came to tell you what I know, and to protect you. I know Fletcher will come for you again. He'll get the job done if the money's big."

"This whole long story and I still don't have an answer to who'd want me dead?"

"I did warn you what I had to say was a long story."

Rea ran his hands through his hair. "Yeah, you did." He had no idea what he was going to do now.

"What we both need is some luck, you know." Karma tilted toward him.

Rea was about to tell her that he didn't believe in any of that mystical voodoo, but he stopped himself. Right now he kind of agreed. Some luck would be great.

Chapter 17

Rea was doing random activities around the bedroom. He cleaned the main light near the vent. It wasn't dirty. He pressed buttons on his computer, but nothing happened. He wiped off his spotless counter and swept his clean floor.

It seemed like he couldn't sit down. Maybe he thought if he sat with her, he'd have to talk to her. If she pushed him to talk about their relationship, all she'd accomplish would be his closing down.

In the last few hours, he hadn't spoken to her once. After she'd told him about Fletcher and The Seemyah, she expected more questions, but he didn't even look at her. He hadn't commented on anything she'd told him or asked her anything more. At the very least, she assumed he'd say something about the fact she had practically begged to stay with him, but no.

Karma rested, sat, waited, and the quiet of the room enveloped them. He acted as if she wasn't worth bothering with, but Karma knew better. At some point, he'd have to talk to her. He just needed to stop being so stubborn.

She angled back against the soft pillows, and Rea began to clean his counter and table a second time. There was clearly nothing on it. She spread out the blanket and arranged it over her body so her nipples were slightly showing. When she did that, it was the only time she caught his eye. She realized as she folded the cover that the blanket was a different one with a busy pink flower pattern. It didn't look like a blanket he would've chosen for his bed. She petted the new quilt. Maybe he was finally decorating and settling into this water base. She couldn't picture him decorating with pink flowers, but maybe he liked pink.

She imagined staying here with him, and the thought was like a welcoming balm on torn flesh.

"This is nice. When did you get a new blanket? It's softer than your old one." She spoke loudly enough so he could hear her, but he'd turned his back to the bed. Karma hoped her comment would get his attention, but she wished she could've come up with a better opening line to break the ice. She was starting to wonder if he was ever going to talk to her again.

Rea looked up from the counter and peered over his shoulder at her. His eyes dropped to her nipples and then came back up to her face. He looked irritated, and she got some pleasure from taunting him. It was good to know he couldn't ignore her forever.

"I had to get a new quilt 'coz you were so gross when you got here that I had to throw my other one in the incinerator."

Karma laughed but then realized he wasn't joking. He didn't even crack a smile.

"I fell into the ocean when Fletcher shot me. It was rank. He was expecting me. I should've known better, but I'm a little rusty since I got out of The Seemyah." Karma knew she owed Rea more than she could ever repay. If he hadn't helped her, she wouldn't be alive. She sobered and met Rea's unflinching green eyes.

"You fell into the ocean?" His eyes flipped back and forth over her. A deep "v" appeared between his eyebrows. That look gave Karma hope. It meant he must care for her. It was a good sign. "That explains a lot," he added, and ran his hands back and forth through his red hair. As he did, his red locks stuck up like little red flames dancing. "You could've died."

He didn't want her dead, another good sign.

Karma didn't know what more to say. She wanted more than anything to assure him that her dying wasn't her concern. Losing him was her only real fear. She needed to convince him she'd stay here if he asked her to, but really, she didn't know how to prove to him she was a changed person. Even with the power to know when people were lying, it seemed like he didn't trust his ability.

When they were younger, he'd never fully trusted his instincts, and now it was obvious to her that nothing about that had changed for him. She didn't think he'd believe her if she told him she loved him. Maybe who she had become was so far away from the girl he knew that he couldn't care for her. He might not ever be able to think about her in the same way again. All Karma was really asking for was for Rea to let her stay and for them to get to know each other once again. She was sure that if they spent honest time together, they'd be happy. She was attracted to Rea, and she knew he liked her. If only they could learn to trust and make peace with their past.

"I don't think it's a good idea for you to stay, Karma. I don't know who you are now. We're both different people."

Rea's words killed her inside, but she didn't let the hurt show on her face.

"Right now Fletcher is coming for you, and I can help you when he shows up. I don't want you hurt or killed.

Fletcher made it clear you were still his hit, and if I got in his way, he wouldn't have any problem killing me as well. He shot me when I told him I wasn't accepting the job. I'm as marked as you are now. I'm not leaving until Fletcher is dead. I have a right to kill him for the simple fact he killed Tad. I may not have liked Tad much, but he was my stepbrother. I'll have the best chance of catching him here. Besides, I still have a little responsibility to the members of The Seemyah, and I'm sure he's doing this job without their approval."

"So, this is about you being loyal to The Seemyah and your brother. Not about me."

"Stepbrother," she corrected and then continued. "No, it's about my loyalty to you. Didn't you hear me? I don't want you hurt or killed. I'm loyal to you now, not them. You have my word." Karma gave him a sincere look to show him she meant what she said, but he looked unmoved. He offered her no encouragement.

She didn't know what to say now.

"Karma, you can't stay here. I can't trust you. You shot me." Rea came over to stand next to her bed, and he looked down at her. His look was frosty. Karma wished she could have him the way he was before she told him about her past.

"And you punched me in the face and sprayed a whole roomful of bullets trying to kill me. I think we're even."

"I knew that would come back to bite me in the ass." Rea put his hands on his hips. "You became an assassin."

He wasn't relenting, and frustration rose within her.

Karma glowered at him. "You became a doormat for your father to wipe his boots on."

Rea's next look was so glacial Karma thought he could've started another ice era in his bedroom.

She shivered and came up with a new plan. She really didn't want to fight with him. She only wanted him to understand they were more than their pasts. She was more than hers.

"All I'm asking for is time, another week. I promise to tell you only the truth while I'm here, and I promise to watch your back until Fletcher shows up. Can't you give me a chance? You'll know if I'm lying."

Rea's shoulders dropped slightly. He was giving in. She wanted to do a victory dance.

"If I say no?" Rea cast a sideways glance.

"If you say no… I'll hide on the base, and you'll spend half the time wondering where I am or if it's someone trying to kill you. All I'm asking for is some time, Rea. Please."

Karma knew she was begging, but she couldn't help it. Rea didn't understand what was at stake here. She wished he could see this was more than merely killing Fletcher and keeping him safe. It was also about them as a couple. Throwing away everything they once had would be a waste. Throwing away a real future was a waste, too, especially when life was short and Karma was sure they could find true happiness with each other.

The idea of real happiness filled her with hope. Hope for their mutual future, a future that was once taken from them. Karma also had hoped she could become someone better. Together she and Rea could build a new life.

"You can stay for one week." Rea's face was a flat mask.

Karma couldn't help but let a huge smile spread across her face. She didn't even care he was still glaring at her.

"You can stay, but I have some conditions."

"I figured you would. Go."

"First, you stay within my sight at all times."

"Done." She nodded happily. Her smile was so large her cheeks hurt.

"I'm not finished yet." His face looked like it could've been made out of cement, but Karma didn't care about his dour expression. She was staying, and she'd never been more excited about something so simple.

"You stay with me at all times, and no lies about anything. As soon as Fletcher is taken care of, you leave if I say so. This is my base. The safety of everyone here is important."

Karma's heart dropped when he mentioned her leaving, but at the same time, she was still joyful she'd have some time with him, however short it might be. Now, she had mixed emotions about Fletcher showing up. On the one hand, it would be good to have the bastard dead, but if it took him awhile to make his move, then Karma would have a longer time with Rea.

"You agree to my terms?" Rea crossed his arms over his chest.

"Absolutely, but I want to be armed."

Karma thought he looked like he might strangle her. That wasn't a good sign, but she couldn't help him without a weapon.

"No."

That one word booked no argument, but Karma wasn't deterred. His no-nonsense expressions never fazed her.

"I can't protect you without a gun, and I'm taking baby steps in leaving my former life. You can't keep me unarmed. That's nonsense. I'm a better shot than most of your men. Your guards are novices and kind of lazy. I need some type of weapon. I'm here to help you."

"I can keep you unarmed all I want. People stay unarmed all the time, and they live happy lives. If I wanted to, I could keep you naked and tied to my bed."

"Kinky." Karma saw the slightest smile pick up one side of his mouth, and then just as suddenly as it had appeared, he pushed it away. He went back to being solemn again.

"None of that either. You can stay only 'coz I have someone trying to kill me. That's all. There is no 'we.' Got it?"

Karma shrugged and let the blanket drop lower.

"Perhaps you'll change your mind." She relaxed and shoved the blanket the rest of the way off. He'd change his mind, she was sure.

"You're stubborn. I forgot how you never take no for an answer."

Karma laughed and didn't answer. For now, she was just going to be pleased with her small victory. She gingerly moved her legs until they were poised over the floor. Her hands spread wide on either side of her body for balance. If she had to stay unarmed for Rea to trust her, she could do that, at least for a while. She had to force her legs to hold her up, and she wobbled. It appeared the conversation was over for now.

"What're you doing?" Rea crossed over to stand directly in front of her. He looked at her as if he'd never seen her before.

"I have to use the bathroom." Karma struggled to steady herself on her feet. She held on to the bed as she tried to get her bearings. She wasn't sure how long she stood there before Rea wrapped his arms around her waist. She waited for him to help her to the bathroom or toss her back into bed, but he did neither of those things. He only pulled her close and held her to him like he missed her. As they stood there, his eyes gazed at her naked body. Her skin heated where his eyes traveled.

His eyes spoke of anger and concern, but it was clear by his embrace that his body wanted her. She didn't like seeing him so confused. He dropped his head to her shoulder and inhaled. She wanted him to accept that he was attracted to her, and maybe, he always would be. It wouldn't be so bad if they were together. Why couldn't he see he was being damn obstinate about this? The sooner he got over what had happened and came to terms with their relationship, the better.

Rea finally broke the silence. "You have to move slowly at first. Gears said it'd take time for you to get all your strength back. Your body needs time to recover from the drugs he gave you."

Karma nodded, but she didn't want to talk. She was basking in the excitement of Rea holding her. For this moment, even if his actions were only because he was helping her, it didn't matter. She wanted to enjoy having him touch her again. Cautiously, she let her hands slide up and around his neck to cling to him even tighter.

"Don't," Rea whispered and swallowed hard.

"Do you mean that?"

"No"

She gently pulled his mouth to her seeking lips. She gave him every opportunity to pull away, or shove her back onto the bed, but he didn't. Defeated, he dropped his mouth to enclose her lips. His warm breath filled her.

A knock on the door brought them both out of their trance. Rea pushed her toward the bathroom. She stumbled and then stood holding onto the door frame. She heard Rea mumble something about being stupid, and she gripped the door handle while he headed to his computers.

"It's Ken. I was expecting him. Get into the bathroom. I'll call you when he's gone. I need to find you some clothes."

"I thought naked and tied to your bed was an option."

That drew a grin out of him, but he didn't respond. Instead he waved his arm at her in a gesture that she supposed was "get moving."

Karma nodded and slowly shuffled into the other room.

As soon as the door closed behind her, she could vaguely hear Rea and another deep male voice in the other room. She tried hard to listen, but she couldn't make out anything and gave up. She decided she didn't care right now. She'd take a long, hot shower and get clean. Then she was going to come up with a plan. She needed to figure out how to get Rea to keep her with him after Fletcher was dead.

Her father had told her once that if she put her mind to something, she could figure out how to get it. He said nothing was out of her reach. The first thing she wanted was Rea. She wanted him with all his weaknesses and strengths. She understood him in a way she was sure no one else ever could. She believed that with time and effort, they could be a real "we."

Karma considered whether if she acted fragile it would force Rea to take care of her. They would spend lots of time together if Rea thought she was still weak. Karma discharged that idea as soon as it came to her. No, if she wanted Rea, she'd have to play with all her cards on the table. No lies, that's what she was sticking to.

Karma took her time brushing her teeth and using the entire bathroom. She was exasperated at how the easy act of showering was now so difficult. As she moved around the best she could, she made sure to not push herself too hard.

When she'd finally grabbed a towel, she heard a rap on the door. The thump echoed off the tile walls, and she reached out for the towel bar to support herself.

"Karma? Ken's gone." Karma heard Rea's muffled voice as he opened the door a sliver. She was having a hard time moving quickly enough to answer. She expected him to burst in to make sure she wasn't breaking his rules.

Sure enough, after about a minute, the door opened. Rea stood in the doorway like an avenging angel. Karma ignored him and kept drying her body off.

"What're you doing?" He looked her up and down.

"You know—" She stopped herself from laughing. "I think, you've a knack for asking silly questions in the bathroom. I'm drying off after my shower. It's slow, my muscles hurt."

Rea shook his head at her and snatched the towel out of her hands. She expected him to be rough with her because his mood seemed to be as stormy as the wind on the surface, but his actions were gentle. Gingerly, he patted her skin and then scooped her up in his arms.

"Don't get used to this," he muttered into her hair. She smiled as she held onto him more tightly.

"I was thinking how lucky I am to have a big strong man take care of me. It's all very romantical, being swept off my feet." Karma laid it on thick, and her comment drew a reluctant smile out of him.

Rea set her down on the bed and arranged the blanket over her before sitting down next to her hip. She was thrilled he was staying by her side, but she didn't want to say anything in case he changed his mind.

"Why do you always mention luck? You know it doesn't exist. Hard work and perseverance are how you survive in the world. Luck is as useless as faith. Those things aren't real."

Karma regarded him thoughtfully. He meant what he said, but it sounded like his father talking instead of him.

"My dad totally believed in luck. So much so that before I'd go on a job, he'd play one hand of poker with me. If I beat him, then I left; and if I didn't, he'd postpone the job until Lady Luck had returned to my side. I know life is about hard work, but it made him feel better, and honestly, it made me feel better too. Sometimes when you're scared, it's nice to feel like something or someone is on your side."

"That's nuts." Rea fluffed her pillow. She could see he was thinking more about what she'd said. "The cards you had on you when you first showed up make sense now," he added.

Karma smiled and thought about her father.

"Yeah, those cards were my dad's. I agree it is a bit silly, and it's not really a good way to live your life, but I think life is a mixture of luck, hard work, and faith in something. Maybe it comes down to finding all three."

Rea leaned back against the headboard and was silent. He looked lost in thought, and she hoped this didn't end up in an argument. Right now, fighting with him was the last thing she wanted to do.

"Ken says he believes in luck. Gears is always going on about faith, and my dad thought hard work was a religion. When I think about it, none of them seems any happier than I am. We're all looking for something, but we don't know what we want. Does that make sense?"

"That's an altogether different question, isn't it? What are you looking for? Are you looking for happiness?"

"Happiness is out of my reach." Rea sounded so sincere it made her heart hurt. She didn't want him to ever think that.

"That's your dad talking. You can have anything you want."

"Anything I want?" His eyes studied her face. A smile almost touched his lips. She saw it right before it vanished.

"Anything." She giggled now that his mood had lightened some.

Both Karma and Rea fell silent again. He sat with her for a few minutes. After a short while, he got up, hiding a yawn.

"Where're you going?" Arranging her face into a disinterested mask, she kept the note of desperation out of her voice. She kept it out, but only just barely.

"I can't sleep with you, and it's late, and I'm tired. I'm going to get comfortable in my chair." He gestured to the office chair in front of his computer. Karma glared at it like the seat was a beckoning female rival.

"You're not sleeping in a hard, uncomfortable desk chair. That's silly. The bed is big enough for both of us, and you're sleepy. Just lie here with me."

Rea's face showed his indecision, and she could see his fatigue all of a sudden. She wasn't sure how she'd missed it before, but now she saw his haggard appearance. He hadn't shaved. Dark circles stood out under his green eyes. She wasn't drowsy, but then again, she'd been sleeping for days.

"Rea, what's the problem?" she asked when he kept standing.

"I'm not going back to sleeping with you." His voice had a thread of doubt in it.

"It is sleep only. We've lots of issues, but it doesn't mean you should be kicked out of your bed."

Rea reluctantly climbed onto the mattress with a sigh. Once his head was on the pillow, he turned his back to her.

After a second, he turned to face her and then switched again.

"Now what?"

"I'd hate for you to stab me in the back." One of his eyebrows rose and sarcasm dripped from his lips.

"Very funny."

Rea sighed. "I don't want to put my back to you, but I don't want to face you. If I face you, you might think I'm making some kind of move on you." He appeared so torn that Karma had to dig deep not to laugh at his logic.

"I won't knife you in the back. I'm naked and unarmed, remember." She put her hand on his shoulder and the action stopped his spinning.

"I've not forgotten." He yawned.

Karma reached out her hand and carefully ran her fingers through his hair. He didn't stop her. He murmured nonsense sleepily and snuggled closer instead.

"You're drained, aren't you?" she commented more to herself as he relaxed.

She continued to run her fingers over his head and neck until he was completely pressed up against her body.

"I stayed up with you while you had that fever."

Those words lifted her spirits, and she wanted to tell him that they were a "we."

"How very romantical," she murmured instead, as she kept her smile to herself.

"Ken wasn't shocked you came back. After I'd told him everything about you, he said you sounded like quite the girl, a real keeper." Rea's murmur was languid, and Karma wasn't even sure he realized he was talking.

She didn't comment again. Instead, she thought about what she should do to protect him while she was here. She also tried to come up with a way for the two of them to heal as a pair.

It was a bit of a struggle to heal a relationship after you'd shot someone.

Still, she'd had struggles in the past, and she always got it figured out. If anyone could do it, she was sure she could. All it would take would be faith, luck, and a lot of hard work.

Chapter 18

"Brice," Rea hollered, "you shot the door. That's not a target."

Rea started grinding his teeth together so hard he thought they might turn to dust. The young man dropped his weapon on the floor of the training room and shrugged. Rea thought he might strangle him.

Karma appeared at his side when he yelled. She put her hand lightly on his arm. Just the feel of her warm fingers settled his budding rage. He glanced down at her upturned face, and an abrupt thought struck him.

He was… dare he think it? He was happy.

The idea momentarily blindsided him. It was an unsettling and foreign experience for him. He didn't know where it had come from, or how it had happened, but in the last week, that's exactly how he'd felt. With Karma back in his life, even this hellish training was now tolerable.

"At the beginning of training, I told that blond kid he was shooting like an untrained monkey. I saw a monkey in a cage on the Equator once. It looked about right," Karma whispered. Her comment brought a slight smile to tug on his lips.

"Correcting Brice is like beating your head against a wall. It won't help."

"I know. Actually, I shouldn't have said anything. You're in charge, but that guy is what my dad would've called... stupider."

Rea sighed and scanned all the men around the training room. He was done for today.

"I'm calling it," he yelled to the group.

Most of the men nodded as if calling an end to the training was the most reasonable instruction he'd given all day. The mix of guards shuffled off toward either the mess hall or the locker rooms, and as they left, he picked up the two M16s that Karma and he had been using.

"Let's go."

Karma immediately followed him out into the hallway.

They were both silent as they began to walk back to his room. He became lost in thought as they fell into step. Karma was being true to her word and what she'd promised. Everything they talked about, whether it was about her past or what she was thinking about for the future, everything was honest. It was only a small amount of time, but he'd gotten used to her loyalty practically overnight. What should he do about it? He ran his hand through his hair as he considered all his options. Should he ask her to stay another week? After all, Fletcher still hadn't shown up.

"Are we going to clean out the pig stalls?" Karma adjusted the strap on the rifle as they walked toward the rooms that held the animal pens.

"No."

"Are we picking up more weapons to clean?"

"No."

"We're really just going back to the room? This early, really? Typically you come up with some tedious job to give me. Are you starting to forgive me a little bit?" She looked at him hopefully.

"No."

She laughed.

Rea turned the corner and headed straight for his room. He should've known she could read his emotions. She watched his back and never complained about any disgusting job he gave her. He'd already given her the job of cleaning out the pig stalls, and she hadn't said anything other than that she was glad to help.

Rea had decided at the beginning of the week to give her the most annoying things to do on the base so she'd get bored, or frustrated, and leave. He expected her to move on. She didn't want to be tied down. He knew that, but she never left. In fact, every project she did, she did with the same amount of laughter and joy he remembered. Karma made him smile when she thought he was severe. When he asked her to focus, she was alert and attentive.

They'd talked about everything these last few days, and Rea didn't know what to make of her acceptance of him and the lifestyle of the base.

He reached his room and unlocked the door. Karma stopped him and checked the lock to make sure no one had tampered with it. He could do it, but she always insisted, so he let her. She was always looking out for him, whether he thought he needed it or not.

After they'd entered his quarters and set the rifles down on his kitchen table, it hit him that she'd changed his room again. She'd brought in a new wooden dresser and organized his clothes. When had she done that? They were always together.

"Did you put this here?" He gestured to the clothes cabinet.

"I thought you might like having your clothes clean and put away in a system that doesn't involve broken plastic. Besides, I ran into a harvester who owed me a favor. He came to sell some new items at the market stalls near the train tracks. You were talking to Brice and doing a security check at all the exits. I was only away from you for like a minute." Karma smiled at him.

"A minute?" He raised one eyebrow.

"Just one." She smiled again and then retrieved the weapon cleaning supplies from under the sink. She set them next to the rifles.

After the table was to her satisfaction, she pulled out one of his larger sweaters and put it on. She treated his room like they were living together. She added things like soft rugs for his feet and chairs that were comfortable. She acted as if they'd always been together and always would be, but this time, she did it knowing exactly who she was, with all her memories intact.

Rea thought he was missing something when it came to her. No matter how hard he tried to scare her away, nothing worked. The more he told her about the things he'd done with his father and the life he'd been living, the more she stayed, listened, and understood. He couldn't shake the feeling of contentment she brought to his life, and he was no longer sure he wanted to.

Karma plopped into the chair nearest the door, an act that she explained showed she was in a more vulnerable position. Once seated, she removed the bolt from the first rifle.

"Are you going to sit with me?"

Rea didn't answer her. His eyes followed the graceful movements of her fingers, as she removed the handguards.

Most nights, he'd sit with her while she'd talk about her former life, as they cleaned weapons from training. She could dismantle anything he brought to her, and she'd have an exciting story to go along with the gun. She was an amazingly fast learner, as well. If he explained how he wanted things done, she did it.

Tonight he was on edge. The knowledge that he was conflicted about her staying was eating at him. He couldn't sit, not when he felt like loving her would spin his world upside down. What if he told her he loved her and she left again? Would she only stay until Fletcher was dead?

"You're not very talkative tonight. Do you want me to do something else with my hands?" She batted her eyelashes at him playfully, and all her love was shining in her eyes. It frightened the hell out of him. She was trying to tease him, but realizing how much he was starting to care for her, chased away his good humor.

Last night, in desperation, he'd told Ken and Gears how much he was falling for her, but all they did was laugh at him. Gears even had the balls to say that if Rea was happy now, he'd be ecstatic when they started having intercourse again. Rea ignored that realization and instead lied to himself repetitively. At best, they were becoming friendly acquaintances. Having sex was out of the question, but every time she gave him an I'm-all-yours look, he had to fight to keep his hands off of her.

"Leave the weapons."

She looked at him quizzically, but didn't press the odd statement. He was thankful. He didn't know what to say to her right now. It occurred to him that maybe he should just go to bed early and not try to solve his feelings about her.

Karma left the table. She moved to sit in an overstuffed red chair she'd added to his room this morning. She adjusted her body to rest on the plush cushions. Her hands picked up the sewing that waited for her. Yesterday, she'd begun to fix the green shirt she'd ripped in the shower.

She looked comfortable. In fact, she looked *too* comfortable.

He picked up the newly mended socks on his bed. The silence between them was getting on his nerves. He tried to come up with a topic that was neutral. Blurting out that he loved her and wanted her to stay would be absurd. She didn't even know what kind of man he was now.

"I agreed with you about correcting Brice today. I'm surprised the men took to your hanging out with me in the training room."

Restless, he meandered over to the corner of his room and looked at the pile of empty bags shoved there. She'd had half a dozen of her bags brought by some harvesters, and they were stacked up. The chair that she was curled up in had appeared as well.

Although Rea was going to tell her it was presumptuous of her to believe she could have her clothes here, he didn't say anything. Instead, he'd let her unpack. He should've reminded her she was leaving. This relationship wasn't permanent.

"After they saw me shoot Nash, what were they going to say?"

"Good point."

Her fingers slid over the fabric she was sewing, and the action was almost a sensual caress. She looked domesticated, as if she was his wife and they lived together. Damn, but more and more of that thought was being hammered into his head. It was like when he was younger, and he imagined her with him like this. There had been so many nights when he'd picture a world without his father beating him, one where it was Karma and him together. Because of those memories, he didn't have the strength to tell her not to unpack her damn bags. He'd let her unpack and add her chair. He even accepted her fancy lace bras hanging above his sink.

Rea was going to have to fix this situation somehow; he just didn't know what he should do. He wasn't meant to be with a woman. They were a distraction, weren't they? If she stayed, wouldn't it be bad for the building of the water bases? What if he asked and she turned him down?

Karma offered him an unsure smile and handed him the shirt she'd just finished sewing. He looked at the tiny stitches and marveled at how well done it was.

At first, when Karma was being forced by Gears to spend time resting, all she did was sew. For that reason, all his clothes had started to look like new. When she found an item of his that she couldn't fix, she turned the garment into something else. She was caring for him, but a voice in his head reminded him that she might leave at any moment. She'd kill Fletcher and then leave him. If he asked her to stay and she left him, it would break his heart. He'd never recover.

"I think I'm good for the men. I think at times they listen to me only because of the boobs." Karma kept smiling at him, but the idea this relationship wasn't going to last was sticking in his head.

Karma's smile faltered when he didn't respond. "You should've had a woman crash the party sooner. Boobs cheer everyone up. I've used them a time or two." Karma looked down at her dark gray V-neck shirt like she was giving that part of her body a compliment.

Rea's face darkened at her comment. He thought about his father's idea of women joining the bases. She *was* distracting him. The base was not getting finished faster. He could hear his dad pointing that out. It also popped into his head that maybe she had sex with men to get what she wanted. As a killer, she might've done that. The thought instantly made him want to hit something. She was his. No one else could have her.

He didn't want to admit where his mind was going, so he decided to comment on the training instead.

"My father never respected women, not even my mom. He hasn't been dead long, so this is the first group of men I've had to train by myself from the start. I've built bases with Gears, but we had men to move from other more established NEDs. This is the first set of men that I've had from the beginning. I get to do it my way, but I'm not sure I know what my way is. It doesn't matter, really. After this, I'm done. I don't want to train men anymore. I want to, maybe, work in the greenhouses or do maintenance on the base. Is that dumb?"

To say all this was probably stupid. He looked down at his boots. He was like his teenage self, unsure and hoping she wouldn't laugh at him.

"I, of all people, can completely understand your wanting to reinvent yourself. After I'd made my first body suit, and it stood up so well to the elements, I knew I wanted to make clothes that'd stand up to the ice. At the time, my dad wouldn't let me do it, but Gears pointed out I could do it now. I remember how much fun I had creating it long ago. One day, I plan to design a suit that's really long lasting. Gears likes some of my ideas. We talked about the clothes the base guards could maybe wear." Karma paused. "You know, you've always been good in the gardens and designing space. You got that from your mom. It's natural talent. I think you should start doing things you want to do."

"I'm supposed to devote my life to the water bases. I have responsibilities. I'm not free to leave like you."

Karma shook her head at him. "You have a responsibility to make this base run, but after that, you can settle here if you want or move on. No one's going to tell you what to do. I think you should take some of your father's organization and focus, and some of your mom's gardening abilities, and become Rea. Don't be either one of your parents, become you."

Rea turned away from her, feeling more restless than before. He didn't know what to do when someone told him he could do what he wanted. So many years of being told when to eat, sleep, and train.

"Rea?" Karma said hesitantly. When she spoke, he started to wipe off his already clean counter tops. "Are you telling me there really were no women on the base before? I mean, all this time you've been alone?"

Alone. Yes, that is what he was. He glanced at Karma's eyes. She was here now, but that would change. She'd left before, and he had no reason to trust that she wouldn't leave again. All he really had was the base, Gears, and his responsibilities. That's all he'd ever have. He wanted to make Karma understand that.

"My father made sure no women were on the bases after you left. The men who stayed were fine with it 'coz they only had to go through the short training period. Most of them had wives or girlfriends who came to live with them after everything was set up. The single guys would chase scientist's daughters, or some men were gay and their boyfriends were training with them. It was fine for everyone except me. After I think it was our second base or third, my dad thought I did something good, and he got me a woman to have for an hour… as a present."

Rea turned his back. He couldn't face her while he admitted this. He'd never told anyone about this, and he pretended to clean some invisible dirt off one of the cabinet doors. He wanted her to understand. To finally see the man he was now. He didn't want her thinking he was that same kid who blindly loved her. He wasn't the same person. And neither was she.

He took a deep breath.

"She wasn't very good. She'd lie there, and I'd cum. Then she'd leave. That went on for about two more bases. I didn't even know her name, and she was older, maybe in her fifties. She never talked to me, and doing her was like fucking a warm bowl of water. I did her when she showed up 'coz my father would've beaten me otherwise. I guess, I also missed sex. I wanted to get off."

"You missed sex, or you missed me?"

"Are you looking for compliments?" He glanced at her and gave a rueful smile. "Yes, I missed you, but after a while, I forgot you."

Sorrow appeared in her eyes. The words hurt her, but he refused to lie.

He continued, "After a while, I stopped doing her when she'd be dropped off. That wasn't 'coz of you."

"I want to ask why, but I feel I'm snooping." Karma looked down. She began sewing one of her sheer bras. Because she was not focused on him, it was easier to answer.

Rea snorted, "You are snooping." He looked up the ceiling for a second. "I don't know why I'm telling you this. I've never told anyone. The truth is, I stopped 'coz I couldn't get it up for her."

Karma nodded like it was no big deal. They could've been discussing a mundane topic. She returned to her sewing as if it was the most absorbing activity in the world.

"Go ahead. Say it. I heard it from my dad. It wouldn't be anything new."

"Say what?" Karma still didn't look up at him, and now he wanted her to. He wanted her to look him right in the eye. If there was ever a moment that might push her away, he was sure this was it.

"Say how fucking manly that is. Say what a loser I am that I couldn't pop a chubby for a woman spread before me. I get it. I got it when my father found out and beat me senseless over it."

Karma finally looked at him. Her eyes widened, and then her eyebrows came together.

She dropped her sewing and got up from her chair. She was no longer awkward in her gait, and she came to stand directly in front of him. There was no place to escape. She pressed close to him so he was forced to put his back against the counter. Her hips were against his. Her face was turned up so he could look down and know with a slight dip of his head that he could taste her waiting mouth.

"That isn't what I'd say at all." Her voice had a sultry edge to it.

"What would you say?" His voice came out like he'd just eaten gravel. Her beckoning eyes were turning his insides to lava.

"I was going to say your body knew what it wanted faster than your brain did. Sometimes we fight what's right for us." Her voice was no more than a purr. The invitation in her tone was clear.

"Sometimes you have to fight it. There are things that aren't going to work out. Sometimes you know it's all going to fail, no matter how hard you try." He broke away from her. Rea turned and picked up his rag to wipe the cabinets again. He wanted her, and it took everything in him to not kiss her until she begged him.

"What happened after that?"

"My father stopped having her show up. He thought it was a punishment. I didn't. It was better to have my right hand as company than the stranger who was there for the money. I hated that he was controlling my sex life too. There wasn't one thing in my life that was mine."

Now that he thought about it, he faced the fact that he still thought his father was controlling him. It was still new to him that he was in charge of his life. In fact, with Karma, he considered that she might be trying to control him, too. She never took no for an answer. Wasn't that like his dad in some ways? Karma never had anyone telling her what to do. She could leave. Nothing was holding her to him. She could fuck him and then leave him again.

Lost in that dark thought, Rea was surprised when Karma reached around him and took the rag he was using to clean. She hung it out to dry on the faucet.

"I bet you think because I was the one carrying the gun that I spent my life doing what I wanted." Karma rested her hip against the counter, as her eyes scanned him.

Yes, he did think that. He reached out and traced the words on her arms. She could do whatever she wanted. It seemed unfair somehow. If he decided to have sex with her again, it would be his decision.

"I didn't say that."

"You didn't have to. I can see what you're thinking, and you're always saying I can leave."

"You can walk away at any time."

"So can you."

"You don't get it." Rea dropped his hands to his sides.

"Don't say responsibilities again." Karma laughed, then sobered. "I get it. You know, I wasn't running around doing whatever I wanted, either. It wasn't like that in The Seemyah. I had to answer to my father. Then after my dad died, I was stuck corralling Fletcher. After my father's death, the family incinerated him before I even had a chance to say goodbye. I never got a say in anything. I always felt like I was at someone's mercy. It was always either the client or my father. It was never what I wanted to do that came first." She paused. "Weapon or no weapon, I get not being in control. I'm free now, but it wasn't always like that. I went after what I wanted. Go after what you want, Rea."

Rea understood what she said, maybe better than anyone. His life had always seemed like it was someone else's. Now with her here, he felt like he could chase his dreams. Karma shared who she was with him, without holding anything back. Her determination to have her freedom was inspiring to him. Their closeness made him feel more comfortable in his own skin.

There was something more as well. He wanted her to be in his life. He wanted to make a permanent place for her. His connection with her was growing stronger with every piece of her she shared.

These feelings were unstoppable, yet he kept up the fight. Giving in to this love would only cause suffering, wouldn't it? He couldn't lose her again and survive the hurt. He had to keep his distance if he didn't want to be left here shattered to pieces.

As his eyes swept the new furniture and her clothes, he faced that these thoughts could be his dad's.

His fingers moved over her tattoos again as he tried to decide if he should ask her to stay. Would she give up her freedom for him?

"What's on your mind? You're tracing my tattoos again. Are you thinking about getting one? A tattoo artist is hard to find. We'd have to go to the Equator."

"We?"

"Yeah, you know… you and me. If you ever want to take a trip, I'm with you all the way. I can help you navigate the place. It's insane. It's lots of mixed countries, fights over land, and language barriers. The money is messed up as well, but I'd help you."

"Stop liking me so much, Karma. There's no 'we.'" Rea sighed and let go of her arm. He stalked over to the bed. It was getting late. There was a whole day of training tomorrow. He needed to get some sleep.

He glanced over his shoulder when he realized he wasn't as tired as he thought. Mostly, he was troubled thinking about Karma. He had to step away. Sleep would be his diversion.

"Why fight it, Rea? I don't see a point in this. I accept this thing between us, so why can't you?"

"I have to look at 'this thing between us.' I don't just jump in."

Karma pushed the chairs in around the table.

"Why don't you take a break from looking at things?" She turned off the lights, casting the entire room into darkness.

Rea swore because she could see perfectly in the dark.

"Knock it off, Karma." He gave her the best warning tone, but the lights stayed off. "This isn't funny."

"I didn't say this was funny."

Just as he turned to back his legs up against the bed, her breath was hot on his neck. He turned to get his bearings and grab her, but it was like trying to catch the wind. He decided to yell at her for the childish games. Before he could, her mouth settled abruptly on his. She started to sip from him like he was an excellent wine and she was a drunk.

The power of her insatiable desire made his defenses crumble. Rea involuntarily started to kiss her back, as if unable to stop himself. She guided his hands to her breasts, and he squeezed them softly. He ran his thumb over the hardened nipples and pinched them through her shirt.

As soon as she moaned slightly, Rea realized what he was doing. He shoved away from her and blindly hit the sun lamp on the headboard of the bed. The light turned on and gave the room a soft radiance. He stared at her in the low light. Karma looked at him like a woman waiting for her man. Her skin looked softer and silkier in the warm glow. Her lips looked enticing. He could still taste her in his mouth, and he ran his fingers over his tingling lips.

"Stop this. My father told me when and where to have sex. I'll be damned if that's going to happen again. You're trying to control me."

"You think that's what I'm doing?"

"Yes, that's what you're doing. I'll decide what I want." Rea thought he probably sounded like he was throwing a temper tantrum. If anyone knew he was stopping a beautiful woman from having sex with him, they'd think he was out of his mind. Right now, he knew he was acting insane, but he wanted sex on his terms for once, not the other way around.

"You're right. I'm sorry."

Puzzled, he was instantly wary. He could tell she was contrite, but he could also tell she didn't want to back down. That was Karma, a mix of stubbornness and flexibility.

"I hear what you're saying, but I want you, and nothing about that has changed."

Rea put his hand up, but she kept talking.

"Every day I'm feeling better, and with every moment, I get to know you, I come to care about you even more. I'm not attempting to control you. I'm trying to be with you. I understand your not trusting me right now, but what I'm offering is…" Karma paused as if searching for the right words. "Whenever you're ready, you can have me any way you want. If you need to dominate to feel in control, then that's fine. I want you to know you can always count on me."

Rea looked at her suspiciously. "This seems like a calculated move to get what you want." He felt a little like he was being snowed.

"I just want to show you that you can trust me in and out of bed. If it would help, you can tie me up or hold me down or give me a command, and I'll do it. If you don't want to have sex, then I'll wait. Whatever you say."

"Sex on my terms?" Rea raised one eyebrow.

"Yes."

Chapter 19

Karma wasn't sure she had made the right decision. On the one hand, she'd say her luck was running high. She was getting what she wanted, sex with Rea and the opportunity to show him she could be trusted no matter what they were doing together.

On the other hand, she wasn't sure she could give Rea the kind of submissiveness he was after. After what Rea had told her about his dad, she could see why he wanted control, but promising to follow orders wasn't really her strong suit. It was worth trying, though. This was her last effort to get Rea to see she could make sacrifices for him. Her time with him was up.

When they were younger, she'd had no problem with how she and Rea had sex, but back then, they did acts they chose to try together. Back then, he was stronger than her physically, but mentally they were always on the same page. Now things were different.

Now she was familiar with where the guns were and how to hurt him if she didn't like what was going on. She could stop him if she wanted to, but she didn't want to stop him. In fact, these last few days, she'd been strung tight like a bowstring. Her body was begging for her to give in, and that's what she told Rea she'd do.

"I like you like this. I should keep you naked and on my bed all the time."

"Naked and tied to the bed was an option when I first got here." Karma could hear Rea somewhere behind her, but she didn't move her head.

He chuckled.

After he had her strip naked, he'd told her to wait on all fours in the middle of the bed. He asked her not to move. A second ago, he'd come out of the bathroom, and she could hear the swish of the rug under his feet. He'd probably gone in there to test if she'd wait. She was doing her best, and she wasn't going to move an inch. If this was what he needed to prove she could be counted on, then she was going to do whatever he asked her to do. Being honest with him and telling him about her life had only healed a small portion of the hurt between them. This obedience might make real amends.

While she waited, her pussy contracted at the mere thought of him entering her from behind. She hoped he could see the wetness that slicked her lower lips and dampened her inner thighs. Even if this was about building trust, her body was alive and excited. Heat was starting to twist through her, and her heart pounded.

She was almost positive he was behind her somewhere, and soon she'd have what she'd been craving for days. The idea made her nipples bead tightly. Her breasts ached for his touch. She realized she was breathing heavily.

"You're ready for me, and I haven't even touched you yet. I like that. Close your eyes."

Karma heard his voice closer this time, and she did as he asked. As soon as her eyelids lowered, a piece of soft fabric slipped over the top of her head.

His scent came to her first. The item over her eyes smelled of his soap and his skin. He must've placed one of his shirts over her head. She thrilled at being surrounded by his smell, and she sucked in a deep breath through her nose.

"You said I could have what I wanted. Remember?" His breath fluttered the hair at the nape of her neck as he dropped one kiss to the sensitive spot at the top of her spine. "I don't think you've ever actually experienced the dark, Kitten. Will you do that for me?"

"I'm not sure I'll like it, but I won't take it off." She tipped her head down and took a steady breath. Whatever he put over her eyes didn't move.

"You can't turn off the light now." Rea sounded smug. "You're enjoying yourself, aren't you?"

"Yes." He dropped another kiss on her shoulder.

Inside she was exhilarated. If he was happy to be in charge, then she was happy, even if she hated not being able to see. She balled up her fists into the blanket as he tightened whatever cloth he was using to cover her eyes.

As soon as he seemed to accept she wasn't going to move, he brushed against her. She waited as patiently as she could. She could feel his tongue make lazy circles starting at the nape of her neck. His moist lips trailed down her spine as he kissed every rib. By the time he reached the top of her ass, she was shivering with pleasure. She was doing her best not to let go of the blanket and pin him under her. Karma held on to the bed like it was a lifeline, and a tingling sensation ran all the way up to her scalp.

"This does mean something to me," he said gruffly, as Karma heard the rustle of clothing behind her. She hoped he was taking off his clothes. She wanted to thank the heavens for that. He must've noticed how tightly she was holding the sheets to stay still. No, she'd promised to do what she was told and give him a reason to believe in her again. At least when it came to the bedroom, she was sure she could be everything he could ever want or need.

When the bed dipped down, she figured out he was in front of her. She could hear the hum of the sun lamp, and she felt his fingers trace her knuckles. One by one, he forced her to let go of the blankets. He spread her fingers out flat against the mattress. As he leaned over her, his cock touched her shoulder once, then twice. It'd be so easy to reach out and capture his hardness.

Her jaw clenched when he moved around her. She didn't even incline her head toward where she was sure his large shaft would be, even though she wanted to. Keeping still was hard, but she was doing it.

Once he had her exactly where he wanted her, he let one of his hands slip over her stomach until his fingers dipped between her parted legs. The smell of her wetness reached her as he parted the slippery lips of her slit. Finally, she thought, she could have him. She hated waiting. Patience was always a hard battle for her to fight. Every moment seemed to light her skin on fire. His knuckle rubbed over her clit, and a lance of pure sensation shot through her. She bit down on her tongue to not make a noise. She heard him chuckle.

"You can moan for me, Kitten. I love hearing you beg."

Karma let a noise escape that was part sob and part moan. She pushed her pelvis forward to make him stroke her again. As her hips twisted, he lightened the touch until it was just the tips of his fingers. She was instantly aggravated. He was teasing her. She wanted to give up and tackle him. At this point, his other hand hadn't even touched her yet, and she was getting crazy on the inside.

He brushed his mouth over her skin. His lips started at her ear and moved to her shoulders. Karma felt him smile. If she ripped off the blindfold, he'd never let it go. He'd say this was proof he couldn't trust her. Her head dropped, and she forced herself to stay perfectly still.

He must've noticed she'd stopped wriggling, and once again his hand was on her. He flicked her clit only slightly, and her breath caught. Passion was making her muscles tense and flex. Her arms were shaking. A desperate longing filled her veins. Sweat slid off her skin, and she could feel his chest vibrate with some type of groan.

"Beg me, Kitten. I want to hear you say it."

Karma didn't have any qualms about begging, at least not begging for him. She wanted this torment to end. She needed to feel him inside of her. She wanted to feel him explode with her wrapped around his body.

"Please, Rea. I want you." The last of her words came out as a garbled groan. It was cut off abruptly when two of his fingers plunged into her pussy. He worked both fingers roughly in her channel, giving her a measure of satisfaction. She could feel him stroking the sensitive spot inside of her with hard, sure movements.

She bucked and tipped her hips out to make him move deeper. Helplessly, she turned her head toward him.

"Please."

His fingers caught her chin, and he held it. With her head turned, he shoved his tongue abruptly into her mouth. Blindly, she started to suck on it. He grunted and pinched her clit, leaving her empty of his fingers.

Open and unfulfilled, she whimpered. Soon his mouth, which had been so unrelenting, became soft and wild. His lips, teeth, and tongue ravaged her until she could no longer remember a time before this. Her body still felt deprived, but she was captivated by his endless consuming kisses.

Just when their panting breaths mingled, and she was sure he'd take her, he stopped. His mouth left hers to feel all alone and exposed.

"Please, Rea, don't leave. Let me have you. Anything." She meant it as she stayed there waiting for him. She wanted any part of him that he'd give her. Only after a few seconds, he gave in.

He moved to press his thigh against her cheek. The drop of the mattress near her hand made her smile. She heard his breathing stop, and she wanted to laugh. This might've been about trust, but right now it was fast turning into an avalanche of lust.

The head of his straining prick brushed her chin, and she didn't need to turn because he started to press his prick against her lips. She flicked her tongue against the broad head, catching the salty taste that was uniquely him. The thick moisture that beaded out was darkly carnal. It gave her a feeling of power to know he was breaking down.

Opening her mouth to take him, she suckled the head before she sank down onto his entire thick pole. She licked and sucked, letting her mouth pull on the firm warm flesh. The groan that echoed in the quiet of the room made a vast warmth blossom in her chest. This time, the sex between them was honest. There were no lies or confusion this time. He understood who was going to be wrapped around his body. Who was wrapped around his heart.

Without being able to control it, her hips pumped as scorching desire rolled through her. Her pussy clenched on nothing. She quivered as she sucked hard. His palms came up to cup the side of her face, and he wrapped his large hands around to the back of her head. He dug his fingers into her thick hair. He guided her head in a rhythm he liked, and she followed it, enjoying her Rea.

This was where she should be, back in his bed where she belonged. She was right, at the beginning of the night, when she thought her luck was running high. This was good luck; actually, it was better than that. This was, for once, everything being right in the world.

Chapter 20

"No more," Rea's voice came out in a gruff command.

Before she could stop him, he savagely pulled his dick from the hot suction of her mouth. He didn't know why, but he didn't want to come in her mouth right now. An urge inside of him was demanding he give her more. He needed to give himself more, too. He needed to be inside of her and feel her body milk his cock.

The more he thought about it, the less this was about being in charge. Instead, this was fulfilling a connection missing between them. He was going to force Karma to climax for him and in the process release all his pent-up sexual tension. He'd have Karma give herself over to him. It felt right this time with her. He was free to indulge his darker appetites because she accepted him.

Karma murmured her annoyance when he moved away from her mouth, and he smiled. He came around the bed, behind her, to her spread legs. He knelt and stared down at the smooth white flesh of her rounded bottom. She looked so beautiful displayed for him like this. She was pretty, yet salacious, a mixture of beauty and erotica all laid out before his eyes.

Karma was like that, always a combination of opposites.

"I have to have you," he whispered. He meant more than her body. He had to have all of her. He wanted all of her.

"You can have anything," she whispered back.

He lined up his throbbing cock at her slick entrance. She didn't seem worried about what he was doing and arched her back at him. Without warning, he grabbed her ass and dug his fingers into the soft flesh.

Like a man possessed, he plunged his aching erection into her slick enveloping pussy. He swore she was heaven. Karma cried out, and he couldn't stop the deep groan that poured out of him as he pounded her. She was so tight, and the same as he remembered. Every time with her was piercing and exceptional. It was like the past, but it was also new.

Rea rammed into her with all his power as his eyes closed. Ecstasy filled him. He flexed the muscles of his thighs and forced her to cry out his name with every thrust.

Mindlessly, he ran his hands frantically over her ass. He'd let his fingers linger over her legs and then move to her clit. Of their own volition, his fingers started up from where her dripping pussy and his cock met, and gently spread her liquid heat over her puckered asshole. He held his breath as he licked his fingers to taste her. He wanted to make her scream. He was going to open her ass and make her never be able to forget him again. No matter what happened in the future, he wanted her to never forget his hands, his mouth, and his cock. Jealousy was eating at him. He wanted to make sure that once she left, she'd always want him and only him.

Before he began playing around with the tight fissure, he wet his thumb. Slowly, at first, he pressed into her anus.

Another moan and incoherent word came out of her. He didn't stop. In fact, her nonsense words spurred him on. Soon, he could feel how his wet thumb was pushing her closer to her breaking point.

"Do you remember this? I used to fuck you here."

She didn't answer. Rea barely got the words out as her passage gripped him tighter. He pulled his thumb out and again licked his fingers.

Carefully, as he rocked his dick into her, he added his first finger. He could feel his prick being massaged inside of her body. Her body was so perfect for him. That would never change.

Her wet channel was pulsating. Never before had his shaft been so eager. Even when he tried to recall the sex they had in their youth, never had it been this good. He rocked his hips forward, making a gentler rhythm.

His finger was pressing deep inside of her. Carefully, he pulled it out before adding a second finger and pushing back in. He could feel her orgasm, which seemed to be calling to his member, and he wished this could go on forever. Again, she would beg for him to fill her with his seed, to make this sweet torture end.

"Please," she whimpered like she was crying, but he knew better.

He slowed the movement of his pelvis, letting his fingers match the speed. He started a slow in-and-out action that was meant to drive her over the edge. Back and forth his fingers moved until he thought they'd both go mad.

Just as he was sure she was going to give up and start fucking him back, some of his control snapped. Blindly, he wrapped his other arm around her waist and then drove into her with real domination. His cock was stretching her. The penetration was perfect. The action made her cry out, and he could feel her whole body shaking. He stilled when she was close to exploding. A feeling inside of him washed through him. To know he was holding her orgasm hostage was a heady feeling.

"Faster."

"We'll go as fast or as slow as I want." Rea's words came out gravelly. He thought she might've heard the catch in his voice.

He too was at his breaking point. He wasn't hiding it well.

To prove he was going to do what he wanted, he resumed his movements with his fingers. He let his other hand go from around her waist to pinch one of her nipples.

He stopped and rolled one nipple before squeezing her whole breast. The mixture of his forceful hands, hard prick, and the delicate way he was probing her ass seemed to have broken the last of her willpower. Her body gave in to him. Her pussy squeezed down hard of its own accord. A gush of warm liquid flowed to the base of his cock.

The amusement was over. Her quivering pussy forced him to surrender the contest of wills. He grabbed her hip and his hand tightened. His other hand started to work her ass in earnest now. He pumped his fingers in at a vigorous speed. The waves of her climax washed over him.

Karma threw her hips back. Satisfying rapture ripped through his chest as her panting became screams. Her yelling his name filled his ears.

His skin felt too hot and too tight. He was going to break apart. With a bellow behind her, his hips matched the milking of her channel.

I love you. The words swirled around in his brain and time stopped. He had the feeling his body was no longer his, but hers to have. He had the overwhelming feeling they could do this forever and never stop. They belonged to each other now. No one else would ever be good enough for either of them.

He shuddered as Karma slammed into him again and again. His pelvis rotated to grind into her, and he hoped she could feel his cock swelling to its fullest. His prick filling her completely made her sex clench around him, and she began to orgasm again. He had no self-control left, and he bucked his hips as explosive sensations catapulted through his veins.

His orgasm seemed to go on and on. He would've collapsed on top of the bed if it weren't for worrying about crushing her.

As Rea bucked his hips twice more, his seed filled her passage. He pulled his one hand from her body and pushed them both down on the bed.

Spent, he felt the sweat on both their bodies seal them together. Fatigue gripped him like never before. He didn't speak as he arranged her back against his chest. He held her tight. Sleep saturated him, and he let it wash over him. He held her so close he could feel his softening penis between her legs.

"Karma, that was incredible. I…" Rea was stupefied. What were the right words? "Thank you" didn't seem right.

Out of the corner of his eye, he could see the lift of her lips. Did she think it was funny he couldn't speak? If he spoke, he'd pour out his love for her. He might tell her to stay with him and never leave. He brushed his hand over her arms while he held her. He didn't want her to leave, but he wasn't sure if he was making the right choices for the base. Normally, he was a problem solver, but right now, he didn't have a clear idea of what he should do. What if he asked her and she said she didn't want to be stuck here? He couldn't blame her if she didn't want to live in the same place for the rest of her life. Her freedom was hard earned.

Giving it up for someone you knew back when you were a teenager was nuts.

This also might not be the right moment. For the first time, they had some honesty between them, and he wasn't going to ruin it by saying empty words he hadn't thought through.

Rea couldn't explain what was different about this or what had happened. He needed some time to think. He needed some rest and some time.

Once he slept, he could figure it all out in the morning.

Chapter 21

As Karma woke, she realized she was still next to Rea. They'd fallen asleep. She pushed at the makeshift blindfold, which was caught in her hair, and her eyes alighted on the digital clock on the computer. She guessed she'd only been out for a short time. Her face turned to Rea, and she saw he was awake.

Rea's green eyes blinked slowly in the soft light. She was so sexually sedated that unless Fletcher showed up at this moment to kill them both, she wasn't moving. She wanted to stay snuggled next to Rea for a year. She didn't remember ever being this content even when she and Rea were first together.

"You wiped me out," she whispered.

Rea took one hand and ran the tip of his finger over her eyebrow, and then down over her nose and chin. His hands smelled like soap, and she noticed his hair was damp. He must've gotten up and showered. She'd slept right through it. She wanted to laugh when she realized he indeed had knocked her out. She never slept this hard.

He traced her face slowly and let his hand wander over her chest and stomach.

Whenever he hit a scar, he paused and ran his fingers over the raised skin before touching some other part of her.

He looked at her beaten body, but he wasn't disgusted by her scars, merely inquisitive.

"Why don't you leave? I've nothing to offer you. I'm tied here."

"You know why I won't go." She studied his features.

"I've tried to get rid of you." Rea frowned and rolled onto his back. He stacked his hands on his chest.

"I know you've tried."

"I wanted you to know who I am. What it's like here."

"I get it."

"I've told you every horrible thing I could think of. I've even given you jobs my men find irritating. Hell, Karma, you've cleaned every weapon I own, yet you're still with me. The way I fucked you a bit ago, it was hard. I'm hard on things. I'm hard on you. I don't know how to be with someone. I'm happy alone."

"I don't believe you're happy alone. I don't think you'll ever be happy without me. I wouldn't be happy without you, either." Karma chose her words carefully, and she let them sit in the air between them.

"Damn it, Karma, are you going to leave again?"

"I'll leave if you tell me to go, and you mean it. I do want you happy, if nothing else. Please believe that."

"I told you to go when you first showed up," Rea muttered uncertainly.

"But I knew you didn't mean it." Karma grinned and snuggled closer.

Rea wrapped one arm around her. She could tell he didn't want her to go away. He stated it because he thought he had to. He thought he was ruining her life by keeping her here, but it wasn't real. He needed more time to see that they could be happy wherever they were. The sex had helped as she'd thought. Now, all she had to do was give him a little more time.

"What about your life before? Do you miss the action? Do you miss the Equator and all the sex with strangers? I bet men loved you."

Karma laughed out loud, and then realized he was serious.

"You haven't heard one thing I've said all week. My life was like oil-filled ocean water. It was garbage, Rea. When I left you, it was like you'd thrown my sexual thermostat off. After you, I could only ever reach lukewarm. And I told you I'd quit long before I even came here. I wanted to do something else with my life. I'm happy here. You've a built-in lie detector, but you won't see the truth."

"You're just saying that."

"You're the worst lie detector ever. Do you want to know about other men, Rea? Is that what this is really about?"

"Oh, God. No." Rea's tone was a mix of disgust and demand. Karma couldn't help but laugh at the sour expression on his face.

"Too late. Now I'm going to tell you."

Rea turned suddenly and flipped her over so she was face down on the bed.

"No," he repeated sternly. He was amazingly fast sometimes, and Karma marveled at how strong he was.

He laughed low in his throat when he had her pinned. She didn't struggle under him, even though she could probably get out from the position. Once he had her pinned, he took both her hands and held them behind her back.

"I mean it, Kitten. Don't tell me." He breathed the words harshly into her hair at the back of her neck. It tickled.

He was trying to scare her, but she wasn't afraid. If she tugged, he'd let go because that was the kind of man he was, but she didn't move. She just thought about how he kept insisting she wanted freedom. That she didn't want to be tied to him because of the base. No matter how many times she insisted she was choosing to be here, he seemed to think this was still about Fletcher. He really thought they couldn't be mended, and she didn't know why. Was jealousy part of the problem?

"Rea?"

He murmured incoherent words as he shifted down her body. He began to spread her legs apart as he rained kisses down her spine and tried to make her squirm. It worked, but she wasn't going to forget this conversation. She needed him to know she wanted to be here. Fletcher, and The Seemyah, and all that be damned.

"Rea, there hasn't been anyone but you, no other men."

He stilled his actions behind her and let go of her hands suddenly. She shifted to look over her shoulder. He was giving her the mesmerizing stare he gave people when he was trying to decide if they were lying.

"It's not that out there if you think about it. Everyone in The Seemyah knew my dad. He was the kind of man that had a quick temper. Anyone I liked, he frightened away, and the rest, I'd no interest in. Like I said, I couldn't get past lukewarm. We were so in tune. I could never find that again."

Karma felt Rea breathing behind her. She rolled over and shifted her legs to go on either side of him. After she'd arranged the pillow so she could look at him, she waited for him to speak.

He was now kneeling between her legs, and he looked like he was thinking hard. He traced the muscles on her abs.

His fingers circled her belly button in an absent way. Actually, Karma had noticed Rea touched her when he was lost in thought. It was as if he wanted to make sure he wasn't alone.

Finally, he broke the silence.

"You're telling me the truth, but it's hard to believe. Your life has been intense. You've told me the stories. For every scar, you tell me about a thing you did or someone you were with. I don't picture your father as being so frightening that men would run away from you. If I were after you, no one would stop me. Not your dad. No one."

Karma wrapped her arms around the pillow near her head and arranged her hair on it. He kept up the touching, but once in a while, he'd let his fingers drop between her parted legs to slide over her tender flesh. His hands danced over her thighs to her stomach and then moved between her legs again.

"If you'd known where I was… would you've come for me? I mean, you said no one would be able to stop you. Does that include your dad?" Karma was nervous to ask.

Rea had a ready answer for her, like he was already thinking about that himself.

"Hell yes, I would've blown off my dad. I could've blown him off lots of years back, but I didn't have anywhere to go. I couldn't cut the strings."

"You were responsible, and you helped Gears. You've helped a lot of people. You're a good man, Rea. You had a reason to stay. I didn't."

"Don't say that. I'm not some honorable, noble person. I couldn't do what you did. I couldn't leave, and I thought you were long gone. My father said you'd left, and you didn't say goodbye 'coz you were done with me. He said you couldn't watch me be beaten anymore. He wasn't lying. I could tell, but now that I know the story, it changes what he told me. You thought I was dead. You couldn't watch me get beaten, but not 'coz you were ashamed of me. I gave up on leaving when my father told me that. After my dad died, I stayed, and I devoted my life to the water bases. I stayed 'coz I wanted to leave this world knowing I'd done something other than wander around being lost."

Rea had a faraway look in his eye, and Karma hoped he wasn't in the past. The two of them pondering what might've been wasn't good for this relationship.

"You're no longer lost, as you put it. The water bases are quite a legacy." She paused. "But in the end, having a bunch of future historians yammer about how great you were means nothing if your life was miserable. My dad said that once, and I think it's true."

"I think I'd have liked your dad. He doesn't sound that bad, other than the fact the man taught you to kill people."

Karma smiled and touched his shoulders when his hands came up to massage her breasts. He was leaned over her now, and he caressed her nipples softly.

"My dad would've hated you. He tried to kill anyone who even thought about sleeping with me. I told you he had a temper. It never bothered me, however. I wasn't afraid of him. We were close, him and me. I miss him a lot. I don't miss being told what to do, but *him* I miss."

"There are a few guys I know who have a temper like that. Ken, who watches the office, can fly off the handle. Gears has a temper, too. He doesn't seem like it, but he can be unbelievably scary. He gets pissed about shit, and he can really screw you over if he wants to. I don't worry about either of them. They're good men and good help. If it weren't for the two of them, I wouldn't be here to take care of you."

"After Fletcher shows up and I kill him, and after everything is settled with you and me, I'll have to remember to make a special trip to say thanks to them," Karma said with a languid sigh.

"It's surprisingly good to have you around to meet the men I train." Rea paused, and she could almost hear his thoughts getting wound up again. "It's nice right now, but I know how this will go. You'll leave when you get bored here. The base is very day-to-day. That's what happens. There is no adventure here for you."

"'We' could be an adventure."

Rea touched another scar.

"Do 'we' really have a chance? So much time has passed. We can't go back."

Karma didn't want Rea to live in the past and wonder about all the what-ifs. The what-ifs could kill this new relationship she was so carefully trying to build.

If only Rea could see how rare second chances were and how lucky the two of them really were.

"No, we can't go back. I wouldn't ask that of you, and I don't want to. But I also don't want to waste time on regrets. I want…"

"What?" Rea's eyes searched hers.

"For now, I want less talking and more rubbing," Karma said dreamily. She scooted her body closer to his legs and wiggled.

Rea's hand dipped lower between her legs. He let his fingers run over the wet flesh that was still coated with his cream. She wanted him over and over again, and the rest of the night was going to be hers. When he was inside of her, all the problems of the world dropped away.

"I can do that." His voice was eager.

She could tell his thoughts were no longer on either one of their dead fathers, the water bases, or training.

Karma purred and lifted her hips to give him better access. No matter what Rea did, she'd stay if he asked. He was so worth it to her. She could never go back to a lukewarm existence again. Being with Rea made her count herself very, very lucky.

Chapter 22

Rea crawled out from under the dark-haired beauty sleeping next to him. She was curled around his body like a well-fed kitten.

Rising, he placed his feet on the floor, expecting the rush of cold from the cement. Instead of chilly concrete, his toes dug into soft fibers. Karma had put a runner of thick carpet from his side of the bed all the way to the bathroom door.

He turned and adjusted the blankets over Karma and stopped himself from laughing out loud. This was the kind of thoughtfulness and understanding that made Karma unique. She always did things to make his life better, and she never thought anything of it. He kissed her forehead and went to the kitchen still naked.

"What's going on, handsome?" she murmured groggily. "What time is it?"

"It's 1:05 a.m. Nothing's going on. I'm getting a drink of water. Go back to sleep. I'll be back in a minute. We don't have to be up for training for hours yet."

Karma nodded and sank back into her pillow.

He liked that she was so worn out. He loved that he could sap her energy by making love to her. For a second, that thought hit him hard, like a frying pan over his head. Making love was exactly what it was. There was a difference between fucking and making love. Even when he was rough with Karma, and she was screaming his name loud enough for everyone on the base to hear, it was still making love compared to what he'd had in the past.

Karma was all kinds of fantastic. At this point, he'd made up his mind. He was going to ask her to stay. He had to plan the right moment and figure out the right words, but he was going to ask her. She wanted to build trust between them, and he was starting to believe that was possible.

Rea grabbed a forgotten plastic cup on the side of the kitchen sink and turned on the water. Once he had a quick drink, he was going to climb back into bed. He had to admit that even though it was fun to zap her energy, she did it right back to him. He was tired, and he couldn't wait to get under the warm covers.

Before Rea could fill his cup, a loud knock sliced through the silence of the room. The sound was so unexpected that for a moment Rea didn't move. From behind him, Karma sat straight up in bed.

"Something's wrong. I feel it." Karma grabbed his blanket and pulled it over her naked chest. She then bent down and grabbed his pants that were lying on the floor. She tossed them to him with a flick of her wrist.

"Me too." Rea's eyes followed her movements as she slipped on a shirt. Something didn't feel right about this disruption at one in the morning. He didn't know what it was, but it was special that Karma could feel it as well. He tugged on his pants.

Rea checked the cameras. He saw Gears in the hallway. His friend's head was tucked above a series of coats, and he was playing with his glasses.

"It's just Gears," he told Karma just as another knock sounded.

"At 1:05 in the morning?"

"Gears has no sense of time."

Rea unlocked his door while behind him Karma started to load one of his pistols. He was going to tell her not to, but a piece of him said to let her be. In fact, her getting armed was a comforting sensation. She probably thought she needed to protect him. She was always saying things like that.

After a quick glance to check that she was dressed, Rea opened the door.

Gears stepped into his bedroom and gave an awkward smile at Karma before looking at Rea's bare chest.

"I'm sorry to wake you, or not wake you if you were…" He looked down at his coat and touched one of the buttons. "I forgot that you could be doing…" He stopped again. Rea exhaled with frustration. For a man who was considered a genius, Gears wasn't good with simple things, like talking.

"We were sleeping, Gears. What'd you want?" Rea closed the door.

"The power is out in my room."

Rea reached over and flipped the light switch. No light came on.

Karma got up from the bed and went to the bathroom. He heard the click of the switch in there, but nothing illumined.

Frowning, he pointed to the camera on his computer.

"That's working. I can read the time, and I can see the hall—" The word "hall" died on his lips just as the computer screen went dark. The last of the light in the room had disappeared. The room was thrown into complete blackness.

A sinking feeling settled into his gut. Fletcher was here. There was no question.

Rea took a deep breath as he tried to quell his frustration. He should've been ready, but here he was, half-dressed and in the dark.

"Don't panic." Karma's voice was soft next to him.

He gritted his teeth. "I'm not going to panic. I'm pissed. I should've known he was here. Where the hell are Ken and all the men? Damn it, I should've been ready for this." When Rea paused, Karma cut in.

"You can't know everything and always be working. You have a life, Rea. We have a life," she ended softly. "And I was telling Gears not to panic, not you," she added.

Karma grabbed his hand in the dark. He felt the familiar shape of his Glock being pressed into his palm.

Rea nodded. That's what he wanted, a life. He wanted a life where the men did their job, and he was able to do a different job on the base. He wanted a life with Karma in it—him and her cuddling in bed and building a home.

Was something as simple as that out of his reach?

No. He wanted her and he'd figure out a way to keep her. He was going to trust her, and after Fletcher was no longer a threat, he'd convince her to stay. He'd ask her to give up her freedom for him.

"How did you know that the power was out, Gears? Did someone tell you?" Better to ask Gears about the power so he didn't pour his heart out. There was no way he was going to bare his soul while they were in the dark waiting for an assassin to show himself.

"I was sleeping, but I knew the power went out when the incubator lights turned off. I was worried about my lizard babies, so I came here to talk to you about it."

"Why do you have lizard babies?" Karma asked next to him.

"Don't ask Gears about his projects. It'll only make you want to rip out your hair," Rea quickly muttered before Gears could answer. He then tucked his gun into the waistband of his pants as he gestured to where he thought the bed might be. "Karma, under my bed is a flashlight. I also need a shirt."

Rea saw his flashlight come on. It cast a yellow glow in the room, and he could once again see Karma, Gears, and the furniture.

"You won't need to rip your hair out. If you keep rubbing it like you do, you'll be bald in no time." Gears bent down and picked up a shirt off the floor. He handed it to him. Rea pulled the garment on over his head.

Rea glared at Gears after his comment and ran his fingers through his hair. "We need to get to the electrical panel and get the lights back on. Some of the security is hooked to the panel, and we have to check that first. If it's not damaged, then we'll have to check where the main power comes in from the surface of the planet. There are battery terminals that are hooked to the wind generators."

Karma shook her head. "I know Fletcher. This is what he does when he's desperate. He shoots out electrical panels and then goes on a killing spree. It's what he always does when he can't have his way. It's a child's tantrum."

"Some child," Gears whispered.

"The emergency lights are working in the halls. So there's still some battery power," Rea said after he opened the door a crack. After his eyes adjusted to the red lights in the hall, he listened for gunfire. No killing spree yet.

"We need the camera to see where Fletcher is on the base. Otherwise, we'll just be guessing," Karma suggested.

Rea found it hard to believe Fletcher would attack a water base alone. His men weren't great, but they were all armed.

"We sent the electrician on to the next base that's planned to be built. And I'm not an electrician." Gears nervously pushed up his glasses. "Maybe it's not Fletcher. Maybe it's nothing."

It wasn't nothing, but Rea couldn't explain why he thought that. Instead, he looked at the pistol in Karma's hand. "We're going to the panel, and we'll check it out. And we'll go expecting Fletcher."

Karma nodded, and when she noted where his eyes had traveled, she held the gun out for him to take. "I know, I know, unarmed."

Rea could almost hear the defeat in her voice. He didn't like it. If he was going to trust her, he might as well throw himself all the way into it.

"We can be a 'we.'" He took the Beretta from her outstretched hand and pressed the gun into Gears' chest. After Gears fumbled with it for a moment, he then regarded Karma.

"Karma." Her eyes went from Gears' shaking hands to his face. "Under the bed are my assault rifle and your MP5. Grab all the ammo and I'll wait until you get your body suit on."

Karma's eyes lit up like twinkling holiday lights. "You mean it? A real 'we'?"

"Are you as good a shot in the dark as you are with the lights on?"

A smile lit up her face. "Better."

"Then get dressed and *we* can protect Gears while *we* head to the electrical room."

Karma dashed to the bathroom. He heard the rustle of her clothes. After he hunted for a couple of bulletproof vests, he grabbed his radio. So far there hadn't been any chatter about the base, but he expected that to change.

"You're arming your trigger-happy girlfriend. Are you sure this is a good idea?" Gears asked as Rea laced up his boots.

Rea tossed his friend body armor and the radio. "Don't worry about my girlfriend. She just wants to help me," he answered, as he put on the other vest. He didn't add that he loved her. It was probably not the right time for that.

Karma appeared out of the bathroom, dressed to kill. She immediately retrieved his M4. She filled hidden pockets with ammo and pulled her hair back into a ponytail.

"I'm ready." She smiled.

"I'm not." Gears frowned.

Rea picked up the flashlight and slung the MP5 over his shoulder. He adjusted the weapon to lie on his chest. All they had to do was make it to the panel, fix it, and then find Fletcher and kill him. After that, he could tell Karma he wanted her to stay. He'd tell her he had faith in the two of them to make their relationship work. He hoped she'd still be willing to stay after everything that had happened between them. He'd told her to leave before. He couldn't undo that.

Rea opened the door and looked out. Gears hung back and Karma brushed against his side. "You called me your girlfriend," she whispered as she scanned the hall.

"Yes, I did."

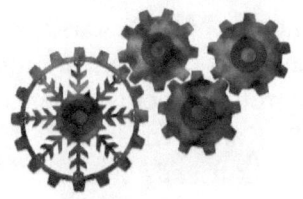

Chapter 23

The halls glowed a dull red from the emergency lights. For Karma, the halls might've been as bright as ever. She could even see some things better, like where there was even a little adjustment of light. If anyone was carrying a flashlight up ahead, she'd notice that change even from a distance.

Scanning behind them, she looked around Gears. Rea was behind her. Gears trailed after them. Rea was protecting the doctor. His compact rifle was at the ready. She tried to spot anything that might tip her off to a trap. Fletcher never did like traps. He'd said once that they were too time-consuming when you could just walk up and shoot people. Just because he said that didn't mean that he wouldn't set any. It had been a long time since she'd worked with him, so she wasn't a hundred percent sure what he'd do next. If it was the same old Fletcher, then he'd shoot out an electrical panel and start mowing people down.

They turned down the next hall. She took the lead. Directly past the cement column, she heard shots. The sound reverberated off the walls. Behind her, Rea pressed

Gears to the wall. The area in close proximity to them looked safe, but the noise was loud. The gunfire was coming from behind them.

Rea took the radio from Gears. "Status report."

She heard a muffled voice followed by static.

Rea nodded at her. "The base is being attacked at two points—where the trains enter and at ground level near the wind generators. Ground level is under control."

"Two points?" Karma whispered.

"Fletcher brought friends along."

"He doesn't have any friends," she muttered more to herself.

She waved her hand silently to indicate that Rea should take point. She put the doctor between them. The assassin part of her wanted to ditch Gears and Rea. She felt driven to hunt down the shooter, but she'd told Rea she'd stay with him. She wasn't going to let him down now. As much as she recognized that Rea could take care of himself, she knew that looking after Gears was like herding cats. Rea was putting faith in her. She wouldn't desert him.

Rea came to the next corner of the hall. He angled only a small portion of his body around the smooth stone. The radio was passed to Gears. He lifted his weapon. Behind her, Karma heard more shots. Several pops bounced off the walls. Semi-automatic.

Wishing they had better cover, she ran into Gears. He'd come to a complete stop. He was cowering behind Rea.

"Karma," Rea whispered. "Who's ahead of us in the hall? I can see movement."

Karma bent around Rea. She dropped to a knee to make a smaller, lower silhouette. She peeked around cement that capped the corner of the wall.

As soon as she saw Eric, she tucked her head back. She adjusted her rifle to aim at the floor again.

"It's Eric."

"Is he armed?" Rea asked.

Karma wished she knew what he was thinking. Was he not trusting Eric now?

"No. He looks worried."

Rea gave a curt nod. He stepped slowly around the corner.

"Who's there?" Eric called out.

"It's just Karma, and me, and Gears," Rea responded.

Eric's shoulders relaxed. "Thank God."

"I'm not thanking God yet," Gears muttered behind her.

"What's going on? The lights are out, and I can't find anyone."

Eric was right. They hadn't seen anyone. Actually, with the kind of men she'd met on this base, she'd have expected to see some of them cowering by now. Either that or ignoring the situation with the "we're all gonna die anyway" attitude.

"You should've stayed in your room. It'd be safer," Karma said.

"I know. That's what Ken told me to do, but after he left and didn't come back, I got worried something was going on. I was afraid he was hurt or that maybe…" He paused. "I was feeling like I was waiting for someone to bust in and kill me."

Karma nodded and asked herself what she knew about Ken. Rea had mentioned him before, but what did she really know about him? It wouldn't be totally outlandish if he were someone Fletcher was paying for information about the base. She should've asked more questions about him sooner.

She moved out of the way as Rea asked if Eric's dog was safe. As she kept a lookout down the hall, Eric assured him the pup was fine.

"We need to get to the electrical room. We can fix the panel, and it'd be safer than standing out in the hallway." Rea's sentence brought her head out of her thoughts about Ken.

"I know some electrical wiring. I can help," Eric volunteered.

"No. You stay here. We have Gears."

Gears pushed up his glasses. "I'm not an electrician. I can stay, and Eric could go. I'll hide under his bed."

Karma almost laughed at the picture of Gears under Eric's bed but stopped herself.

"No." Rea checked his ammo.

"Don't dump me here. Please. I can help, really," Eric begged.

"Karma, what do you think? Should we take Eric with us?" Rea asked after a second.

This surprised her. He was asking her for her opinion. She thought carefully about what she wanted to say. She remembered all the things Fletcher said when he was setting up this deal with her. He said he was going to handle Gears and Eric. At the time, she'd thought maybe Eric was the client, but now she wasn't so sure. In fact, now she was starting to question all this work to kill Rea.

Why had Rea been the target in the first place? She never had figured that out.

"I think you need to ask Eric if he hired Fletcher to kill you."

"I never hired a hit man!" Eric put his hand to his chest like he was having a heart attack. "I came here for help. I told you that. You of all people would know if I was lying."

Rea nodded. Karma figured that was him indicating Eric wasn't lying.

"Fletcher said he was going to handle Eric and Gears. That could mean one of them hired him to kill you, or they're on the hit list, too. This whole time I've been looking after you, but maybe they're involved in some way."

"I can't afford a hit man," Gears tossed out casually.

Karma, Rea, and Eric all turned to look at Gears, who was pulling on gloves while trying to hold the Beretta under his arm.

When Gears noticed the silence, he looked up.

"I'm not saying I would." Gears' brow furrowed. "I didn't mean like I'd do it. I didn't hire anyone. I'm just saying I don't have a bunch of extra money, and if I did, I wouldn't hire Fletcher. Besides, it appears he isn't even a successful hit man. Shooting out a panel and killing everyone isn't a well-thought-out plan. I'd hire someone better if I had that kind of cash. Maybe, I'd suggest poison."

The silence continued. Everyone kept staring.

Gears looked even more uncomfortable. "For Pete's sake, stop staring at me. I never hired anyone. I like Rea. I like the base. I don't hire assassins to kill my friends. Stop it!"

Rea scrubbed a hand through his hair.

"Gears didn't hire him, Karma." He looked at her. "And we have to get moving to the panel. We can talk more about it once we aren't sitting wide open in the hallway. Eric, you can come."

Karma nodded, but Rea didn't start walking again.

"I want to know why you didn't tell me any of this before."

She tried to read Rea's expression. Did he think she'd kept this from him intentionally? Actually, she just hadn't thought about it until now.

"I was focused on protecting you. I didn't think Eric or Gears could be a target. I never knew how they were involved. They were names Fletcher gave in passing."

Another round of gunshots ended her explanation. Gears ducked behind her. More than one weapon was being fired. They needed to find a safe place for the doctor and Eric.

Rea grabbed the radio. He checked with Brice. He then tipped his head toward the next walkway.

"We need to move," he commanded. She agreed.

Rea took point down the hall. Eric and Gears hurried after him. She kept her ears and eyes open.

Karma scanned every corner they approached. More noises filled the halls. A man hollered. Several shots were fired. The radio kept up constant dialog. Rea put the volume on low.

When they reached the maintenance area, they heard more gunfire. It was closer this time. They all came to a halt. Gingerly, she moved ahead of Rea. She peeked down the last corridor. On the right side was the electrical room. A large man had his back to her. Something about him seemed oddly familiar. The stranger was trying to open the door. Another man flanked him with his gun at the ready.

She crouched down next to the wall and aimed her rifle while she looked down her sights. Next to her Rea dropped to a knee.

He whispered in her ear. "Who is it? Is it Fletcher?"

"No, it's not Fletcher. It's two men trying to get into the electrical room." Karma paused. She studied the large man's frame. "He has dark hair, and he's tall." Karma stopped speaking and took a deep breath.

This was unbelievable.

"It's Ken. Don't shoot him. He works for me," Rea said as he stood.

"That's not Ken. That's Keith, my father."

Chapter 24

"Did you say Keith? Your father? I must've misunderstood you," Rea had the feeling he'd just missed something. Karma had said her dad was dead. Had that been a lie? No, he had faith in her. This must just be a mistake, and Ken just looked like her dad.

Karma didn't answer him.

Rea called out a hushed "Ken" and came out past the wall. Ken was attempting to get the door open. Young and useless, Brice was with him.

"Boss-Mac, we need to get in here. I have a key, but the lock has been damaged." Ken's eyes went past Rea to Karma standing behind him. "Hello, Kar, glad you're here."

Ken produced a small dark-colored case from his pocket and handed it to her. When the flashlight passed her face, Rea noticed her eyes had gone as cold as ice. She snatched the case from Ken and then put her rifle on her shoulder.

"Were you expecting me, *Ken*?" she snapped.

"I didn't think I could hide from you forever. There are a lot of cameras on this base, and I'm not stupider." Ken nodded at Karma. "Give her a minute and we'll be in. She can crack any lock, even broken ones."

Karma stepped forward.

"We don't have time right now, but I've got questions, Ken." Rea acted as a lookout on one side of the door. Brice did the same on the opposite side of the hall. Behind him, Karma opened the case. He glanced over as she picked the lock to the door. The whole time, she didn't say a word. Her silence made him nervous. Actually, a lot of this made him nervous. She said this was her father. He wanted to question everyone, but silence was his friend right now. He couldn't have a big long conversation in the hall. Not when they were being hunted and they had no lights and no idea where Fletcher could be.

Gears huddled close to Eric. Both men moved behind Ken's large frame. If it was bothering Ken, he didn't let it show. He just kept his gun up, his mouth closed, and his eyes open.

Much to Rea's surprise, Brice did the same thing. He wasn't prattling on or looking worried. Considering what a bad shot he was, Rea thought he wouldn't be as calm and relaxed as he was right now.

Karma made a triumphant "ahh" sound at the door the same moment Brice let off two shots. Rea turned in time to see a man who'd just come around the corner get hit in the head. The stranger fell to the ground.

"What the hell was that?" Rea couldn't hide how flabbergasted he was. The shot was amazing, especially in the low light. Two in the head, perfectly between the eyes.

"Brice works for me. I got the best men I could find," Ken said. "He's a great shot."

"A great shot? You ruined four doors in the training room." Rea scanned the lanky youth. "And three lights." He very much doubted that.

Brice smiled. "Ken asked all of us to pretend to be novices, so you wouldn't think something was up. He thought it'd be best if we just went along with your training. Actually, you're a good trainer."

"I didn't think it was the right time to put all my cards on the table." Ken shrugged. "I was waiting for—"

"For what? For hell to freeze over? For Earth to melt? This is my base. I've a right to know what's going on." Rea's eyes looked to Karma for a second.

"Don't look at me. I don't know what's going on either." Karma opened the door and stormed into the electrical room.

Gears and Eric hurried after her. Rea gave Brice orders to check the men who were guarding the area where the trains parked. While he gave instructions on vulnerable points, Ken got on his radio. Karma helped Gears open the panel. Eric held the flashlight.

After Brice left, they closed the heavy steel door.

The room the five of them entered was a simple square. On the center of the far wall were three sub-panels. Eric pointed the flashlight at the largest of the three. He could see random bullet holes peppering it.

"Fletcher never did listen to me. If you're aiming to cut the power, then you should do it where it comes in from the surface of the planet. This is a… what's the word? Shortcut?" Ken took out a pistol and checked the clip.

"Could I have a brief explanation?" Rea looked to Ken and then to Karma. How could he have missed the similarities?

Karma frowned. "I know what this looks like. You think I lied when I said my father was dead. Well, he was. I was at his funeral. I was handed his ashes. I'm as confused as you are."

"Mac, you always knew I was lying about my name." Ken slipped his weapon back into a holster on his thigh. "And I don't know who was incinerated, but it wasn't me."

"Yeah, I knew about the name." Rea studied Ken or Keith. "I thought it might be 'coz you were hiding from an ex-girlfriend or a crazy wife. Maybe you had a rough past. We always worked well together, and you never lied about anything else. I just thought I knew who you were."

"Boy, you're right. I did have a rough past, and the name's Keith Davis."

Rea studied Keith's dark eyes and his large impressive form. He started to feel the burning in his gut. His stomach felt like he'd eaten fire. It was a lie.

"Your name's not Keith Davis." Rea wished Karma would say what she was thinking too. He wanted to have faith in her. She couldn't have known about all this. He refused to believe everything between them had been a lie.

"Yes, I've had a lot of names, but I think the Keith Davis part is the only one that's important here."

Rea glanced at Karma again. Did she really not know her father was alive? And more importantly, why was her dad here? Why did Keith have men working for him and pretending to be new at guarding? He'd actually realized some of them were pretending, but he figured it was just most of them dodging work.

"I thought I could trust you, Keith." A sinking feeling nudged at him.

"You can trust me. It hasn't been easy keeping things from you, but by the time I wanted to tell you who I was, the situation had changed."

Before he could get more out of Keith, he heard Gears behind him. Gears was singing a tune to the electrical panel. The doctor's back was to them.

"The black wire goes to gold, and the white to silver, and don't forget the ground."

Eric, Keith, Karma and he all turned to watch Gears as he continued to hum. Finally, Eric spoke. "What're you doing?"

The words stopped Gears' singing.

Gears spun around holding a screwdriver in his hand. His cheeks were red. "I told you before, I'm not an electrician. The song helps me keep this straight."

Rea nodded. "I can see that, but can you fix it?"

"Yes, but I need time."

"We need light. The men coming in at the train station are wearing night vision." Rea looked to Karma.

Karma pinned her father with a hard look. "We can't check the cameras and pinpoint Fletcher until we have power. While we wait, I want to know the whole story, Dad. I want to know all of it. Start at the beginning."

"Fine." Keith nodded. "Let me start by saying I'm not planning to make apologies for The Seemyah or the choices I made. I've been doing what I think is best."

"What do you mean by best?" Rea studied Keith. Sure, Rea had talked to him many times before, but this was different. He kept asking himself how he had missed Karma and Keith's resemblance.

"It all began when I faked my own death."

As Keith spoke, Rea glanced at Eric and Gears, who looked captivated by that starting sentence. Gears stopped working. Eric nudged him back to what he was supposed to be focused on.

"You see, I had to do it. I made it no secret I wanted Karma to have my empire. I'd hoped Fletcher would become her second, like he'd been mine. I wanted the business and The Seemyah to prosper under their joint leadership. I had to keep The Seemyah and the building business on top."

While Keith continued, Rea opened the door a crack and scanned the hall. This wasn't the time to talk, but Karma was like a dog after a meaty bone. She wasn't going to let this go. Rea was sure of that.

"To keep the business on top, you thought it'd be best if you pretended to die?" Karma pulled extra ammo from one of her many pockets.

"I thought Fletcher loved you, Karma. I figured you cared about him, too. I thought it was only a matter of time." Keith produced about half a dozen extra magazines for his pistol. Apparently he liked pockets as much as his daughter.

Karma crossed to the door and peeked out just as he'd done. "Only a matter of time until what?"

"Fletcher thought I was... what's the right word? Overbearing? I started to assume it was me that was keeping you both apart and stopping you from taking a leadership role." Keith handed Rea ammo for his Glock. He looked at him. "I faked my death so Karma could become a real leader without me around."

Karma ran her hand along the M4 on her shoulder. She looked pissed enough to shoot her dad.

"I never cared for Fletcher. I told that to you both repeatedly. Neither one of you could accept it. I wanted my freedom." Her eyes blazed in fury. "Get to the point."

Keith sighed at his daughter. "This is a long story, Kar."

A fight was brewing between daughter and father. He didn't need or want that right now.

"Maybe this isn't the right time for long stories," Rea interjected.

"You told me you liked long stories," Karma snapped. "Keep talking."

He was right. She wasn't about to let this go.

Chapter 25

"After I faked my death and left, Karma surprised me and left too," Keith continued.

Karma stared at her father. This was un-fucking-believable.

All of this because she didn't love Fletcher and didn't want to run the family? She understood her father had built his business from nothing, but she had dreams of her own.

"I told you what I wanted. You didn't listen." She heard gunfire a long way off. Everyone eyed the door. Footsteps could be heard. She waited. Silence finally settled over them again.

"Yes, I didn't listen." Keith gave Karma a sad half-smile. "Instead of working with Fletcher and taking over, you vanished. By the time I got back from my fake death, no one could find you. I also found out when I returned that Fletcher wanted to force you to marry him. I knew he had designs on The Seemyah, but I didn't know to what extent he'd go to control the family." Keith paused. "Fletcher knew no one would be loyal to him without you at his side. He was angry when you left, and he swore to destroy The Seemyah if he couldn't run it."

Rea opened the door again. "I'm going to check on the hall. Gears, hurry up. Eric stay here with Keith, and Karma, you gotta wrap up this conversation."

"Fine." She took the radio from Rea. As Rea stepped out, she turned the volume to low. She was so angry that the idea they were trapped in this room didn't even matter to her right now.

"So, where did you go?" It was hard to imagine her dad just sitting around a pool on the Equator.

"I came here. This was the one place I knew no one would look for me. I'd also heard that Mr. MacBain had been put on a hit list. There was someone who wanted the head of the water bases dead, and Gears, what's the word... vulnerable. I came to check it out."

That wasn't the answer Karma expected.

"What?" Both Gears and she spoke in unison. Gears stopped working. He looked at Keith.

"I was waiting for word from my men." Keith shrugged. "They were looking for you, Kar."

"If you're here to kill Rea, then you're not doing a very good job," Gears commented wryly.

Rea poked his head back in. "Are you done yet, Gears?"

Gears jumped. He spun back to the panel.

"I won't let you kill Rea." Karma swallowed hard. She'd never gone head-to-head with her dad over a job before. The idea of pointing a gun at his head didn't sit well with her.

Everyone stared at her. Rea stepped back inside. He frowned at all of them.

"I'm not trying to kill Rea, even though I could. I was... what's the word... we'll just use babysit. I was babysitting him." Just a hint of a smile appeared on Keith's face.

"Could you use a different term than babysit?" Rea looked up at the ceiling for a moment.

"Why were you babysitting Rea? I know you wouldn't do it out of the goodness of your heart." Karma didn't believe her father was looking after Rea. Her father was a lot of things, both good and bad, but benevolent wasn't one.

"Let me finish explaining. I was babysitting Rea—"

"Pick a new term," Rea interrupted. He opened the door again. "Or maybe you could talk about this later."

Her father ignored him. "Because when I talked to The Seemyah they told me that Fletcher had agreed to take a job killing him. The men refused the hit. Without Karma by his side, he was on his own. He left."

"So, you wanted to stop Fletcher?" She crossed to the door and looked out as well. The hall was still empty.

Rea shook his head at them. He listened to the radio for a moment. When he realized the volume was on low, he turned it back up. He barked out some commands to Brice on the other end. She heard a few more shots. It was still distant.

"Fletcher had agreed that The Seemyah would kill two men. One was the head of the water bases, Rea, the man I babysit—never mind. The other was the man that the Canadian Prime Minster had chosen to be the next president of the C.T.O.N.A."

"Me," Eric said from where he was next to Gears. "I came here thinking I'd be safe, and the head of the organization trying to kill me has been with me this whole time."

So that's what Fletcher was talking about. Fletcher had taken one job, Rea, and then taken another, Eric. Karma thought the money must've been fantastic, either that or he thought the kill was going to be easy.

"After the men explained, I looked into the big question of who was Eric Bennett." Her father inclined his head toward Bennett. "Through my sources, I learned Canada is having a problem far north near the old Alaska area. In some of the small underground communities, there is an outbreak of some type of illness. It's something no one has ever heard of. They say the sickness is carried in the snow. When the snow melts the virus becomes airborne, and people breathe it in. After they breathe it in, they die."

"They nicknamed the virus 'Snow Flu,'" Eric said as he fidgeted with the collar of his shirt.

"You knew about this?" Karma was shocked. This kind of thing should be all over the news. Why was no one told about this?

Rea attached the radio to his belt. He then glared at Eric. "You came for my help, but you didn't tell me this?"

"The Prime Minister wants to close the border between the old U.S. and Canada to make sure the illness stays in one place. The virus can be passed along, and he doesn't want it to spread. The United Nations wants to make sure Snow Flu doesn't reach the Equator until they have a vaccination. Everyone is working on a cure as fast as they can, but nothing has been figured out. Canada was told by all the other nations to get a president for the C.T.O.N.A. and close the borders. The UN wants someone everyone can look up to as the new president. No one is to know about Snow Flu because they don't want people to panic. The Equator is about as crazy as it can be. Add people panicking even more, and it will be complete chaos." Eric spoke quickly, like he was finally confessing a scary topic that had been hanging over his head.

"Why did they choose you, Eric?" Gears asked, pausing from the wires again. Everyone turned to look at him. "Not that I don't think you are presidential material."

"Work on the panel, Gears." Rea pointed at the wires. "We can talk about this later. We need to move."

"I also want to know why they chose Eric." Karma frowned. She wasn't going to let everyone leave here until she knew everything that was going on.

"They asked me because of who I know, mostly." Eric took the flashlight from Gears and held it up to the panel. "The Prime Minster thought I'd network and keep things moving forward. I knew the man who held the water bases in the palm of his hand." Eric nodded his head at Rea. "I could meet the brilliant scientist who cleans water." He then tipped his head to Gears. "I knew the harvesters because of my dad. While Canada solved the health problems, they wanted someone who'd keep the progress. I do know a lot of people, but I didn't know if I should take the job. I asked for time. I came here to talk to you, Rea. I hoped you'd give me advice. I'd need the water bases behind me. If I choose to do this, I'd need a group to keep order. You were the only person I could think of that had a team."

"This doesn't answer the question of who wants Rea and Eric dead, and Gears alone on the water bases," Karma cut in.

"I'm getting there." Keith held up his hand to silence her. "First, I learned about Eric, and after doing research, I discovered that if Eric doesn't choose to accept the position or if he's unable to take it…" Keith trailed off.

"Like if he's dead?" she asked.

"Yes, if he's dead, then Canada has a second choice. They asked a man who's head of a criminal organization known as 'The Originals.' This scum lives near the border of Mexico and the old Texas area surrounded by an empire of more scum. They call themselves the Mexican Government, but that's not accurate. They're not Mexican or government. They're nothing more than hit men and thieves. They've been rivals of mine for years. The Canadian government just doesn't see it. They hide behind their government influence and their money. They use terms like government like I use underground building."

"It's a cover." Karma nodded.

"Yes, if Canada passes this president job to the head of The Originals, they'll take over the C.T.O.N.A. and crush anyone who stands in their way. Because being stuck under these men would be awful for business, I made it my personal mission to ensure Eric takes the job."

"But you were with me, not Eric." Rea moved next to Gears. He bent down and picked up a piece of wire off the floor.

"I'd a stroke of good luck," Keith smiled broadly. "I had my men tail Eric and then he came to me. I had everyone here that I wished to babysit."

"You're right, Rea," Eric muttered. "I don't care much for *that* term."

Rea went back to the door. "Why not tell me or Eric?"

"You don't give your trust easily, and by this time, Eric was cautious. I knew he wouldn't trust just anyone, either. He was safe with my men. That's all that was important."

"I was moving around a lot." Eric dropped the flashlight he'd been holding for Gears. "I thought the moving was what was keeping me safe. I didn't know I was being followed. I feel dumb."

"Don't feel stupid, Bennett." Karma adjusted her rifle. "Fletcher tossed in Gears' name and yours right before I came here. At the time, I just didn't care. I wanted to be done. I should've paid attention."

"You can't know everything and always be working," Rea whispered to her.

Keith turned to Eric. "The Originals are not to be underestimated. They're attacking this base because a takeover of the NEDs is a huge part of their goal. They want you and Rea dead, and they'll kidnap Gears. Controlling the C.T.O.N.A. has been their mission for years. They'll use whatever they have to do this."

"So, you're helping Eric because of money? This is about his death being bad for business?" Karma thought that was more like her dad. He was protecting his territory, not Rea and Eric.

"The world is about money." Keith shrugged at her. "It's about money and sex. People do things for two reasons. Love for someone or for what they can get. I've never seen anything different than that."

Silence reigned after her father's statement. All that could be heard was Gears humming.

Rea talked into the radio for a moment and then looked at her dad. "Are we done now? We should get out of here. How are we doing, Gears?"

"One more minute." Gears responded.

Keith looked at her and Rea. "I guess I've one other thing I should tell you."

"I know what you're going to say," Rea said. "When Fletcher was kicked out of The Seemyah, he started working for The Originals. We can talk about that later."

Karma nodded. She'd thought that too. "That's why Fletcher is still involved in killing Rea and Eric. That's where he's getting his team." Even if she saw that coming, it still kind of hurt. He had been family, after all.

"That's not what I was going to say, but that's right. The Originals offered him a position. The only problem was that he was having a hard time getting his targets. All of The Seemyah knew how he worked. They stopped him from killing Eric at every turn. To my surprise, he did something I didn't expect."

"He hired Karma to kill me." Rea's eyes looked tired. She wanted to hold him. "Right now Brice said he has the surface under control. We need to get the power up for the men attacking with night vision near the trains. Gears, how you doing?"

"Almost." Gears tipped the flashlight back up.

Keith sighed. "I've thought about Fletcher, and I think his plan was to have Karma kill Rea while he was off trying to find Eric and kill him."

Keith took out a second pistol and checked the clip. "When Karma got here, I'll admit I didn't know what to do. When she lost her memory, I guessed I'd have to wait and figure it out when she was better." Her dad slipped his gun back into its holster. "I locked this base down tight and kept Rea safe. I thought I knew what to expect out of Fletcher. I was looking out for Eric, and so were all the men I hired."

"All the men on the water base are your guys?" Gears asked.

"Gears," Rea snapped. "We need light."

"All but the two Mac fired the day they hurt Karma. And Nash, the bastard. His paperwork was perfect." Keith nodded.

Karma considered all the men she'd met on the base. They weren't as good as The Seemyah, but she didn't kill Rea, and she was thankful for that. They weren't totally useless.

"Your guys are kind of lazy," she mumbled.

Keith gave a short burst of laughter. "My men have been working many hours and are tired. Tired is different from lazy. They were told to protect the base, look after Eric, watch Rea, and make sure Gears didn't get taken.... or hurt himself."

"I don't hurt myself," Gears piped up. The words weren't even past his lips before a spark flashed at the panel. He promptly winced and put his finger in his mouth.

Rea shook his head at Gears. He then looked to her. "I could tell they were trying. If I'd thought they were a lost cause, I'd have fired them all, but I just kept hoping it was going to get better."

"It did get better," Keith smiled.

"No, *it* didn't." Rea exhaled. "This isn't better. Fletcher's here. We're pinned down in a room with no power." Rea glanced at Gears.

Gears jumped guiltily.

"It's better. We're not dead," Keith insisted.

"Wait." Karma held up her hand. "What was it that you wanted to say? You said there was one other thing."

"No," Rea interrupted. "We're done talking."

Keith looked uncomfortable, a look she'd rarely seen. "When you showed up, I didn't want to meddle in your life anymore." He paused. "I waited for Fletcher to make his move." Another pause. "After I took care of my business, I thought maybe I'd move on." A third pause. "I considered letting Rea have you this time."

Keith stopped talking abruptly. It was as if he thought he had given all the explanations.

"I could have Rea *this time*?" Karma had a terrible feeling she wasn't going to like the answer to that question.

Chapter 26

Keith started to pace the small room. His eyes jumped first to Rea and then to Karma. Rea's stomach rolled slightly as if afraid of what her father was going to say next. Didn't he realize this wasn't a good time?

"I say 'this time' because after Karma had come to me, I checked up on Rea and his dad." Keith faced him. "If you remember, Davis Construction worked on parts of the water bases. I've been taking contracts for the bases for years."

Rea gave a slight nod. He didn't recall the name Davis Construction on documents, but he'd never thought much about the workers that did the building. His father had handled most of that. Mostly Rea just made sure the training got accomplished.

"You knew Rea was alive," Karma said softly. "You were lying to me from the start."

Rea wanted to reach out and hold her, but he also didn't want to move. He wanted Keith to stop talking. They could work it out later.

"I met you back then, Rea. I met you and your father. I saw how things were."

Karma glared at her father. "He was just a teenager."

"He was no type of leader, Kar. He was so beaten down. I didn't want my girl to have any part of that. I told Rea's father he should be more careful in guarding him. I convinced him to protect Rea's identity. They moved from base to base, so for the most part, I didn't have to worry about it much."

"You told Rea's dad to hide him so I'd never stumble across him again." Karma looked over at Rea. He didn't know what to say.

He shrugged at Keith. "He's right. I was no type of leader. I'm still not. I train men and keep an eye on Gears." Admitting this in front of Karma felt like the world was crushing him to the ground. "I'm always going to be tied here to the bases. I get that. It makes sense that your dad wanted a better life for you. Let's just get the lights on and we can talk about it later."

"I want to talk about it now," she spat. "Let's be clear. I don't want The Seemyah."

"But you do want your freedom. That's something I can never give you." Rea couldn't ask her to trade her dad's organization for the water bases. It was the same responsibilities. Both The Seemyah and the bases were about cohesiveness. She'd be stuck with a family either way. Freedom was a way of living that she coveted. It was why she'd left The Seemyah.

Rea realized he wanted her to be happy. Even if that meant she'd leave him.

"What if I don't want freedom? Maybe I changed my mind." Her smile made him forget about Fletcher, the gunfight near the trains, and the lights.

Her words settled over him like a warm blanket. She still wanted to stay. He thanked God for her stubbornness.

Keith's voice broke in before Rea answered. "The Seemyah is yours, Kar. You can have the world at your feet."

Rea swallowed. He couldn't give her the world. All he had to offer was his heart.

"Ask me to stay and I will." She paid no attention to her dad and Rea's heart melted.

A silence stretched between them. Was he enough? Was they being a "we" enough? Their relationship had been so hard up to now. If she stayed, could he make her happy here? Damn it, he'd try.

"Is it that easy? I just ask you to stay and you will?" A smile tugged at his lips.

"I told you that from the start."

"Then please stay with me." Rea held his breath.

Gunshots hit the door. Rea pushed Karma to the furthest wall. He put his whole body over hers. It was a natural move to keep her out of harm's way. Rounds passed through the sheet metal and insulation. Bullets struck the cement blocks near one of the panels.

Keith grabbed Eric by the collar and threw him down on the floor. "Stay there," he commanded.

Gears spun around. He glanced at everyone. "I did it!"

"Get down!" Rea barked at him. Gears obediently dropped to a knee.

Karma shoved away from him. She'd only moved for a second when the overhead lights came on. She was standing next to the light switch checking a pistol she'd just produced. His friend had indeed done it. Power was back.

Gears crawled on the floor to him and glared. "I was hoping for a thank you."

"Yeah, in a minute." He pulled out his Glock and moved closer to the door.

The squawk of Keith's two-way radio drew everyone's attention. The voice on the radio belonged to Brice.

"What's happening?" Rea only caught a few garbled words. Keith's radio fell to the floor.

"Fletcher got the drop on Brice at the tracks." Keith shoved a gun at Eric's hand. "He's hit. Everyone is stuck where they are. Fletcher and a few of his men are coming toward us."

"Or they're already here," Eric muttered with his face squished to the floor.

Gears stood up. "We've got to go. I need to get my medical bag. I need to help Brice."

More bullets hit the door. Rea threw Gears back to the ground. So far, the door was holding, but the metal was beginning to look like Swiss cheese. He needed to problem-solve.

Rea stood up. He slid to the side of the door. He pressed his back to the cement. He'd have to take Gears to Brice. He'd also have to get out of this room before the door broke into tiny pieces.

"Gears, turn off the lights. All of them. Security included."

Karma was crouched on the ground. She glanced up, surprised. "Really?"

"Gears, turn them all off, give Karma one minute, and then bring them up again. Ken, Keith, whatever, warn the men it's about to happen. The dark will give Karma time to kill whoever is outside this room. Hopefully at the tracks it'll throw off the guys wearing their night vision. Is one minute enough?"

Karma smiled. "One minute is great."

Keith barked out the information to Brice. He waited until he got the okay back. Rea looked at the time on the radio. He waved to Gears.

Gears stood up and turned off the sub-panels at the main breaker.

Darkness enveloped him. Next to him the door opened. He heard it shut. It was the longest minute of his life. Shots sounded. He prayed to a God he didn't believe in that Karma wasn't hurt. He didn't know what he'd do if she died. The seconds ticked by at a snail's pace.

The lights came on. He quickly noted his surroundings. The doctor stood next to the panel. Eric was flat on the floor. Keith stood on the other side of Gears.

The silence worried him.

"Karma?" he whispered. No response.

The door was slightly open. Cautiously, Rea tilted his body around the opening. He swept the hall with a quick look. On the floor were three men, all shot in the head. Further down the walkway was another assassin, facedown.

Keith came up behind him. "I'm sure Karma is further down the hall. She's got luck to spare."

Another volley of shots rang out away from them. Rea stepped out into the walkway. Keith was probably right. Hopefully, Karma wasn't hurt. He had to get to her. More shots ricocheted off the bricks.

Rea hurried to the end of the walkway. Keith followed. He moved pretty fast for an old man. Keith pushed past him when they reached the end of the corridor. Still trying to babysit him, Karma's father stuck his head out mere inches.

Instantly, a tall, well-dressed man skidded to a halt at the other end of the hall. Rea only got a brief glance at him before he was slammed backward against the cement.

Keith had shoved him aside. He fired his 9mm. The other gunman did the same thing.

Rea knew the moment a bullet hit Keith.

Keith stumbled. Rea grabbed him around the waist. Blood spurted from Keith's leg. He yanked hard until Keith fell back onto him. Rea put both arms under Keith's armpits. He heaved the large man backward. Keith's legs dragged on the floor.

Once he was around the corner, he propped Keith up against the wall.

The stranger stopped shooting. The halls were silent. Had Keith hit the other man?

"Dad." Karma came up behind them. Rea had never been so happy to see someone.

"He was shot by the other gunman down the hall. I think the fucker is injured as well. Where were you?"

"I followed one of Fletcher's men down the hallway, to the left." Karma leaned over her father. "Dad, you okay?"

"Tough as nails," came the older man's response. "It's Fletcher, Karma, go get him."

Karma didn't spare either of them another look. She stepped around her dad and began shooting down the hall. The zing of the bullets bounced off the cold cement walls.

"I'll try to put pressure on this wound. If only Gears was here."

Rea set down his weapon. He pressed his palms to the blood gushing out of Keith's leg. Keith did the same. He fumbled with the torn fabric. Together they ripped a larger hole in his pants. Rea had just started to think he might have to create a tourniquet when he heard a noise behind him. Both he and Keith picked up their guns.

Gears was jogging down the hall. Eric was right beside him. Both men were holding weapons. As happy as he was to see the two of them, he was also furious. Gears and Eric didn't need to be in the middle of this. They needed to be safe.

"I told you two to stay where you were. What're you doing here?"

They came to a halt in front of Rea and Keith. Eric held up Keith's radio. Rea didn't even known they had it.

"Keith left his radio on. You said you needed Gears. We heard you."

Rea's eyes spotted a shooter who'd just turned the corner behind Gears and Eric. Rea snatched up his gun. It was sticky with blood. He came to his feet over Keith.

"Down." Rea shoved Gears to the floor. The doctor dropped next to Keith. Eric did the same thing. Rea was thankful his friend was wearing a vest. Still, he should've never left the safety of the electrical room.

The stranger behind Gears shot. A bullet hit Rea in the left arm. He ignored the pain. He returned fire. It struck the gunman in the chest. He fired off two more shots. They hit the stranger in the head. Rea's eyes shifted down to the doctor. His friend was bent over Keith. Eric was helping him. They looked unhurt to Rea. He exhaled. He needed to get them all to safety. He also needed to help Karma.

Gears glanced up. "You were hit."

"I'm fine. Just look after Keith."

Rea gripped his gun. He disregarded the burning in his upper arm.

"I'll take care of Keith." Gears didn't look at him again. "Go help your trigger-happy girlfriend."

He didn't know if he should leave Gears. His eyes jumped to Eric and then to Keith.

The old man smiled at him. "I'll babysit. I was shot in the leg, not the hand." Keith held up his pistol. Rea nodded.

He was desperate to see that Karma wasn't hurt. He started to jog after her. He quickly recalled where she'd gone.

When he came to the first hall, he tipped slightly around the wall. He saw Karma advancing down the corridor. Her back was to him. When she came to the end of the walkway, she began shooting around the next corner. Rea rushed over to her position as soon as he spotted her. She flipped her eyes to him and then knelt. Dust from the cement was floating in the air. Bullets were striking the stone directly above her. She ducked; then fired back.

Rea got to her position. He looked down his sights. "Is it just Fletcher?" He fired a round toward where she was aiming.

"Yes." She put a new magazine in her rifle. "Is my dad okay?"

"Gears is an experienced doctor." He couldn't say yes. He didn't know.

Rea leaned around the cement a little more. He wanted to get a good look at the man they'd all been waiting for.

Fletcher wasn't what he expected. He was tall, well-built, and polished. He could be a salesman. He was wearing a tailored black suit. Even ducking behind the doorway, not a single hair was out of place.

Karma called out to him. "It's over, Fletcher." She shot again. "I've killed everyone around here. No one's left to help you."

Fletcher's voice was smooth and unruffled. "The Originals will destroy all of you. I've told them every detail of the family. You can kill me, but it won't matter."

Rea pressed himself against the wall. The Originals sounded like a cult.

"I'm going to go out into the open." Karma looked at him. "I'm wearing my full body suit. As soon as he leans out to shoot, you hit him."

Rea shook his head. "No. The men will show up. We'll just keep him busy until they get here."

Karma stood. "This is my fight. Trust me. I've done this before. Please, Rea?"

The "please" pierced his heart. He held his rifle at the ready.

"Fletcher won't shoot you in the head?"

"Probably not."

Before he could tell her that "probably not" wasn't an acceptable answer, she stepped out past the wall.

Rea aimed. Karma was right. Fletcher leaned too far out past the doorframe. His arm and head came into view. As soon as Rea got a clear shot, he took it.

His bullet tore through Fletcher's hand. But Fletcher's weapon had already flashed. A bullet screamed toward Karma. She rolled to the other side of the hall. The bullet missed her. Rea could see where the round hit the wall. Fletcher's gun dropped with a clatter. Karma lifted her rifle. She didn't pause. She unloaded her entire magazine.

Most of her bullets were direct hits. Round after round struck Fletcher's chest and head. She didn't stop shooting until the magazine was empty. "Click" went the trigger.

It was almost strange when Rea could only hear the sound of his breathing.

He came out past the wall. Karma went over to Fletcher's body. She swung the M4 onto her back. She pulled a small pistol from one of her many pockets. Her hand shook only slightly as she clutched the gun out in front of her. A single bullet left her sidearm. It struck Fletcher in the head—right between the eyes.

Rea raised an eyebrow. He'd thought Fletcher was already dead, but it appeared Karma didn't take any chances. Her eyes glistened with tears. She turned away from the lifeless body. With a shake of her head, she slid her weapon back into a mystery pocket.

"Are you okay?" He wanted to hug her, but she didn't give him a chance.

"Bullets are cheap. Lives are expensive."

Rea nodded.

"We have to see if my dad's alive." She brushed away tears from her cheeks and started to sprint back down the hall. He chased after her.

They reached her dad at the same time. He was still on the floor with Gears fighting to stop the bleeding.

"Dad?" Karma dropped to her knees. A few more tears slipped down her cheeks. "I'm rusty. I'm sorry."

"I'll be fine, Kar. Why the tears?"

"I can't do this anymore."

Rea wrapped an arm around her. She tipped her head to his chest. He wanted to say comforting words, but he didn't know what. Keith thought he was going to be fine, so it wasn't a lie, but it didn't mean it was true.

"Gears?" He looked at the doctor.

Gears spared him only a brief glance. "I have to stop the blood loss, and he won't be dancing anytime soon. Eric is going to help me get him to the medical wing. Brice is there already. I'm told he's stable."

"Are there a lot of men hurt?" Rea needed to get a status report.

"A few." Gears eyes went to Rea's arm. "You need to get looked at too. Your arm is covered in blood."

"I have to check the base."

"Are you okay?" Karma noticed where he'd been shot. She frowned at him.

"I'm fine." Rea expected Gears to argue, but Keith had all of his attention.

Karma nodded at him. An acceptance, he guessed. She held her father's hand. Rea took Keith's radio. There was a lot of work to be done, and the only thing he wanted to do right now was wrap his good arm around Karma.

"Kar." Keith looked at Karma and then to Rea. "I know you want to quit, but I need you. You have to go. You have to warn The Seemyah. Only you know where they are. You must tell The Seemyah about The Originals."

Eric started to help Keith off the floor. "Tell them what?"

"We have a protocol for when one of us has switched sides." The words struggled to find their way out of Keith's mouth. He grunted.

"I know the deal, Dad. I'll go." Karma sighed.

A crackle came over the radio in Rea's hand. "We got one of Gears' medical gurneys. We're passing the electrical room now."

Rea and Karma turned their heads toward the rumble of a small flat cart they could hear close by. After a minute, one of the water base guards appeared. Immediately, they helped Keith onto the cart.

Karma squeezed her father's hand again, as they started to hurry down the hall toward Gears' medical room.

"I'll check on you right after I check on the men," he called out after Keith. Keith barely acknowledged him.

Karma didn't follow her dad. She stayed in the hall with Rea. When everyone left, and it was just the two of them, she looked him in the eye.

"I'm leaving." She reached out and brushed her fingers lightly over the blood that was along his bicep.

Rea swallowed. For once he wanted to feel the pain in his arm. It was preferable to the torment of her leaving him.

Was he supposed to beg her not to go? He wanted to do that but he couldn't. He understood responsibility. He'd heard Fletcher say The Originals had all their information. He couldn't blame her for helping her family. He couldn't ask her to abandon them. Just like he couldn't abandon Gears and the water bases.

"I'll come back," she declared quietly.

Rea wanted to have faith in her. Faith she'd return to him.

"I'm not strong enough to see you leave again."

"Don't be silly. The first time you didn't *see* me leave." Karma gave him a smile, but it didn't reach her eyes.

"I woke up without you. That was plenty hard."

"And the second time, I shot out the light so you didn't have to see it." She was trying to sound light. She was teasing, but it didn't work. He felt her absence already.

"I almost wish I was in the dark again." This hurt. He couldn't push the misery away.

Karma gave him a sad smile. She linked his fingers with hers and pulled him down the hall. Maybe he should give her a kiss goodbye? Why did words leave him when he needed them the most?

When they got to the electrical room, she walked in and he followed her. She let go of his hand and closed the tattered door.

She gave him one more of those dazzling smiles and then turned off the light. The room was almost entirely dark.

"I'll come back. I love you," he heard her whisper. He couldn't see her move in the dark, but he felt her lips.

She kissed him. It was everything that he loved. Her warm breath, her soft lips, and her tongue timid and wet.

He reached up and brushed his fingertips through her hair. Then, like the flutter of the wind, her lips were gone.

He opened his eyes, and in the dim light, he didn't even see her shadow. The door opened; then closed. A brief flash of light, then he was alone.

Chapter 27

Karma dropped onto the thick dirt below her and stepped over a flower. She swiftly scanned the back of the greenhouses. Noting that some of the plants were new, she dashed a few wayward hairs away from her face.

After taking off her gloves, she stuffed them into the bag on her back and stood up. The room was quiet and serene. She walked around the first plastic-covered house leisurely. Her fingers petted some of the soft petals of the flowers. She'd been gone one month, yet not much had changed. She hoped Rea hadn't changed his mind about wanting her.

Her eyes closed for a moment and she took a deep breath. The room smelled of fresh rosemary. The smell of this room reminded her that she'd almost killed Rea here. Nothing about their relationship had been easy. She willed away the tears that formed whenever she thought about this place. Not this place, she reminded herself, but Rea. She wished she'd been able to come back sooner.

Karma calmed her ragged nerves and reminded herself he'd asked her to stay. Maybe he didn't use the word love, but it was implied. Right?

She decided she'd visit her dad first to make sure he was doing well. Then she'd talk to Rea.

The door to the greenhouse squeaked when she opened it. Her eyes scanned the walkways. The hall was all the same. The base was peaceful. She swiftly began to stride down the corridor. Karma passed some of the rooms and navigated her way straight to the medical wing. She could still remember every aspect of the base. At night, she dreamed about it. Well, not the base so much as Rea

Outside the room, sitting on a wooden chair, was Brice. Brice had his head propped back against the wall with his eyes closed. His deep breathing told her he was probably asleep. She slipped silently up to him and put the barrel of her gun at the nape his neck.

His eyes popped open.

"You shouldn't be sleeping if you're protecting my dad."

Brice's shoulders dropped slightly, and he looked up at her. He gave her a relaxed smile.

"Nice to see you're back. Your dad missed you."

Karma slipped her gun back into the holster on her thigh and nodded. She then turned to the door and entered the small room.

When she entered, she noted her dad first. He was sitting up in a narrow bed pushed against the furthest wall. He was shuffling an old deck of cards.

Gears was sitting at a computer to her right. A row of six label makers were on the desk by his keyboard. A snake was draped around his neck like a thin, ugly brown scarf.

Her dad noticed her first. He sat up a little straighter.

"I've been waiting for you, girl." A hint of his Russian accent was present. Whenever he said the word "girl," she could hear it. His accent reminded her of her youth. He didn't sound surprised to see her. He acted as if he always knew when she was going to show up.

Gears jumped at the sight of her and grabbed at his chest. "You scared me."

"Hi, Gears." She tipped her head to him and set her bag down. He nodded and got up from his chair.

"Your dad kept saying you'd be here soon. I didn't think he meant *now*." Gears took the snake from around his neck and put the serpent in a nearby cage. He then regarded her again. "I'm almost getting used to you being armed and sneaking into rooms."

Karma glanced at the cage of snakes. "I'm almost getting used to you, too."

Gears smiled. "I'll let you and your dad talk. I have to go and check on a few of the guys." He picked up a backpack off the table, a label maker, and headed out the door.

After Gears departed, she grabbed Gears chair and pulled it up next to her dad's bed. Her father kept shuffling his cards and didn't look up.

"How's the family?"

"Team One is red." She was glad her father wasn't looking at her. She hated to admit she hadn't gotten there before they were all murdered. They were family. They hadn't deserved to die like that. What had been done to them would haunt her nightmares for a long time.

Her father frowned. "And the other teams?"

"I beat The Originals. I moved faster. All the other teams are green."

Her father visibly relaxed. "Did you give them a new directive?"

"I did."

"Thank you."

She nodded. When he didn't say anything more, she took out her gun and switched it to safe. She wasn't surprised that her dad was silent. He was probably thinking about his next plan. She was thinking about her next plan, too.

"Are you staying here?" He asked her after a minute.

She didn't answer. Only the shuffling of cards broke the silence. The red diamond pattern passed through her father's fingers.

"I'm afraid," she whispered after a while. It was funny, but she'd never said that to her dad before. All the hits, all the dangerous situations, yet this was the time that anxiety was gripping her. She didn't want to be tied down, but she did want to be tied to Rea. She didn't want The Seemyah, but she didn't want to leave here. Damn.

"You know that I've always tried to get you to take over The Seemyah. I say we play a hand." Her father began to deal the cards. "If I win, you take over The Seemyah. I'm bringing them here. They're going to guard Eric until his position is set. You'll oversee the operation."

"So, if you win, I have to stay here?"

"Yes, run The Seemyah, make roots, you lose your freedom. You'll also have to work out your relationship with Mac."

"If I win?"

"You do as you wish. Go or stay. I'll stay out of your life. I won't meddle."

"You've meddled enough." She let the cards cool before her. Her father was going to stay out of her life. That was unlikely. She'd have to see it to believe it.

Picking up the cards in front of her, she arranged them in her hand. Her father did the same, but his expression was blank. He gave nothing away and sat without moving.

"I'll take one." Karma slid one card toward him, and her father gave her a new card. Once again, she arranged them in her hand. She could get up and leave. She didn't have to play.

"Dealer will take one." Again, he adjusted the cards to his satisfaction and relaxed his shoulders back on the pillows at the headboard.

"So?" she asked when the silence between them started to stretch on to the absurd. It was merely a deck of cards. She could do what she damn well wanted.

She sighed. What she wanted was to see Rea.

"I have a pair." Her father set his cards on the blanket. "Kings."

Karma set her cards down.

"Four aces. I win." She looked over at the door.

"Go, if you like, have all the freedom you want." Her father spoke offhandedly, but Karma could hear the disappointment behind the words.

"No, thanks. I think I'll go talk to Rea instead. It's not often I get such a great hand. I must have good luck right now. I shouldn't waste it hanging around the Equator."

Karma got up from her seat. "I'd best use this luck while I have it."

Chapter 28

Rea was covered in mud, sand, and clay. In his entire life, he was sure he'd never been this dirty. In his whole life, he was also sure he'd never been this depressed.

The flats of his palms brushed sand from his face. He used his fingers to dust chunks of mud from his hair. Keith was going to holler at him when he saw the mistake he'd made in the new hallway.

Cursing his distracted thoughts and his poor ability to focus on underground building, Rea opened the door to his bedroom. After he'd entered, he slammed it using his boot. A slab of mud fell to the floor. He ignored the mess.

The door closed with a loud thud, and Rea closed his eyes. He relaxed against the wood panels. He really liked building underground. He loved leaving the training and guarding to Keith. He had all the spare time he wanted now. So, why wasn't he happy? He knew the answer. He wasn't focused on building because he was thinking about her. He wasn't happy about having the time to himself because of her as well. Spare time was useless if he didn't have her in his room waiting for him. Freedom from training men was what he'd been after his whole life. Now that he had it, he didn't have anything to use it on.

He thought about going to the Equator to find her. Maybe she was somewhere having the time of her life. He pushed that thought away. She'd said she'd come back. He'd wait.

His fingertips scratched at the whiskers he'd forgotten to shave earlier, and he considered all the words he'd say when she came back. This time, he'd say the right thing.

On the day she left, she had said she'd return. He should've told her he loved her then. If he had said the words, then maybe he'd have no regrets.

Frustration was a living, breathing creature in the room with him, and he let it wrap its claws around him. His hands went to the bottom of his shirt. He swept the garment over his head. Rea threw it to the foot of the bed, without bothering to turn on the light. He raked his hands through his hair to dispel some of the mud and then reached for the light switch in the bathroom.

"You enter a room without turning on the lights? I'd think you'd know better by now. Someone might be waiting here to kill you." Karma's voice washed through him like the hottest, most relaxing shower he'd ever had. Keith had told him to be patient. Her father had said she'd be back and to have faith. He'd tried so hard, and now like magic, she was here. She clicked on the sun lamp by the bed. The light cast a warm, comforting glow over where she stood next to his bed.

After she'd left here, he'd taken the vent cover off, wishing that she'd come in again. He'd added softer sun lamps around the room, and a new blanket. He wanted her to like them. He had prayed every night that she'd sneak into his room one last time. Since she'd left, everything he'd done was as if she'd return, and she'd stay. Her staying was all he had thought about.

She glanced up at the light, the vent, and then back to him. He kept his eyes glued to her. She looked healthy to him. She looked fit and not bleeding.

"Are you hurt at all? Shot or injured?"

"I'm not hurt," Karma said slowly. Her eyebrows knitted together, showing puzzlement.

"Good." Rea crossed the room and crushed her to him.

He held her so tight he thought he was making it hard for her to breathe. He could feel her cheek pressed against his chest. Her body close to him was enough to make him feel alive again.

"I'll say it," he whispered into her hair.

"Say what?"

"I'll say that I should've never told you to leave in the first place. I hate when you're gone." He breathed her in. "I'll beg this time."

Karma laughed lightly, and the sound was muffled against him.

He let go of her and looked down at her beautiful dark eyes. Running his hand up into her hair, he pulled out her ponytail. He wanted her ready to go to bed. He wanted her to climb into his bed more than anything. Her hair would be around her shoulders, and she'd take off her body suit and never leave.

A chunk of mud fell to the floor from his hair.

"Why're you so muddy, bad training day?" She reached up and took another piece of dirt still clinging on some of his locks.

"Your dad took over the training. He plans to bring The Seemyah here to guard the base full-time. I'm overseeing some of the transition, but the men are solid. They don't need me much. I'm learning underground building." He wanted to add that he loved her, but he wasn't sure if he should just blurt the statement out like that.

"You agreed to have The Seemyah on the bases?" Karma asked offhandedly.

She didn't fool him. She was interested in what had been happening while she was away.

"It was put together by Gears, Eric, Keith, and I. I told Eric to hire The Seemyah as his official government protection. He asked for my advice, and that's what I thought would work. Keith is his head security officer. The family helps safeguard the bases when they aren't on security detail with Eric. No more contract killing. They're going legitimate."

Karma raised her eyebrows but didn't say anything.

"Eric told the Prime Minster he'd take the job, but only if he had his security detail with him. The Prime Minister agreed. This way Eric feels safe and Keith has a respectable job for all of the family. The Seemyah are working, and I get to learn underground building, so I can take over Davis Construction."

"Except it looks like building is harder than you thought." Karma pulled away from him.

Rea let her step past him. He eyed her cautiously, and he measured how close she was to the ventilation grate.

"It's rough going, but only 'coz I have a hard time keeping all the instructions in my head. Keith wants me to master this, and he yells at me a lot, but not like my dad."

"He can be hot-headed, but why can't you keep the instructions in your head?" Karma had her back to him and was looking at the new blanket on his bed. The quilt was a heavier material with a purple diamond design. She bent over and traced the pattern with her fingertip.

"I never think about anything other than you." It was a now-or-never moment. He stopped procrastinating. "I love you." Now, he'd have to find out if she still loved him. "Do you think you could still love me? Maybe even grow to love me like you used to?"

Rea's heart was about to beat out of his chest. The pounding was so loud he thought she must be able to hear it. He had to know if she was here to be with him or not. If she was, then this time, he was with her all the way. If she told him she needed to decorate every wall in his room with weapons, then he'd start hanging them. He remembered what Gears had said. He'd be damn happy to have a trigger-happy girlfriend. Good or bad shot, he wouldn't care as long as that woman was Karma.

When Karma didn't respond, Rea tasted abject fear. He'd made too many mistakes.

"Karma, say something," he finally got out.

Karma turned around and held out her gun and clip. "I like it better when you call me Kitten."

Rea held his smile while he took her gun and set it on the table. He came back over to where she was standing and wrapped his arms around her again.

"Stay with me, Kitten. Or if you want to leave, take me with you. I'll abandon the bases for you." He buried his head into her hair and thanked whoever was looking down on him.

"I think I'll stay… but am I staying as your girlfriend?"

"No."

She immediately tried to pull out of his embrace. Rea wouldn't let her go and waited until she gave up moving. He could tell she was annoyed with him because she was no longer hugging him back. Now her arms fell limp at her sides.

"I don't think you should stay here as my girlfriend. Your father said if I didn't marry you when you came back, he'd kill me. He meant it; he would literally kill me. He told me he'd cut me up into little pieces and hide the body where no one would ever find it."

Karma burst out laughing and hugged him again.

"Kitten, how can you laugh?" Rea pretended real alarm. "Your dad was serious. Gears told me your dad said he was going to kill me and make my death look like an accident."

Karma laughed even harder. It drew out the smile he'd been trying to hold back. He grinned down at her. She was even more beautiful than he remembered.

"I hate to tell you this, but I think it sounds like we should get married." She smiled up into his eyes.

"I better not take any chances with my life, especially now that it's getting good." Rea nodded. "Keith is basically forcing me at gunpoint to build you a home on the other end of the water base. The rooms are going to be big enough for the two of us, and maybe if anyone else should come along…"

"Like if Gears wants to move in with us?" Karma asked. "I overheard a few guards saying dad calls Gears a real Davis now. I think he adopted him."

Rea chuckled. "I don't think that's what your dad had in mind."

Karma nodded and then pulled out of his embrace. "Rea, do you know what you're asking me? I mean, all jokes aside, I have a colorful past and last time we tried to make this work, it didn't go so well. Both times, actually."

"I'm going to make us work. We're going to be a real 'we' this time. I love you. Say you love me too. Say it like you used to."

"Fine, I love you."

Rea slanted his eyes at her skeptically.

"Okay, I love you a lot?" She smiled a little when his face was still solemn.

"No."

"I love you more than anything in the whole world. I'll stay here with you. We'll work everything out. We can be a 'we.' It's the least I can do since you're building me a new home and all."

Rea laughed. "That's the truth."

He kissed her. His face was muddy, but he couldn't wait even one moment longer. Her tongue entered his mouth. He gripped her thighs as he crushed her to him.

When they finally parted, he tugged her along to the bathroom. From past experience, he was sure he could convince her to take a shower with him. He glanced down at his pants. He'd have to make sure he wasn't wearing anything he liked when he got into the shower.

"Karma?" He paused with her following behind him. "You could've had your freedom. Why did you come back here?"

Rea turned to look into her eyes. There was no doubt in his mind she loved him and wanted to stay like she said, but still, he was curious as to why she'd decided to give her freedom up for him.

Slipping her arms around him, Karma paused. She studied his face.

"I guess, I came back because… you're one very lucky man."

Epilogue

The time was five after one in the early morning hours. Karma leaned against one of the entryways that led into the water base. The harvester she was to meet was described as "The Tall Indian." Karma waited along the train tracks for all the men to get off the arriving trains. There were men everywhere setting up stalls to sell their items from the surface. The cement platform was chaotic. If Rea knew she was down here, he'd be hopping mad.

Since he'd found out she was pregnant, he'd gone back to watching her all the time. It wasn't that he was concerned she'd leave, he was simply afraid for her. He'd been worried since Gears had described her giving birth. As far as she was concerned, he'd used one too many details. She'd told Gears a real Davis wouldn't have screwed her over like that. She wasn't apprehensive about the birth, and Rea shouldn't be either. Besides, she needed to pick up this new blanket from this particular harvester. Supposedly, only he could find things that were unique. There was no way just any present would do to celebrate their one-year anniversary. Even if Rea discovered she was here, getting his gift was worth his irritation.

Karma pressed closer to the stones next to the door and then tipped her head to see around some crates. She recognized the man she was supposed to meet the second he lumbered off the train. Brice had said he was tall, had a long black braid, and was an Indian. She'd questioned if the man was from India or native to the Americas. Brice said he didn't know. Honestly, she didn't care. She'd only asked for clarification to be able to recognize him faster. As far as she was concerned, as long as he was willing to sell her items, it didn't matter.

"You Karma?" The stranger asked as he crossed the cement platform away from a group of men unloading what looked like coffins filled with bolts of fabric.

"Yeah." She set her hand lightly on her gun. She never trusted harvesters, not even her uncle when she was young, but they were the only people who could get the really good items from the surface of the planet.

"My name's Soaring Hawk," the tall harvester announced.

She guessed American Indian.

"Do you have the blanket I want? Brice said you could get it."

The huge muscles of his biceps flexed as he reached behind him. He started pulling what appeared to be fabric from his pack. A relaxed smile appeared on his face when he handed it to her.

Karma pulled out a corner of the folded fabric and petted the fleece. It was perfect. A massive king-sized feather comforter that supposedly came from a real store. She squeezed it and thought about how much Rea was going to love the blanket. For a second, she pictured him and her and their new baby cuddling wrapped in this.

"It's not free. I had to trek far to get that, all the way to the Beyond," Hawk said.

Karma rolled the fabric up. She tucked it under her arm. "Here." She tugged out the money she'd brought from a pocket in her jeans.

"I got a little girl at home, and a new baby boy."

"Spare me the negotiation tactics. You're not getting more." Karma sighed.

Hawk shrugged. "Can't blame a harvester for trying."

Karma chuckled and headed back into the water base.

Once she was back in the water base halls, she started jogging. It was the middle of the night and she figured that no one was going to be up. She had to hurry back so Rea wouldn't wonder where she'd gone. If he woke up without her, she'd get twenty questions. She couldn't have that. Particularly with a human lie detector. She didn't want him to find out about his present until tomorrow night when she gave it to him at their anniversary dinner.

Switching to a full run, she spun around the corner. She ran directly into Gears. He reeled backward and then righted himself. She dropped her blanket on the floor. Gears recovered his balance and adjusted his glasses. He gave her a wide-eyed stare.

"What're you doing?" Gears asked her. "Do you know what time it is? You should be asleep. You need more rest now."

Karma picked up the blanket from where she'd dropped it. "I got this blanket for Rea. I wanted to give it to him at our anniversary dinner tomorrow. I'm just going to hide it. But I have to hurry back before he catches me. Wait, why are you up?" She paused. In a mocking tone, she added, "Do you know what time it is?"

Gears frowned and adjusted his glasses again. "I'm up because of my rabbits."

"Rabbits?" She could never keep up with what Gears was working on.

"They keep reproducing. I have to get this figured out. They just keep…" Gears put his hands together and intertwined his fingers. He then pulled his hands apart again and stared at her. "Never mind what they do. I just have a lot of bunnies."

Karma laughed at the anxious look on his face. She also thought his way of explaining his rabbit's mating amusing. "I get it. You're an odd duck, Gears."

Gears' face brightened. "Ducks. That's a much better idea than rabbits."

Karma shrugged. She needed to get back to bed before Rea sent out people looking for her. Even though Rea was a builder now, The Seemyah still respected him highly. He could get a search party together quicker than anyone she'd ever met—including her father.

"I've got to go. I'll talk with you later about ducks."

Gears nodded. "Let me take the blanket. I'll hide it in my room until your dinner tomorrow."

That was good luck. "Thank you."

As soon as Gears took the bundle, she quickly dashed down the hall again. From behind her, she heard Gears call out the word "rest."

When she got to their bedroom, she opened the door as silently as possible and entered.

Rea was sitting on the side of the bed. He'd put on a pair of pants, and a shirt was in his hands. He looked up when she came in.

"I was just coming to look for you. I was…" He trailed off.

"Worried?" She finished his sentence.

"Fucking scared out of my mind. I'm trying, but I don't know what I'll do if you get hurt, or if the baby gets hurt. Gears said women can die in childbirth. He also said if you fall you can lose the baby."

Karma crossed the room to stand between his legs. She took the shirt from his hands and tossed it to a nearby chair.

"Gears should've never talked to you about me having this child. The baby and I will be okay. I love you."

She climbed into his lap and snuggled under his chin. Slipping her hands over his bare chest, she tipped back so Rea could put his hand on her belly.

"Where were you?" Rea asked.

"I was talking to Gears." That was the truth, so she went with it. "He's having problems with his rabbits making a lot of babies and—"

Rea cut her off. "Forget I asked."

"I guess I told him to get ducks instead." She looked up at Rea. He was shaking his head.

"What your dad said was worse. He told him to get owls. He told Gears that owls would eat the rabbits. You should've seen Gears' face. He was horrified."

"Is Dad home again? I thought he left to meet the Prime Minister."

"He returned yesterday, but he was in a meeting with The Seemyah. You were perfecting your new cold weather suit with Gears." Rea wrapped an arm around her and scooted so he was resting his shoulders against the pillows.

"What did I miss?"

"The Prime Minister is really impressed with Keith. He thinks The Seemyah shouldn't only protect the acting president, but also protect the underground population after the borders close. Their job description is all about protecting the people, so we can flourish."

"What did all the men say?" She kissed Rea's neck. Her tongue slid out and caressed the sensitive spot under his ear. He shuddered.

"I think they wanted your opinion about it, too. Your dad went over radon poisoning, Snow Flu, and weather safety that might need to be addressed. The Prime Minister also wants a new official government name. Let's see if I can recall it. It had a lot of words and they were using an acronym by the end of the meeting."

Karma licked his ear again.

Rea sighed. "I'm never going to remember if you keep distracting me."

Karma giggled. "I love distracting you."

She slid her shirt over her head and then removed her bra. His eyes hungrily ate her up. It always amused her when he did that. She tugged off her jeans next and then curled around Rea once more.

"I know. It was the H.S.P.C.," he announced suddenly. He pulled their quilt over her chest. "It's the Human Survival and Population Care. Your dad wants a set of gears to be the symbol for the group."

"Sounds like a government name to me." Karma had stopped listening and was considering how to get him out of his pants. She pushed the quilt down again.

"I think your dad is only staying a few days. Then, I think he's planning on talking to some of the other teams that have settled onto the other bases. He also told me he asked Gears to change his last name to Davis for protection purposes. It'll be helpful if Gears has a little more protection and privacy. We all agree on that."

She sighed dreamily and pressed her body close to Rea. "Is Gears going to go with Dad and Bennett?"

"Yes. He's going to get the research they have on Snow Flu."

"I guessed he'd do that. Once they're gone, we could have a few romantical months together, just you and me, before the baby gets here."

Rea murmured yes and pulled the quilt up to her chin.

Karma spread her hand flat on his nipple and toyed with his sprinkle of chest hair. She didn't want to talk anymore. What she wanted now was Rea, and then she'd follow Gears' advice and get some rest. She nuzzled his neck.

"You know what I think?"

"What?"

"We should stop talking about my dad, and the H.S.P.C., and copy Gears' rabbits."

Rea laughed and batted her hands away when she reached for his pants.

"I don't know. It's late, and you should be sleeping. Gears said lots of rest and plenty of water and—"

"Have faith in me. I'm going to be okay, and so what if it's late," she murmured into his neck, as her hands found the buttons of his pants again.

"What time is it?" he asked absently. Her hands slipped into his waistband, and he didn't swat them away. He'd promised her he'd never turn her down or tell her to leave for the rest of his life. It appeared she remembered that. She unsnapped the buttons.

"It's almost two."

~ The End ~

Thank you for reading **1:05 a.m.** If you enjoyed this book and would like to give back to the authors, please consider writing a review! Reviews are a tremendous help for authors. So if you were moved and enjoyed this book enough to write even one sentence of encouragement it would be a huge boon.

https://www.goodreads.com/book/show/32790952-1

Want more of The Ice Era Chronicle series? Join the exclusive readers group for GIVEAWAYS, Advanced reader opportunities and Pre-order notifications!

http://eepurl.com/cg9ip1

Connect with C.M. Moore:

Facebook:
https://www.facebook.com/profile.php?id=100010442116825

Twitter: https://twitter.com/time_for_snow

Google+: https://plus.google.com/101755128915251195131

Tumblr: http://c-m-moore.tumblr.com/

Pinterest: https://www.pinterest.com/cmmooreauthor/

Website: http://www.authorcmmoore.com/

We often update our books when grammar errors are found, so please let us know if you've found one at:
stephanie@trollriverpub.com

Other Great Books from Troll River Publications

KINGS OF GUARDIAN
BOOK 1

KRIS MICHAELS

Lovely

ELITE DOMS of
WASHINGTON BOOK 1
ELIZABETH SaFLEUR

For every woman who's ever desired...

More

The Evermore Series
Rachel De Lune

THE KEY
CLASS

THE KEYS TO JOB SEARCH SUCCESS

John J. Daly, Jr.

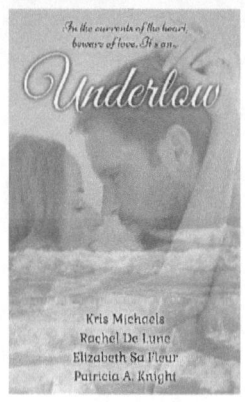

In the currents of the heart,
beware of love. It's on.

Underlow

Kris Michaels
Rachel De Lune
Elizabeth Sa Fleur
Patricia A. Knight